an open marriage

TESS STIMSON is the author of numerous novels,
including *The Adultery Club* and *The Infidelity Chain*,
as well as one biography, and writes regularly for the
Daily Mail and several women's magazines. Born and
brought up in Sussex, she graduated from Oxford before
spending a number of years as a news producer with
ITN. She now lives in Vermont with her American
husband, their daughter and her two sons.

www.tessstimson.com

By Tess Stimson

Fiction

An Open Marriage

The Lying Game

The Wife Who Ran Away

What's Yours is Mine

The Nanny
[previously published as *The Cradle Snatcher*]

The Infidelity Chain

The Adultery Club

Hard News

Soft Focus

Pole Position

Non-Fiction

Beat the Bitch:
How to Stop the Other Woman Stealing Your Man

Yours Till the End:
The Biography of a Beirut Hostage

tess stimson

an open marriage

PAN BOOKS

First published 2014 by Pan Books
an imprint of Pan Macmillan, a division of Macmillan Publishers Limited
Pan Macmillan, 20 New Wharf Road, London N1 9RR
Basingstoke and Oxford
Associated companies throughout the world
www.panmacmillan.com

ISBN 978-0-330-52204-5

1 3 5 7 9 8 6 4 2

A CIP catalogue record for this book is available from the British Library.

Typeset by Palimpsest Book Production Ltd, Falkirk, Stirlingshire
Printed and bound by CPI Group (UK) Ltd, Croydon, CR0 4YY

For my brother, Charles:

love you beyond words;

proud of you beyond measure

1

Mia

There's a secret to getting older: a low-watt bulb over the mirror. Scrutinizing your image too closely and minutely dissecting the creep of the years is a recipe for disappointment. There's a reason our sight gets blurred as we approach middle age.

I slick on a smear of lipstick and stretch my smile to check my teeth. Not that I'm middle-aged yet, I hope. An unknown twenty-something PR cutie sent me a free sample of menopause cream last week, along with a perky little note exhorting me to try it out and write about it in my weekly column. Given I've only just turned thirty-nine, I clearly need to change the byline photo on my website.

Maybe I should rub the cream on my mirror, I ponder idly, as I twist my blonde hair into a neat pleat. Or on my boobs. Or possibly my husband.

'Ready?' Kit asks, catching my eye in the glass.

Gesturing down at my navy jersey wrap dress and nude

L.K. Bennett heels, a homage to the Duchess of Cambridge, I give a twirl. 'Smart? Or just dull?'

'Appropriate,' Kit says, pleased.

Appropriate. No higher praise. Screw looking chic or sexy, or even just *nice*; I've long since learned the only sartorial criterion that matters to the Brits is *appropriate*. Better to look like the rear end of a truck in dated, ill-fitting taffeta and blend in than dress like a *Vogue* model and stand out. Kate Middleton is a sweet girl, but as per the strict British caste system, her blood isn't exactly blue. Which means she can't stray off-message with so much as a sparkly hairclip in case people start remembering her mother once took drink orders in Business Class.

Kit's usually more eloquent in his compliments, but today's a special case. He picks up my pearl necklace and I dip my head so he can fasten it around my neck. The pearls were a wedding present from his mother, who's been giving me *appropriate* gifts since I took up with her son in the hope of training the brash American out of me. Her distinct lack of success has dampened her enthusiasm not one whit. But today I'm playing it her way and dressing à la Middleton because I'm finally about to cross the aisle and become One of Them. (Much to my father's horror, I might add. A rabid Bostonian, to him the events surrounding the Tea Party of 1773 are still raw.)

Kit holds the bedroom door open for me and we go downstairs. My husband, of course, looks appropriate as always: a tall, bookish, handsome-behind-his-glasses tweedy English professor straight from central casting. (If you know your movies, think Robert Redford in *Three Days of the Condor*.) Greying blond hair a tad too long on the collar, leather patches on the elbows of his houndstooth blazer, beneath which he's surprisingly muscular, piercing blue eyes ablaze behind those specs. He's not quite a professor, not yet; he teaches English to unwilling teenage minds at an expensive private high school just outside Oxford. But he *looks* as if he should be rubbing shoulders with Tolkien and C.S. Lewis at one of those famous dreaming spires down the road; and in this country, appearances, as we know, are everything.

My mother-in-law, Ruth, glances up from her *Tatler* as we come downstairs straight into the cramped sitting room. A converted labourer's cottage dating back to the eighteenth century, our house is quirky and full of character, but so small you can almost stand in the middle of any room and touch both sides. 'You look nice, Mia,' she says approvingly. 'That extra weight suits you.'

'Did you want some Scotch with your vinegar?' I mutter under my breath as I walk in. 'Or were you waiting till after breakfast?'

'Given the circumstances, dear, I'd call this medicinal, wouldn't you?'

The woman has ears like a bat. Without missing a beat, I pour Ruth a double measure from the wet bar – a 'vulgar American habit' of which she deeply disapproves – and hand it to her without the benefit of ice (a far more heinous British habit, if you ask me). Kit glances at his watch, then at his mother, but wisely says nothing. Ruth can drink all of us under the table and is a borderline alcoholic, but she does it with such unapologetic determination, you can't help but admire her.

The first few muffled bars of 'Hail to the Chief' ring out from my purse. I scrabble for my phone and dart back into the hallway, holding up one finger to pacify Kit. 'I'll be quick, I promise.'

'You still going through with it?' Lois demands in my ear.

'Don't try and talk me down. This is a heady, romantic gesture.'

'Abandoning your job and running off to England for some guy was a heady, romantic gesture. This is just patriotic suicide.'

'I'm doing it for love,' I protest. 'For my man. And as a mark of gratitude to the generous country that's taken me to its heart—'

'And will now give you cheaper taxes,' Lois points out.

'Well, yes. That too.'

'You're doing the right thing,' she says unexpectedly.

'Am I?'

'Your life is with Kit. Lock, stock and barrel. You don't need me to tell you that.'

There's a sudden lump in my throat. I've known Lois for more than fifteen years, since I first started as a lowly intern at CNN's HQ in Atlanta. Nine years my senior, a native New Yorker who's been there, done that and bought every T-shirt, she ran the International Desk with a fist of iron for a decade before jumping ship to start her own media consultancy. Widowed at just thirty when her cameraman husband was shot and killed in Bosnia, she singlehandedly raised their infant son whilst growing her business into one of the top five media firms in the country. She's my best friend – the smart, savvy, streetwise older sister I never had. Point of order: she's my *only* friend.

It's a chicken-and-egg thing. Did I become a lone-wolf, hard-edged international journalist because I have few friends and no ties; or did I end up with few friends because I was never in one place for more than a day or two at a time?

Either way, I have Lois to thank. She gave me my first break when I landed in her lap as an unpaid gopher, wet behind the ears and way too full of myself and my post-grad in journalism from UC Berkeley. She helped me cut my teeth and later gave me my first paid job as a producer. I earned my place on screen via the traditional journalistic combo of hard work (eighty-hour weeks, no vacations for two years) and dumb good luck (on the morning of 9/11 I happened to be just four blocks down from the World Trade Center interviewing a megalomaniacal IVF doctor who'd inseminated seventy-two women with his own sperm). I worked my way up from house fires and deer trapped on icy lakes to embassy bombings and Afghanistan. By the time I met Kit, seven years after starting at CNN, I'd finally joined the official war correspondent roster. I hadn't quite made it to the big league yet, but I was just one civil war or African genocide away.

However, three hundred twenty days a year on the road is a bitch if you want to have anything approaching a personal life. Sex life, sure: there's nothing like a war zone to ratchet up the libido. Bombs as aphrodisiacs; it's a recognized condition. Some of my romances even made it onto Main Street, but they never lasted more than a couple months. What man wants to play second fiddle to an unpredictable, insatiable, all-consuming job? The only guys who got it were those in the business themselves, and two highpowered, high-maintenance egos under one roof isn't exactly a recipe for domesticity.

When Kit and I met at a wedding in Scotland nine years ago (he was bartending; I was the reluctant family rep for the nuptials of a second cousin), I was just looking to get laid. We had a great hook-up on the ninth hole of the hotel golf course, and the sex was so good I couldn't resist repeating it (in bed and out of it) numerous times over the remaining four days of my visit. But I never considered it might lead to something more permanent. Sure, he was great company: then thirty-one, a year older than me, he was smart, thoughtful and amusing. It didn't seem either to faze or to impress him that I was on TV earning ten times what he made tutoring kids while he put himself through school after several years' travelling across America, and consequently I was able to relax and be myself with him – something I hadn't done in a long time. But there was no way a relationship could ever work. Not given the different lives we led. Not with four thousand miles between us.

Kit, however, thought differently. Even then he knew me better than I knew myself.

By the time my plane landed in Atlanta, there was already a witty, self-deprecating email waiting for me. It was impossible not to respond, out of politeness if nothing else, though I still couldn't see any future in it. What as? Pen pals?

And yet somehow, over the next few weeks, I found myself in the midst of a quaint Victorian courtship conducted entirely through the written word. We exchanged emails on subjects as wide-ranging as Melville and crème brûlée (Kit having trained as a chef during a brief marriage to a high-maintenance divorcee eleven years his senior). Gradually our emails became more frequent and more intimate as we slowly revealed ourselves to each other as if performing a biographic striptease: fragments of our childhoods, lost loves, sexual fantasies. I loved the elegant way Kit thought and wrote. His arguments were measured and scholarly; he was open-minded and responsive, and (uniquely in my experience) never afraid to admit it if there was something he didn't know.

Soon our emails were supplemented by phone calls, the two of us talking well into my night and his early morning, sometimes for several hours at a time. Three months after my first trip to Scotland, and at Lois's urging, I flew over for a long weekend, just to put what I was beginning to admit could be *It* to the test.

We passed, with flying colours.

For nearly a year I shuttled between Atlanta and Edinburgh trying to decide whether I wanted to make the move permanent. Kit still had three more years of his doctorate to go, and besides, he wasn't one of those people who can willingly transplant themselves halfway round the world. If one of us was going to relocate, it had to be me.

Career-wise I could certainly do it – I could likely swing a posting to CNN's London bureau; but more interestingly, I'd recently been approached by a Boston newspaper that wanted me to write a syndicated column. I still loved my job, no question, but for the first time in my career I was feeling battle-fatigued. Maybe it was the prospect of a different kind of life with Kit. Maybe I'd just seen enough kids maimed by landmines or emotionally scarred by years of civil war. Some time away from the front line could be just what I needed to return fresh to the fray in a year or two. I felt sure I could sell the Boston paper on the idea of some kind of *Letter from America* in reverse. The question was, did I want to make such a seismic change in my life for any man, however wonderful?

For there was no doubt in my mind by then that Kit was very wonderful indeed. He was the first civilian I'd dated since I'd joined CNN, and the first Brit; he was different from every other man I'd known. He had no ego, or at least not the macho, thin-skinned kind that had problems with successful women. He had a quiet inner strength: he knew who he was, and what he was worth. I knew he'd keep me on the straight and narrow. That, in the end, was why I quit my job and moved four thousand miles to marry him. I didn't need thrills and trouble from a man; I created enough of my own.

It was a wrench, though. Admittedly I had few family ties: Mom had died a few years earlier from stomach cancer, Dad had just retired to Florida, and I was an only child with – as we've established – few close friends. But giving up your homeland isn't as easy as it sounds, even for someone as rootless as me. If I hadn't found out I was pregnant the month after I moved to Edinburgh, I'm not sure I'd have stuck it out. But Emmy's arrival six months later sealed the deal; and I've never regretted it for one second.

Emmy scampers down the stairs now, her long chestnut hair streaming over her shoulders, green eyes dancing with excitement. She gets her colouring from Ruth; both Kit and I are fair-haired and blue-eyed.

'You look beautiful!' she carols as she skids to a halt beside me. 'You don't look like you! You look like a *proper* mummy!'

She takes after Ruth in other ways, too.

'Lois, I have to go,' I say into the phone. My voice catches. 'I'm so glad you called. I really appreciate it, you know?'

'I do, kid. Go do your duty. Queen and country and all that. Just remember you're a Yankee at heart. Born and bred. Fourth of July and the Red Sox all the way.'

Emmy tugs at my hand as I put my phone away and go back into the sitting room. 'Are you going to be English from now on?'

'I think it'll take more than a piece of paper to achieve *that*,' Ruth says tartly.

'We should get going,' Kit intervenes. 'The ceremony starts at ten.'

The four of us cram into his car, doubling up like pretzels to fit into the toy-sized seats. Cars in this country are so *small*. Like the roads. And the houses. And the parking spaces. (Don't even get me started on the subway. Not for nothing do they call it the Tube: when the doors open at a station, people burst out onto the platform like popcorn from a pressurized can, having shared more intimate body contact with complete strangers in ten minutes than they have with their spouses in ten years.)

But small cars or not, tepid alcoholic beverages or not, weird accents and stiff upper lips and smug sense of superiority or not, I love the Brits. I'm married to one. My daughter is one. And I'm about to sign on the dotted line and become one myself.

The citizenship ceremony is surprisingly moving. Twenty-five of us file into the Council Chamber of Oxford's County Hall along with our families and sign the Oxfordshire Citizenship Register. (Kit and I moved south from Edinburgh five years ago when he got a job teaching English at a secondary school just outside Oxford, shortly after he finally finished his PhD.) A speech from the local Mr Big, and then finally the Oath of Allegiance and the Citizenship Pledge.

'I didn't know we had an Oath of Allegiance,' Ruth stage-whispers sniffily. 'That sounds a bit *American* to me.'

As I stand with everyone else to recite the oath, I'm hit by the ramifications of what I'm about to do. I'm legally renouncing the Land of the Free, officially throwing my lot in with the inhabitants of this foggy grey rock in the middle of the Atlantic. It's not just about paperwork. I've lived here eight years, and superficially I've acclimatized: I watch *Corrie*, I know a bonnet is part of your wardrobe, I've learned to speak 'English' (though I'll never completely renounce my own language: to me a tap will always be a faucet). I've come to understand only Brits are allowed to criticize the Royals, and that they much prefer the Germans to the French, despite two world wars. But Ruth is right: no matter how many pieces of paper I'm given, I'll never really be one of them. My childhood was all yellow school buses, *Saturday Night Live*, Thanksgiving, and peanut butter and jelly sandwiches (aka PB&J), not Marmite soldiers and *John Craven's Newsround*. I can dress in head-to-toe Boden, celebrate Bonfire Night and buy my panties at M&S till the day I die, but I'll always be an outsider.

Kit squeezes my hand, and I know immediately he understands. I smile up at him and take a calming breath. Lois is right. My life is with Kit, lock, stock and barrel. I'd give up a kidney for this man, never mind my country.

'I, Mia Allen, swear by Almighty God that, on becoming a British citizen, I will be faithful and bear true allegiance to Her Majesty Queen Elizabeth the Second, her heirs, and successors, according to law.'

It's done. We all sing the British National Anthem (wonderfully solemn, but a bit funereal; if I'd been the one picking the anthem, I'd have gone for a more stirring number, like 'Land of Hope and Glory') and troop outside for a group photo on the steps. As if to demonstrate its very Britishness, the sunny September morning has given way to grey drizzle. Ruth huddles in the doorway with Emmy, waiting for Kit to go get the car. Perhaps, like the Wicked Witch of the West, she'll melt if she gets wet.

A shower of red, white and blue confetti flutters over me, and I turn in surprise.

'Charlie!' Kit cries. 'What on earth are you doing here?'

'Thought someone should welcome the new recruit properly,' Charlie grins, producing a bottle of champagne and four flutes from a Waitrose bag. 'Got to have bubbly, or it doesn't count.'

'You haven't met my boss, have you, darling?' Kit says. 'Charlie, this is my wife, Mia.'

I return her radiant smile as we shake hands. I knew Charlie was a woman, of course I did. Kit has worked for her for six months, ever since she recruited him from his local comprehensive to head the English department at St Alphonsus High School. He talks about her often; I know she's whip-smart, energetic, imaginative, and as frustrated as Kit with the inertia among the faculty at the school.

What I didn't know until now is that she's also tall, blonde, blue-eyed, charming and seriously gorgeous. *Exactly* the sort of girl I could be friends with, in fact.

2

Charlie

There are times I wish I'd married a woman. Just for the sheer joy of a spouse who knows what to do with the pile of stuff at the bottom of the stairs.

I pick up my husband's discarded tie from the floor and add it to the stack of things to go upstairs, then throw my keys onto the hall table. 'Rob? Milly?'

A muffled shriek comes from the sitting room, followed by giggles. I pick up Rob's jacket from the hall table and hang it on the coat stand, place his shoes neatly in a corner, scoop a heap of copper-wire cuttings and plastic tabs from the kitchen counter into the bin, put the pliers, screwdriver and wire-cutter back in the drawer, gather the crumpled pages of today's newspaper and fold them neatly together, collect four spent batteries rolling around the floor and toss them into the recycling bin, tidy a dirty Marmite knife and plate into the dishwasher, screw the lid back on the Marmite jar, put away the milk, pick up Rob's balled socks and score a direct hit into the laundry basket just inside the utility-room door, turn off the radio, put the cat food box back under the sink and sweep up the spilled Friskies, close his yawning briefcase and stand it neatly by the front door, step over the unspooled (and evidently unused) vacuum cleaner blocking the hallway, and open the sitting-room door. When I left this morning, the house was exactly the way I like it – square, light, modern, empty – and looking pristine.

Rob is lying on his back in front of the fire, bare feet waving in the air like an upturned beetle. Milly is flying on them on her belly, arms outstretched, blonde hair tousled, blue eyes sparkling, and shrieking with joy. I can't help laughing with them even as I pick up sofa cushions from the floor.

'Careful, Rob, you'll make her sick.'

'She won't be sick. She hasn't eaten yet,' Rob says, but he lowers Milly gently to the floor, rolling his eyes and winking at her.

I put the cushions back on the sofa. 'You didn't give her dinner?'

'I was waiting for you.'

'I told you I'd be home late tonight because of the staff meeting, remember? You were supposed to warm up the lasagna.'

'Sorry. Totally forgot.'

He follows me into the kitchen as I get the lasagna out of the fridge, running his hand through his thick, dark hair, which is greying just a little now at the temples. His bare feet are still tanned from the summer, and a five o'clock shadow darkens all but the Hollywood dimple in his chin. Clad in old jeans and a faded blue T-shirt, he could still be the twenty-three-year-old I fell in love with almost two decades ago. I feel a sudden hot thrust of desire and turn away quickly before he can see it in my eyes. It's always been like this. No matter how badly he behaves, how angry I am with him, how hurt, I'm undone by how much I always, *always* want him.

It wasn't part of my plan to end up married to my first serious boyfriend. At twenty-two, which is what I was when I met Rob, I wasn't even sure if I wanted to get married at all. I'd made a point of not getting serious about anyone when I was at Oxford, breaking up with several perfectly nice, intelligent men (including a future Cabinet minister) for making a harmless suggestion that it was time for me to meet their parents. It wasn't that I wanted to play the field; far from it. But my mother had been in the middle of her veterinary degree when she'd met Dad and given it all up to marry him. I'd seen first-hand the corrosive bitterness that had undermined their relationship for the next forty years. I didn't want to make the same mistake.

My talent was for languages; I'd studied Arabic with Aramaic and Syriac at university, and then interned for a year at the UN in New York before securing a job with the Foreign Office in Egypt, scoring among the top five per cent in my year's intake. I dreamed of a glittering future in the diplomatic corps, wheeling and dealing in the shadows. I'd already been taken aside and had words like 'fast track' and 'chosen few' whispered seductively in my ear.

And then I met Rob. I was no smarter than my mother, as it turned out. Bowled over by a chiselled jaw and come-to-bed eyes.

He was on a month-long holiday at a resort in Egypt, trying to 'figure out' what he planned to do with the rest of his life. It seemed he'd been 'figuring things out' since graduating from Brighton with an engineering degree eighteen months before, and his plans had grown no more concrete in the interim. We met on the same scuba-diving course, and had an intense, erotic holiday romance which we both quickly realized had the potential to become something very much more serious. The only issue was one of logistics. He had no job, no plans for the future, while I'd just been offered a career-making posting to Khartoum. Naturally I didn't expect him to follow me meekly around the world for the rest of his life. But surely he could see that I couldn't give everything up *now*? If he could just spare me a year, two at most . . .

But then he told me about David, and of course that put an end to the conversation. Death does that: trumps whatever cards you think you hold.

David was Rob's elder brother by five years. A golden child – and this isn't just rose-tinted hindsight speaking. Handsome and clever, of course, but more than that. The kind of kid who found himself in the local newspaper at nine for coming up with an initiative to help the homeless that was taken up by *Blue Peter*. A boy who took all his Christmas presents to a children's home – *in secret* – while his parents were sleeping off the Queen's speech. The kind of brother Rob didn't have a hope of living up to, however hard he tried.

A drunk driver killed him on his mother's sixtieth birthday. He'd nipped out to the shops for a bunch of flowers because Rob had forgotten to buy her a present. He was hit as he crossed the road back home. They found the bouquet still clutched in his hand, perfect, unharmed, not a petal out of place.

'I can't *leave* them,' Rob said reasonably. 'They need me. Surely you can see that? I can't just up sticks and move halfway round the world. I'm all they've *got*.'

That was the moment. The last moment I ever really had a choice.

I don't regret giving up my glittering Foreign Office career for a single second.

If it hadn't been for Rob, I'd have spent the last twenty years as a professional liar, oiling the wheels of diplomacy and cosying up to the representatives of murderous regimes in the name of political expediency. I'd have earned ten times what I earn now, met kings and presidents, and been unable to look at myself in the mirror.

Instead, I turned down the Khartoum posting, quit my job with the Foreign Office and returned to England with Rob. He took a job at Black Rock, a start-up company in the then-fledgling IT industry. And I turned my back on a career that would have taken me all over the globe and allowed myself to be restricted to a small corner of Oxfordshire; I exchanged embassies for classrooms, taking a series of jobs teaching Arabic at various small independent schools. And I ended up a thousand times happier because of it. I love my job. I teach less than I used to since being headhunted for the post of Head of Humanities at St Alphonsus eighteen months ago, but it's still the most satisfying aspect of my work. This may not be the career I planned, but I couldn't have chosen a more fulfilling one.

And my diplomatic background has stood me in good stead. There are few circles as competitive, as jealous and insecure, as incestuous and thin-skinned, as the academic one.

Shelby Grade, the head teacher, leans back in her chair at the top of the conference table and folds her arms. 'Sorry,' she says shortly. 'It's an interesting suggestion, Kit, but no. I don't think so.'

'I know this will require some changes to the current syllabus,' Kit Allen presses, 'but given the return nationally to a more structured exam system, if we modify our courses to complement each other—'

'Obviously, if you'd been here a bit longer,' Shelby cuts in smoothly, 'you'd know that our courses are already carefully structured to interface together *perfectly*. I've been at St Alphonsus thirty-one years, and our curriculum has been *extremely* successful. I can't see any reason to modify it now.'

A muscle twitches at the base of Kit's jaw. I have every sympathy with his position; like me, he believes wholeheartedly in our school mission, and finds the *but this is the way we've always done it* rebuttal of every new idea intensely frustrating. I respect his passion and commitment to the school – it's why I hired him to head the English department six months ago, and appointed him to the Forward Planning team – but I need him to work collaboratively with the rest of the team if we're to make any progress.

'With respect, Shelby,' I say smoothly, 'I think that given the government's change of academic focus to core skills—'

'We've always focused on core skills here,' Monica Tarrant, the Head of Art, interrupts sharply. 'I find Kit's suggestion that we haven't offensive and unhelpful.'

'Let's not make this personal,' I say.

'I'd like to know how else we're supposed to take it,' Monica snaps.

'Kit is merely making the point that in order to remain competitive in an increasingly difficult market, treading water simply isn't enough,' I say patiently. 'A number of schools in our area are already offering both the International Baccalaureate and American SATs, as well as A Level options, and if we want to do the same, which we clearly *need* to do if we're to retain students, we have to conflate certain courses and expand our syllabus offerings.'

'No offence to Kit, but this isn't Franklin Comprehensive,' Shelby says silkily. 'I'm sure his last school had all sorts of unusual ideas, but we do things differently here.'

'As I understand it, my experience at Franklin was why you brought me in—'

'*I* didn't bring you in at all,' she flashes.

Kit acknowledges the point-scoring with a terse nod. 'I was asked to bring some new ideas to the table. This isn't a criticism of the way things have been done in the past, simply a recognition that the business is changing.'

'But that's just it,' Monica says triumphantly. '*We* don't view our school as a business. It isn't about *money*.'

'You're absolutely right,' I say swiftly. 'It's about the children. I think we can all agree on that. We all want the best for them, which is why we all bring so much passion and enthusiasm to the table. We're all trying to make St Alphonsus the best it can be. We *are* in a business, as Kit says: the business of forming and shaping young minds.' I look around the conference table. 'As you know, the current school fees are twelve thousand a year. It costs seventeen thousand to educate each child at St Alphonsus. The Sisters of Calvary make up the difference from their endowment to keep the fees competitive, but they've been as hard hit by the recession as the rest of us. We either have to raise the fees, which I know none of us want to do, or increase student registration,' I add, spreading my hands. 'It's that simple.'

'The mission of the school *won't* change,' Kit says, leaning forward to make his point. 'It's the administration and academic course offerings that will be updated. Naturally there will be full consultation with the trustees before we go ahead. No one is suggesting we rush into anything. But we do need to streamline some—'

'I knew it!' Monica exclaims. 'And I'm sure it won't be the English department that comes in for this *streamlining*, not given the support *you* get in certain quarters!'

'Monica, as Kit just pointed out, this isn't personal,' I say evenly.

'Absolutely not,' Kit adds. 'In fact, Monica, one of the things we'll be looking at is augmenting the art department budget to allow you to bring online the various new media we'll be looking to offer under the new curriculum.'

Monica subsides, mollified, and I shoot Kit a grateful look. My job is to somehow mould the disparate and prickly personalities around the table into a cohesive team. Shelby Grade has been at St Alphonsus longer than God and is a smart and shrewd political operator, but she's also obstructive and difficult to work with. I admire Kit for his ability to keep his emotions out of the debate despite intense provocation from both Shelby and Monica. In fact, the more I get to know him, the more I like him. Despite the nutty professor look – gold-rimmed glasses, scuffed brogues, corduroy suit complete with unravelling leather elbow patches – there's a strong and rather rugged masculine air about him. I can't quite put my finger on it. I can picture him sitting atop a wagon forging west across America, a pioneer building a cabin with his bare hands. I know he's good at his job, but he strikes me as the kind of man who belongs in the great outdoors, in a different time and place. With an elephant gun in his hand, I think, glancing at Shelby and sighing inwardly.

'Well, let's not make any hasty decisions now,' Shelby says, gathering the folders in front of her and getting to her feet. 'Perhaps you could email me your thoughts, everyone, and we can have another round-table discussion at the next meeting.'

She sweeps out of the room with as much majesty as five-foot-two inches' worth of pink mohair suiting can convey, trailed by Monica and the rest of the Forward Planning team. I collect my own paperwork to the sound of the final lesson bell and join Kit as he stands at the window watching a crowd of boys in grey trousers and burgundy blazers streaming across the cricket pitch towards the horse chestnut trees down by the river. It's good to know that even in this age of PlayStations and Xboxes, the tradition of conkers is still alive and well. Along with smoking behind the bike sheds, of course; though these days it's probably Afghanistan Gold rather than Silk Cut.

'Thank you,' I tell Kit as he picks up his battered leather messenger bag and starts putting away his notes.

He stops and looks up. 'For what?'

'I know how difficult Shelby can be, but we still have to work with her. I appreciate your patience.'

'Rome wasn't built in a day. There's no point antagonizing her needlessly.'

I smile. It makes such a difference to have even one

member of staff supporting what I'm trying to do. The rest of the team are good people – intelligent and hard-working, putting in long hours for rather less than a king's ransom; but none of them have Kit's passion and commitment. They want to do their jobs, go home at the end of the day and switch off. None of them have the inclination or energy to go up against Shelby, but for the sake of the school, changes have to be made. Kit is exactly what St Alphonsus and I need. For the first time since I took this job, I feel I have a wingman watching my back.

A Keatsian autumnal mist slowly drifts across the field from the river. 'I wish I'd gone to a school as beautiful as this,' Kit comments, glancing towards the window again. 'These kids don't know how lucky they are.'

'Ditto. Local comp in Brentwood for me.'

'Brentwood to Oxford? That's quite a journey.'

'I was a scholarship girl. First in my family to go to university.'

'Likewise. My mother almost killed me when I dropped out in my final year. I went back eighteen months later, but at the time I thought she'd never forgive me.'

I knew the bare facts from his CV, but it's the first time he's volunteered such personal information, and out of curiosity I keep the ball in play. 'Why did you quit?'

'I met my wife. My first wife, I should say. Suki. Eleven years older, very glamorous, very sexy, *very* messed up. Our marriage lasted twenty-three months, and twenty-two of those were spent arguing.'

'Well, your judgement must have improved with age,' I smile. 'Mia seems lovely. How long have the two of you been together?'

'Eight years, give or take. You?'

21

'Married for six, but we've been together for nineteen. We met on a diving course in Sharm el-Sheikh.'

'Wedding in Edinburgh for us. Not quite as glamorous. D'you still dive?'

A sore point. 'Not often these days. My husband Rob does, but since we had Milly, one of us has to stay home with her, and it's usually me.'

'Milly's how old?'

'She'll be seven in February.'

'Our daughter Emmy turned seven recently. We must get the two of them together sometime.' He buckles his messenger bag and slings it across his chest like a bandolier. 'It was really good of you to come to her ceremony last week, by the way. We both really appreciated it.'

'No, it was my pleasure. I've been wanting to meet her ever since I started reading her blog.'

He grimaces. 'As the saying goes, don't believe everything you read in the papers.'

'She doesn't pull her punches, does she?'

'That's one way of putting it.' He grins. 'I know she'd love to go for coffee or something if you have time. She's desperate for intelligent female company – she works from home and feels quite isolated sometimes.'

'I'd love to. I thought she was great fun.'

Mia and I didn't get much chance to talk the other day, but I took to her immediately. I don't know why I was surprised at how warm and funny she was. I suppose journalists have a bit of a reputation these post-phone-hacking days. But Kit's a decent, pleasant man, so it would have been a bit odd if his wife was a cast-iron bitch. Though I still wouldn't have put them together if I'd walked into a party and met them separately. He's so quiet and thoughtful, whereas she's impulsive and outgoing. They're a strange match.

What do people make of Rob and me? I wonder as I walk back towards my office. Do we match? Or are people surprised to see us together, too?

3

Mia

I haven't been this nervous since getting ready for a first date, and you'd have to go a long way back for that. Most of my romantic entanglements – Kit included – weren't exactly planned in advance.

I smooth down my skirt, fidgeting uncomfortably. I hate pantyhose; they never make them long enough in the leg for someone my height, so they always sag at the crotch like I'm wearing a dirty diaper. But Charlie will be coming to the restaurant straight from work, so I've upped the ante on my go-to daytime uniform of jeans and black turtleneck. I've even broken out a pair of heels for the occasion. I'd never admit it in a million years, but Charlie slightly intimidates me.

I grab my keys and pick up my purse. It's all very well for Kit to tell me to relax and take it as it comes, but Charlie's the first woman I've met in years – hell, since I arrived in this country – that I can actually see myself becoming friends with. No one will ever take Lois's place, of course, but Manhattan's a long way to go for a Girls' Night Out. I need to find a friend here, someone local, someone I can just hang with. And I never thought I'd say that.

All my life, I've considered myself pretty self-reliant. I had a handful of really close friends when I was a kid, but I never needed to be part of some huge posse to feel good about myself, probably because I was an only child and used to keeping myself amused. I adored my parents and got on well with them, but while most of my high school friends enrolled at Boston U, sticking to the same few square miles they'd known all their lives, I couldn't wait to explore new pastures. I spent four years at Columbia in New York, and then another couple at Berkeley on the other side of the country in California, before completing the geographic triangle and moving south to Atlanta when I joined CNN. After college, I kept in touch with the few people I really cared about, and I still checked in with them when geography permitted, but their lives moved on without me, as mine did without them. We shared headlines on the rare occasions we did meet up, but we didn't know the little day-to-day details any more, the small things that knit any relationship together. Gradually, over the years, we drifted apart.

And thanks to my insane travel schedule, I didn't really make new friends. I simply didn't have *time* for them. I was a girl who travelled light, literally and metaphorically. So when I met Kit, I took a move of four thousand miles across the Atlantic in my stride.

It was only when I quit my job and started writing from home that I realized how much I'd gotten used to the casual human interaction of a normal working day – my camera crew and the people I interviewed, of course, but also the taxi drivers, the coffee baristas, the PRs and agents and editors, the hacks I met for lunch and the government sources I took out for a drink in the evening. We might not have been friends, exactly, but we had a lot in common, and we moved in the same circles, knew the same people. I felt connected to the world, plugged in. Maybe my social life and work life had become one and the same, but my schedule was most always full.

Suddenly all that was gone. Instead of jumping on a plane and zipping halfway round the world at a moment's notice, the most exciting thing to happen in my day was putting out the trash. For the first time in my adult life, I actually had to *live* somewhere, rather than simply pit-stop while I washed laundry and paid a few bills. I'd never needed to put down roots before, because I'd never been home for more than three days at a time – four, tops. Now I was trapped alone in a tiny apartment every day with only my laptop for company, and not one single solitary soul to talk to till Kit got home.

I'm not autistic. Technically, I know how to make friends; it's a journalist's job, after all, to turn a complete stranger into your secret-spilling BFF within a half-hour of meeting. And getting pregnant with Emmy helped some. At least the appointments with my obstetrician and the prenatal classes widened my social circle to include more than just the mailman and the FedEx guy. I made the effort to stitch together some kind of social life with other expectant moms, but at the end of the day, what did I have in common with a twenty-four-year-old hairdresser with two kids and another on the way? No one like me (professional, anal, American) came to these classes. The kind of smart, fast-track women I might have been able to connect with had better things to do with their mornings than hang around clinics comparing haemorrhoids.

It's been eight years; out of necessity I've gotten used to my solitary existence. My real life is out in the ether, in the virtual world, where I blog and file my column and respond to my followers and am still the same street-smart, savvy, put-together journo I've always been. And when Kit's around, I don't notice the loneliness; he's great company, and we always have something to talk about. But since he started his new job six months ago, he's been putting in crazy hours at work, and anyways, it's not healthy for one person to be your whole life. I need a *friend*.

I arrive at the tiny Italian in central Oxford an uncharacteristic ten minutes early, having caught a lucky break and found a parking space practically outside the restaurant. I order a bottle of fizzy water and play with my phone, trying to look New York cool. I have a feeling I just look sad.

I'm losing miserably at Temple Run 2 when Charlie dashes in, bang on time.

'I'm so, *so* sorry I'm late,' she pants, flinging her purse onto a chair and shrugging out of her jacket. 'I was stuck in a meeting that went on *forever*.'

I drop my phone in my purse and pull back the zinc table so she can sit down. 'Don't worry, I just got here myself. Kit said you had some kind of trustee review coming up?'

'I swear to God, if I spent as much time teaching as I do in meetings, I'd have a school full of Einsteins.'

'When you go freelance, you have zero job security, no pension, no health benefits and a strong possibility of bankruptcy, but on the plus side, at least you never have to go to meetings.'

She laughs, her perfect Colgate smile proving not all Brits are allergic to dentists. '*And* you get to go to work in your pyjamas.'

'Has Kit been telling tales out of school?'

'Background check.' She twists in her chair and waves over a server. 'I don't know about you, but after the morning I've had, I need a drink. Thank God today was just a half-day. Please don't tell me you're a born-again Mormon or something equally teetotal and ghastly – oh, shit. You're *not* Mormon, are you?'

'Didn't the background check tell you?'

'Something this important, I like to be sure. Pinot work for you?'

'One bottle or two?'

'Now you're talking.'

I smooth a stiff white napkin on my lap, feeling over-dressed next to Charlie. I'd been aiming for sharp and stylish, but I have the uneasy feeling I look more like I'm on my way to a job interview. Her understated grey-blue pantsuit and cream silk blouse are a little conservative, but she's accessorized the outfit with beaten silver rings on her thumbs and index fingers, and she has three tiny diamonds in the lobe of each ear, giving her an edgy, contemporary look. I've clearly been out of the mix way too long.

Charlie suddenly reaches across the table, lightly brushing my hand. 'Look, before we go any further, I just wanted to say I'm so sorry to hear about your father. Kit said he was sick; I hope you don't mind that he told me. It must be awful for you to be so far away from him.'

My throat closes. Seven months ago, Dad was diagnosed with a benign bladder tumour. He'd need surgery, the doctors said, but not to worry, he'd be in and out in a day, no cause for concern. Except after it had been removed, a biopsy revealed it *was* cancerous, but no need to panic, it was 'only' in the inner walls of the bladder, which made it stage 1, ninety-six per cent survival rate. And then it grew back the size of a clementine in just six weeks, and when they operated again, they found this time it had invaded the muscular bladder wall too (stage 2) and possibly beyond (stage 3). Chemo followed, and all the rest of the miserable oncology arsenal, but that didn't stop it metastasizing to his prostate, lymph nodes, lungs, and who knew where else in what seemed like minutes, which made it stage 4. Survival rate beyond a year, five per cent, tops. There is no stage 5.

I already lost Mom to breast cancer eight years ago. In a year, I'll be an orphan. At my age, you wouldn't think it would matter as much as it does.

Awkwardly, I twist the stem of my wine glass. 'I always knew something like this could happen when I made the decision to move so far away from home,' I mumble. 'Mom got sick a year before I met Kit. She never even met him. It was hard enough juggling work and visiting her when I was living in the same country as she was. I knew when I came over here Dad could have a heart attack or something and I wouldn't make it home in time. At least this way we get to say our goodbyes.'

'Your heart must leap into your mouth every time the phone goes,' Charlie says softly.

I barely know this woman, but suddenly I have to fight the urge to spill my guts and tell her the story of my life. Much as I appreciate her directness, especially as most people tiptoe around the subject as if death is a sexually transmitted disease, soul-baring isn't really my style; I guess all that self-reliance makes it a little hard to open up. Very

29

un-American, Kit says. I'm not about to rip up the manual now with Charlie. It would be like giving a blow-by-blow of your divorce on a first date. But she's the kind of woman I *could* tell. And for me, that's a big deal.

A waitress appears and we order. I'm relieved when Charlie opts for the spaghetti carbonara; I hate women who invite you for lunch and then just order a starvation salad so you feel you have to have one too.

'I love your blog,' Charlie says, gracefully moving the subject away from my father and onto happier ground. 'Some of your riffs on the way we behave are hilarious. I *loved* that whole commuter thing you did last week.'

'I noticed you apologized for being on time when you got here,' I say slyly.

She laughs. 'It's ingrained in us, isn't it? Some bugger smashes your hip with a shopping trolley and you're the one who says sorry as the ambulance men carry you out.'

'I kind of like it. No one ever says sorry back home in case they get sued.'

'No, but they hope you'll have a nice day when they hand you your shopping, instead of shoving your bag in your face and going straight back to texting their boyfriends.'

I dip a piece of bread in the dish of olive oil and balsamic between us. 'Oh, I'm a bit of a fan of British rudeness, too. When I grow up, I want to be the Dowager Countess of Grantham.'

'According to Rob, I already am,' Charlie says ruefully.

'Don't be defeatist, dear. It's so middle-class.'

She giggles. 'Love that line.'

'Julian Fellowes is such a great writer. Remember that quote about not being unhappily married? You're simply "unable to see as much of each other as you would like".

They should put a statue of him on that empty pedestal in Trafalgar Square.'

'I really liked— Damn.' She breaks off as her phone rings. 'Sorry, it's the school – I have to answer it.'

She takes the phone outside the restaurant and I watch her through the window. Much as I appreciated Charlie's invitation to lunch and have been looking forward to it, I didn't really expect us to click the way we have – or so instantly. It was curiosity (well, and loneliness and desperation) that brought me here to meet her – this woman who works with my husband, and spends more time with him than I do. I realize with a jolt as I sit there that she looks just like me – same height, same size, roughly the same age, blonde, blue-eyed, ditto, ditto. Only in her case, she's polished and refined – a nine out of ten compared with my six on the looks score card.

Anyways, click with her I have. It's the platonic version of a *coup de foudre*. Friendship at first sight.

'You're not going to believe this,' Charlie exclaims, dropping back into her seat and picking up her fork. 'One of the substitute teachers at the school called an entire class of fourteen-year-olds – and I quote – "fucking little shits who need locking up". He's right, of course – Year Nine are little swine – but we've now got a posse of parents marching on the school demanding the legal equivalent of a public flogging.'

I wave our server back to our table. 'Another bottle of the Pinot Grigio,' I say firmly. I turn back to Charlie. 'Kit's using his half-day to run a few errands on Broad Street, so I asked him to meet me here after lunch and drive us back in my car. I figured if things went well, we'd have a drink, and if it was a total wipeout and we hated each other, we could drown our sorrows anyway. I'm sure he won't mind dropping you back home on the way.'

'Bless you. As if we'd hate each other. I think we're going to be friends for life.'

I think she's right. There is the teeny, insignificant little issue of her being Kit's boss, of course, but I don't see why that has to complicate things. I'm sure we'll be able to work things out.

There's nothing to worry about.

4

Charlie

The most important thing, when you're expecting guests for dinner, is not that the house is clean. It's not that the carpet has been hoovered and cat hair vacuumed from the sofa, a new toilet roll and clean hand towel placed in the downstairs lavatory, Lego picked up and stored in the toy box instead of its usual place on the landing ready to brutalize unsuspecting feet in the middle of the night, coats and backpacks hung up, counters cleared, the kitchen floor swept, dead flowers thrown out, old newspapers binned, rubbish emptied. Nor is it even the chopping of salads, the marinating of roasts, the breathing of wine or the elegant laying of the table. The most important thing, as any hostess knows, is that the lawn is mowed in neat, Wimbledon-straight rows.

I open the back door. It's already dusk. Kit and Mia will be here with their daughter in less than half an hour, and Rob is currently sitting astride his macho lawnmower, a miner's headlamp on his head so he can see where he's going in the dark.

'Rob!'

He doesn't even turn. In the kitchen a saucepan boils over and hot water hisses against the hob.

'*Rob!*'

'He's got his ear thingies in,' Milly says helpfully. 'Do you want me to go and get him?'

I hold her back. Rob's mower terrifies me at the best of times; the thought of Milly anywhere near its scything blades in the evening gloom makes me feel sick. 'It's OK, darling. I'll get him. Can you go and put the light on in the front porch so Emmy's mummy and daddy can see which house is ours?'

I rescue the potatoes and go back out to corral my husband. He does this every time we have people over: he decides now is the perfect time to fix the garage door or sort out the leaky seal on the washing machine in case I feel the need to throw in a load of delicates between the appetizers and the main course. I've never quite figured out whether it's because he's terrified I might ask him to help with some sort of emasculating domestic chore, such as loading the dishwasher, or if this is his way of getting revenge on me for daring to imply that his company is not the only social life I'll ever need.

Risking my toes, I stand in the path of the mower as Rob comes back up the meadow towards me, forcing him to either stop or run me over. I suspect it's a close-run decision.

He yanks out his earbuds. 'Get out of the way, Charlie. You'll ruin the line.'

'How can you even tell in the dark?' I ask reasonably. 'Come on, Rob. There's no time for this. They'll be here in twenty minutes and you haven't had a shower yet.'

'You're the one who said we needed to clean up the house.'

'The *house*. They're not going to be able to see the garden at this time of night, never mind the field at the end of it!'

'They're not going anywhere near our bedroom, either, but you still made the bed.'

I sigh. 'Can't you just leave this till tomorrow?'

'I'm halfway through it! I can't leave the bloody mower out here all night!'

I don't have the energy to argue further. I go back inside, churning with anger. Rob will count this as his 'share' of the work, as usual. His idea of a perfect weekend (assuming he isn't away diving) involves taking apart as many mechanical items as possible, cluttering up every available surface, ignoring any attempt by Milly to spend time with her daddy, and then expecting plaudits and thanks for the selfless sacrifice of his time and attention 'fixing up the house'. Meanwhile, I shop for the upcoming week, sort out the laundry, clean our home from top to bottom and finish my weekend more stressed and exhausted, if that were possible, than when it started.

Oh God. Will you listen to me? I've played this record so often, I'm boring *myself*. I think what I hate most about Rob's domestic work-to-rule is the point-scoring nag it turns me into.

In the spirit of conciliation, I quickly change into a chocolate knee-length knitted dress I know Rob likes and matching high-heeled suede boots which are uncomfortable but, according to my husband, irresistibly sexy.

'Is that what you're wearing?' Rob asks as he comes in from the garden trailing grass cuttings all over the clean kitchen floor.

'You said you loved this dress last time I wore it.'

'It's OK.'

I look down at my dress. 'What's wrong with it?'

'I told you, it's OK. It's just a bit boring, that's all.'

'Well, I don't have time to change now, unless you'd like me to answer the door in my knickers,' I say, hurt. 'Can you *please* go and get ready? They'll be here any minute.'

'Christ. Fine. I don't know what the fucking drama is. You're *his* boss, remember?'

'Pound,' Milly chirps from the other side of the breakfast bar as Rob stomps upstairs. 'You said a bad word, Daddy. You have to put a pound in the jar.'

We inaugurated the swear jar after Milly spent an entire weekend when she was two chanting the (admittedly sonorous) phrase 'bugger-bugger-bugger' over and over again. Bad words now mean a coin in the jar for her university education. At this rate, she'll be arriving at college in a gold-plated Mercedes.

There's still no sign of Rob when the doorbell rings at precisely seven thirty. I'd forgotten Americans are always punctual. I suppose it takes the guesswork out of trying to pitch your arrival between fashionably late and unforgivably rude, but I could have used the traditional English fifteen-minute grace period right now.

Milly springs towards the front door, throwing a quick glance over her shoulder for my nod of permission before opening it.

'My name is Amelia, but you can call me Milly,' she announces in her clear, bell-like voice, holding out her hand. 'I'm nearly seven, though Daddy always says more like seven-going-on-seventeen.'

'Milly!'

She looks indignant. 'What? He does.'

'I can believe it,' Kit says seriously, shaking her hand with commensurate formality. 'I'm Kit, and according to my wife, I'm forty-going-on-four.'

Milly giggles.

'Please, come in,' I urge, ushering them across the threshold and taking their coats.

On both the previous occasions I've met her, Mia has been rather formally dressed – some sort of dull ersatz Kate Middleton wrap dress for her naturalization ceremony, and a slightly dated skirt-and-heels outfit when we went out for lunch. But this evening, she looks simply stunning in a pair of wine-coloured hipster leather trousers, vertiginous silver sandals and a clingy black cashmere sweater. The look is much younger and funkier and sexier than anything I've seen before, and as Rob finally comes downstairs, I can practically see his tongue hanging out.

'You must be Emmy,' I say to the pretty little girl hanging back behind her mother. She's the image of Kit. 'Milly's been looking forward to meeting you.'

Emmy nods shyly.

'Rob Brady,' my husband says, almost tripping over himself in his hurry to get past me to Mia. 'You must be the writer. I've been really looking forward to meeting you.'

'Do you want to come upstairs to my room and see my Barbies?' Milly asks Emmy. 'I've got thirty-four! It would've been thirty-five but our cat Smellie was sick on one and Daddy said we had to throw her out. Mummy said we could just wash her and no one would ever know, like when she drops dinner on the floor, but Daddy said we'd end up with salamella and it'd all be Mummy's fault.'

'My daughter has a tendency to over-share,' I say faintly as the two little girls disappear upstairs.

'You think that's bad?' Mia sighs. 'Emmy's just started her own blog on the school magazine website. Every parental fuck-up is shared with the world.'

'Fair enough,' Kit says mildly. 'You share everything else.'

Mia grins at her husband. It makes a change to see Kit in a playful mood; at work he's so focused and intense, it's rare you catch him smiling.

'What can I get you to drink?' Rob asks Mia.

'I'm easy,' she says. 'What do you have?'

'Red wine, white, gin, vodka – or would you prefer a cocktail?'

'Dirty martini?'

'You got it.'

I'm quite sure Rob has no idea what a dirty martini *is* – a white wine spritzer is pushing the limits of his mixological expertise. But a gorgeous blonde in tight red leather trousers is saying the word *dirty* to him, which is all he needs to hear.

'You have olives, right?' Mia asks.

He yanks open the fridge, frantically sifting through the bottles and jars in the door. 'Yes! Olives!' he cries triumphantly, proffering some shrivelled black fossils that have been lurking there since our housewarming.

'I'll pass, thanks,' Mia says dryly.

I gently edge Rob out of the way, locate a jar of stuffed green olives I bought last week and tactfully place it on the counter alongside the bottles of vodka and dry vermouth. He makes a great song and dance about finding a proper martini glass, digging out our (virgin) cocktail shaker from the back of the cupboard and spearing the olives on little sticks, channelling his inner Tom Cruise as if auditioning for the remake of *Cocktail*. I watch his performance, thoroughly amused. Kit could be dying from dehydration and pass out on the floor, and I doubt Rob would notice.

While Rob entertains the troops, I plate up the grapefruit and pomegranate salad appetizer I copied from a recipe card in the *Daily Mail*. It's seriously intimidating cooking for Kit, given he once trained as a chef; hence the salad and roast lamb. The first doesn't require cooking at all, and the second gets better the longer you leave it in the oven. Even I can't go wrong.

'Can I do anything to help?' Kit asks.

'There really isn't much to do,' I say – just as the smoke alarm goes off.

I turn on the extractor fan and flap my hands beneath the alarm. 'Sorry about this. It goes off every time the oven reaches gas mark 2.'

'Let me make the salad dressing while you sort things out.'

'That would be wonderful,' I say gratefully.

'I'll need a few things. Balsamic, apple cider vinegar, sea salt . . .'

As I go over to the oven and turn the knob back a bit, he rattles off a list of ingredients, some of which I've only ever seen in a Nigella cookery book and are as likely to be found in my kitchen as Nigella herself. I gently point this out, but he forages through various cupboards undeterred, and I watch with interest as he locates a jug and adds a dash of this, a pinch of that, with the brisk assurance of a TV chef. I hope he's at least checking the sell-by dates.

'Taste,' he says, holding out a teaspoon of his dressing.

I open my mouth, feeling slightly awkward at the intimacy of the gesture. 'My God! That's amazing! How did you make *that* out of what I've got in my cupboards?'

'If I told you, I'd have to kill you.'

I laugh. I have to admit I was torn about inviting Kit and Mia to dinner; I've always made it a policy not to socialize with colleagues, and Rob was full of dire predictions about crossing lines and living to regret it. But picturesque though our particular corner of Oxfordshire is, it isn't exactly dense with interesting couples. Most of my female friends are married to men Rob can't stand, and the wives of his friends tend to bore me to sobs. Our 'best friends' are Gail and Dave; by which I mean Gail and Rob were at school together, and, unlike most of my female friends, he's neither attracted to nor intimidated by her. She's a desperately sweet woman, and even though we're not entirely on the same wavelength, I like her very much. Dave I'm less keen on, mainly because, like many insecure men, he boosts his fragile ego by putting his wife down. They're our go-to friends, slipped on like a pair of comfortable slippers. But every so often, a girl needs a pair of wicked fuck-me stilettos.

I like Kit a lot, and I think he and Rob will hit it off, even though they're very different. Rob isn't stupid – he has a degree in electronic engineering, after all, and works in a highly skilled IT job – but he knows virtually nothing about art, literature, philosophy or politics. However, Kit is smart enough not to intimidate Rob intellectually, and has enough of the man's man about him for Rob to feel comfortable. And clearly Rob has taken to Mia, which, if I want this friendship to go anywhere, is crucial. I glance out of the window. He's showing her his garden now, pointing towards the meadow with evident pride. I smile inwardly.

Clearly I was wrong. Mowing the lawn *was*, in fact, the most important preparation of the night.

'You have a fabulous yard,' Mia says when they come back inside. She bends to brush grass cuttings off her bare toes and almost gives Rob a heart attack as he gets an eyeful of her perfect rear. 'Those roses are amazing! I can't believe you've still got them through September. Ours were over by the end of July.'

I can tell I'm never going to hear the end of the *just as well I mowed the meadow* story. Even without those leather trousers, Mia would now have a friend for life.

There's definitely a connection between the two of them. Kit and I can both see it. Now in the sunniest of moods, Rob is the life and soul of the party at dinner, flirting and joking at the end of the table, and Mia is revelling in the attention, the two of them feeding off each other. She'll need to be a bit careful, though. She's smart and funny, but Rob doesn't always respond well to teasing. It's what comes from not having any brothers or sisters to toughen him up.

At one point, Milly knocks over a glass of water, splashing Mia. Instantly, Rob leans over with his napkin, brushing off invisible droplets from her cashmere-clad breasts and reaching beneath the table to dry her leather thighs.

'While you're down there,' Mia quips.

Kit raises a sardonic eyebrow at me.

'He doesn't mean anything by it,' I reassure him quietly. 'He's just a terrible flirt. Only child. Always likes to be the centre of attention.'

'You and Mia look very alike,' Kit says tactfully.

'Oh, his flirting doesn't bother me,' I laugh. 'With Rob, it's reflexive. I never take it personally.'

He's right, though: Mia and I do look very similar. I noticed that the first time I met her. If Rob has a type, we both hit all the same buttons. But my husband knows where the line in our marriage is drawn.

It's after eleven by the time they finally leave. For once, Rob hasn't been looking at his watch and dropping heavy-handed hints about having to get up in the morning. Clearly the evening has been a hit all round.

I discover just how much of a hit when we get upstairs. I haven't seen him this revved up for a long time. As soon as the door shuts, he pushes me onto the bed, tugs up my skirt and pulls down my knickers without even giving me time to unzip my boots. Within seconds he's inside me, thrusting no more than three or four times before coming with a hoarse groan.

'Jesus,' he pants as he rolls off me. 'I needed that.'

I pull down my dress. I'm not even wet, but this wasn't about me. After twenty years, I know my husband better than he knows himself.

It's the reason I invited Mia over, after all.

5

Mia

I'm so *not* a camping kind of girl. If the human race was meant to sleep on cold, hard ground, pee behind a bush and eat charred-slash-raw food, we wouldn't have come down from the trees, built restrooms and invented memory-foam mattresses and Viking stoves.

'Mia, could you *please* hold your end of the pole properly,' Kit says tetchily. 'I can't put this tent up by myself.'

Did I *mention* I'm not a camping kind of girl?

'It's raining,' I whine pitifully. 'My hands are cold.'

'They'll be a lot colder if we don't get this tent up before it gets dark. Stop complaining – you'll soon warm up once we've got the fire started. Now come on, tighten that guy rope and hook it round the tent peg.'

I just don't get it. What's the point of driving two hours and then spending another fifty minutes hiking through the New Forest weighed down with ten tons of gear, just so we can do exactly what we were going to do at home anyway – eat, drink and go to sleep – only in the freezing cold and without the benefit of cosy sofas and hot showers? How is this fun? Seriously, how?

In fairness, I'm not the diva this makes me sound. I've earned my stripes. I spent years on the road trying to snatch a few hours' sleep in the back of a Hercules transport plane, or bivouacking in a muddy field embedded with the US infantry. (Don't even get me started on the joys of Travelodge hotels.) But that was *work*. Cold feet, wet clothes and crap food are fair enough when you're being paid large sums of money to suffer. Call me crazy, but my idea of downtime and relaxation involves five-star hotels, fluffy towels, Michelin-rated dinners and plenty of sunshine. It does not include driving stupid iron tent pegs into rock-hard ground with fingers so cold I can no longer feel them. And now it's *really* starting to rain.

'Fuck!' I yelp as my hand slips and I whack my thumb with the mallet.

'Pound,' Emmy says happily.

'We do *not* pay for cursing in our family,' I retort, sucking on my bruised thumb. 'It's one of the few free pleasures left in life.'

'God, don't you love this?' Charlie says happily. 'Rob and I used to camp out all the time before Milly was born, but it's been years since we last did it.'

'I'll let you know when I've found the wine,' I mutter, opening the cooler and rummaging around with my good hand.

She drapes her arms round Rob and kisses him. 'D'you remember when we hiked up Scafell Pike and camped at the summit?' she sighs dreamily. 'That view was incredible. I don't think I've ever seen a sunrise like it.'

Corkscrew. Corkscrew. Please, someone, tell me we remembered to pack a corkscrew.

'It's a screw-top,' Kit says patiently, taking the bottle and opening it for me. 'For heaven's sake, Mia, go and sit down. You're no use to anyone. Emmy and I can finish putting up the tent.'

Not to be a princess – but sit down *where*, exactly?

'Hang on, let me get you a chair,' Rob volunteers. He extricates himself from Charlie's embrace and opens out what looks like a pink umbrella, which he flips into a flimsy but recognizable seat. 'This work for you?'

'Any chance you can do something about the weather while you're at it?'

He nods towards my husband. 'I think MacGyver has that in hand.'

Kit spreads a huge blue tarpaulin on the grass and ties parachute cord through the brass eyelets at the corners. We watch him throw the end of the cord over some nearby branches and pull the tarp up overhead, forming a makeshift but effective shelter, without feeling any need to get up and help him.

I move my chair beneath the tarp, out of the rain, and gingerly sit down in the pink canvas sling. It's like trusting your ass to a Venus flytrap. Rob opens out a second chair and parks it next to me.

'Any time you want to head out of here and find a proper bar, just let me know,' I grumble.

'I thought this weekend was your idea?'

'Are you *kidding* me?'

He grins. 'Yeah. I'm still waiting for the Sherpas to turn up with your feather bed.'

I pour two plastic cups of wine and hand him one. 'Kit

told me you'd all agreed to this trip, and I was the only holdout. He said I'd ruin it for Emmy and everyone if I didn't come.'

'Charlie said *you'd* all agreed to it, and *I* was the arsehole who'd ruin it if I said no.'

'I think we've been had.'

'Bastards. I vote they're on latrine duty.'

'Seconded.' I sip my wine and grimace. The last time I drank out of a plastic cup was at a fraternity kegger, circa 1995. 'I thought you were into this kind of survivalist thing?'

'Ten years ago, maybe. Charlie and I used to travel all over the world to dive sites. We spent most of our cash just getting there. We couldn't afford a hotel on top, so we used to rough it, camping wherever we could. On the beach, sometimes. Christ, that seems a long time ago.' He fishes a bug out of his wine and flicks it into the wet grass. 'When Milly came along, it just got too complicated. And to be honest, I was already sick of carting all our stuff around – the tents and the sleeping bags and all the rest of it. One of you always has to stay with the stuff so it isn't nicked, and you wake up stiff as a board in the morning. You can't even have a cup of tea without lighting a bloody fire. It just gets old.'

'Or we did.' I glance over at Charlie, cheerfully banging in tent pegs in the pouring rain. 'She seems to be having fun, at least.'

'Oh, she's in her element. She loves this sort of thing. Never happier than when there's a crowd,' he adds, a slight edge creeping into his voice.

'Not your scene?'

'I like socializing,' he says defensively. 'But you can't dive if you've been drinking. You could get the bends. I wish Charlie would remember that when she invites everyone home.'

I'm still trying to get a handle on Rob. Having met Charlie, who's gorgeous but serious and smart, even a little intense, I'd figured her husband would be an older version of Kit: thoughtful, measured, intellectual, maybe even a little dry. She'd told me they'd hooked up on a dive trip to Egypt, so I'd pictured him as a kind of Jacques Cousteau lookalike (my dad was a major Cousteau fan, watched every show he ever made). I was seriously taken aback when this dark-haired, smoky-eyed god appeared in the door of their house, barefoot and in jeans, all fallen angel sexiness and designer stubble. But more surprising, he's such a *jock*. In his case, it's all about diving, not football or track, but still. He's obviously not an idiot, and he can certainly flirt his way through dinner, but he doesn't do conversation. He doesn't read, not even news-papers or non-fiction; he's not interested in politics, ditto history, literature, religion, art. How in hell does Charlie keep the ball in play with a guy like that? To be honest, I'd have thought she'd have set the bar a little higher. But maybe if you look as hot as he does, you don't need conversation.

He's not really my type, though. I like a man who can stimulate the organ between my ears as well as the one between my legs. And I prefer the Viking look anyways: tall, muscular, blond and blue-eyed. Like Kit. Rob's slight and barely a half-inch taller than me. Plus, I may not know him that well yet, but I can already tell he's way too high-maintenance for my liking.

(And yes, I'm aware of the hypocrisy. But you can't have two captains steering the ship.)

'OK, the tents are done,' Kit says, ducking under the tarpaulin to join us. 'How about a fire?'

We clear a space, and Kit kneels down, burying a wedge of lint culled from the dryer at home into a small pile of kindling, and then striking a flint and bending to blow gently on the lint. It catches instantly; no wonder so many fires start in the laundry room. Once he's sure it's not going to go out, he arranges some heavy stones in a circle to protect the fire from the wind. Within minutes, it's blazing, and Kit stands and deftly angles the tarp so the smoke isn't trapped beneath it. I'm seriously impressed by his Action Man outdoorsy skills. Unlike Rob, he switches effortlessly between worlds. I love it. He seems so masculine and competent and in control: of both the environment and himself. I feel a primal, atavistic sense of pride. *This* is my man. This is *my* man.

Charlie pulls her damp hair back and twists it into a messy braid. 'Anyone hungry?' she asks, opening a backpack. 'I brought some bread and cheese and a few dips to keep the wolf from the door till supper.'

'It's going to be a while before dinner,' Kit adds. 'The fire needs to burn down first, so I can cook the steak over the embers rather than the flames.'

She passes several shrink-wrapped wedges of cheese to Rob. 'Could you open those while I slice some bread?'

'With what?'

Kit hands him his Swiss Army knife. 'Need some help?'

'I can manage,' Rob says huffily.

Charlie and I exchange hidden smiles as he pries open a blade. His masculine pride is clearly smarting with Kit around. He's evidently used to being the alpha male in the group, but out here in the woods, far away from plugs and appliances and all things mechanical, he's a little out of his depth.

'Oh Jesus!' he yells suddenly.

Charlie swings round. 'What's the matter?'

'The knife slipped! I cut my fucking hand!'

He sinks onto an upended log. I've never actually seen anyone turn green before, but Rob looks the colour of guacamole. He must have cut himself pretty deep. Crap. And we're at least an hour's hike away from civilization and the nearest hospital. 'Let me see,' Kit says briskly.

Rob holds out his hand. I brace myself for gaping flesh and the glisten of bone. I'm not a fan of blood and guts – I cover my eyes during the worst bits of *Grey's Anatomy* – but I learned early on to man up when I had to. You can't make a girlie scene in front of a bunch of US Marines and then expect to be taken seriously as a reporter.

I have to look twice to even *see* his cut. Seriously. He's nicked the ball of his thumb, barely drawing blood. A single Band-Aid would be an over-reaction.

'Oh Jesus,' he says again and passes out.

Kit catches him just before he pitches head first into the fire. 'Easy there, Rob,' he says calmly, lowering him to the wet grass. 'Come on, head between your knees. There you go, my friend. Couple of deep breaths. You'll be fine in a minute.'

'What's wrong with him?' I ask anxiously. 'Is he going to be OK?'

'He'll be fine,' Charlie says, sighing. 'He can't stand the sight of blood. Or needles. Faints every time he has to have an injection. It's nothing,' she calls across the glade, as Milly and Emmy stick their heads out of their tent to see what's going on. 'Daddy's fine, darling. He just cut his finger.'

'You should have seen him when I had a nosebleed,' Milly says with relish. 'He fainted right in the middle of the supermarket! Granny Barbie said he was nothing but a big girl's blouse,' she adds happily.

Kit helps Rob sit up. 'Better?'

'Yeah. Thanks.' He smiles shakily. He still looks pretty green about the gills. 'Sorry about that.'

'Forget it. No harm done.'

'Apart from to my pride. Swooning like a girl . . .'

I squeeze his shoulder sympathetically. 'Honestly, it's no big deal. It takes me two Xanax just to get on a plane, and I haven't gone on the subway in years. Claustrophobic. We all have something that freaks us out.'

'Yeah, well. At least a fear of flying is vaguely logical.'

'If logic came into it, we'd all be terrified of cigarettes,' I say.

'Frogs,' Charlie says, shuddering. 'Just a picture is enough to scare the shit out of me.'

'Clowns,' Kit puts in.

Rob holds up his hand. 'Look, I appreciate everyone trying to make me feel better, but can we just drop it? I could use a beer, actually, Kit,' he says, hauling himself to his feet and reclaiming his chair. 'And a plaster for my thumb. Don't want me fainting away on you again.'

He looks much better already. Charlie digs out a Band-Aid, Kit pops a beer from the cooler, and I circle a couple more flytrap chairs round the fire. The rain is beginning to ease off, and I hate to admit it, but I'm almost starting to enjoy myself as Kit throws four steaks on the grill. There's something about being outdoors makes you hungry, and by the time Kit hands me my enamel plate of steak, beans and a foil-wrapped baked potato, I'm starving.

'How long have you had this land?' I ask Charlie as we all kick back and relax round the leaping flames.

'About four years,' she says. 'My godmother left it to me. She was a character. Raging lesbian most of her life, but when she turned sixty-five, she suddenly developed a penchant for young men a third of her age. Had a series of 'little friends', as she called them, who danced to attention in the hope of being left a fortune.' She brushes a stray ember from her jeans and grinds it into the damp grass. 'Luckily for me, she was nobody's fool, and when she died, I got the lot. Well, when I say "the lot", what I mean is a house no one wanted to buy in Wales, six flea-bitten cats, and eleven acres here in the New Forest.'

Kit throws another log on the fire and props his feet on one of the warm stones encircling it. 'It's a beautiful place,' he says, tilting his head back and staring up at the darkening sky. The pale crescent of the moon is just visible above the trees.

Charlie smiles. 'A long way from St Alphonsus, right?'

'Imagine if Shelby saw the two of you here conspiring together,' I tease. 'It would totally chap her ass.'

'Mia,' Kit says warningly.

'We've only been out here once before, to mark the boundaries,' Charlie says, sensibly ignoring me. 'You can't build here, so I didn't really know what to do with the land. But this is really fun. I'm so glad you agreed to join us.'

I'm not entirely sure why we *did* agree, to be honest. Aside from my perfectly reasonable issues with the whole camping concept, we don't really know Charlie and Rob that well. And there's no getting around the tricky fact that, come Monday, she'll be Kit's boss again. But Kit and Rob seem to have found common ground, the two little girls have hit it off, and Charlie is the first woman I've met in a decade I can imagine still being friends with when we're ninety. So yes, camping in the woods may not be my idea of a good time, but I'd suck down a roasted cockroach if it meant making this work.

Sometime around nine, Milly and Emmy finally go to sleep curled up around each other like kittens in Charlie's tent. I check on them, then move my chair closer to the fire and pull a plaid picnic blanket over my lap. The temperature has dropped, and even with the fire, it's still chilly. I share the blanket with Rob when he moves next to me, grateful for the body warmth.

'Ready for a serious drink?' Kit asks, lining up four enamel mugs on a stone.

'What d'you call a serious drink?' Charlie asks.

'Do you trust me?'

'I wouldn't,' I warn.

'Do you trust me?' Kit repeats.

Charlie laughs. 'OK, fine,' she says, smiling. 'I trust you.'

Kit takes a supersized thermos out of his backpack. 'I made this before we left.'

'Does it have bourbon in it?' I demand.

'You won't taste it.'

'No way. You know I hate bourbon. I'm sticking to wine. You guys go ahead.'

Kit pours three mugs of his brew. 'It's called a Wit's End,' he says, handing them round. 'Three parts strong espresso, two parts Lexington Bourbon, one part Santa Teresa Araku rum, and equal parts Amaro and Aperol on the rocks.'

'I warned you,' I sigh.

Over the next hour, the three of them polish off the contents of the entire thermos, most of which seems to end in Charlie's mug. I know from bitter experience Kit's cocktails have a way of biting you in the ass, but what the hell.

She's enjoying herself. I get the feeling she doesn't let her hair down too often these days.

Kit shakes out a second picnic blanket and wraps it around Charlie's shoulders before settling into a chair next to her and putting his feet back up on the warm stones around the fire. I snuggle down beneath my own blanket, getting a good buzz myself from the wine and the warmth. Rob drapes his arm lightly around my shoulder, and I relax against him as a quiet camaraderie steals over the four of us. For a long time, none of us speak, as we just sit listening to the crackle of the fire. Eventually, I realize Charlie and Kit have fallen asleep, her head pillowed on his shoulder.

'Out for the count,' I murmur quietly.

'I'm not surprised, given she polished off most of that drink of his. She's going to pay tomorrow. You did well sticking to wine.'

'Hey, this isn't my first rodeo.'

His teeth glint in the dark when he smiles. 'I can't believe I fainted earlier,' he confesses. 'There's your husband doing his Bear Grylls number, and I'm passing out like a little girl.'

'Honestly, forget it. I thought you were kinda cute.'

'Really?'

'Would I lie to you?'

Weirdly, it *was* cute that he fainted. Up till then, he'd been acting the player, flirting and coming on to me all the time. Flattering, but the one-dimensional performance was beginning to get old. I'd started to wonder what in heaven Charlie saw in him besides the pretty face. But when he made a dick of himself, I got a glimpse of the real person behind the cartoon caricature. If he'd stop trying so hard, I could like him a whole deal more.

'You're kinda cute yourself,' Rob says, lightly dropping a kiss on the top of my head.

I'm suddenly aware of his thigh against mine, the weight of his arm around me. I shift slightly, unnerved by the unexpected pulse between my legs. He may not be my type on paper, but there's definitely something about him that gets to me. Maybe it's just seeing myself through his eyes.

Kit stirs and gently eases Charlie's head from his shoulder without waking her. 'Time for bed?'

'Let me take her,' Rob says, standing up. 'Too many Wit's Ends, I think.'

'She'll feel it in the morning,' I say ruefully.

Rob helps Charlie stagger sleepily towards their tent, where the girls have elected to spend the night. Kit unzips our own tent and we crawl in. He's already opened out our single sleeping bags and zipped them together, so we can snuggle.

'Just kick off your shoes,' he yawns. 'No need to get undressed.'

I slide into the double sleeping bag and let my hand drift down between his legs. 'You sure about that?'

He turns on his side so my hand just grazes his thigh. 'I'm exhausted.'

'Too exhausted to play?'

He puts his arm around me, pulling my head into the crook of his shoulder. 'Yes. What's got you so amorous?'

'I'm always amorous.'

'No,' Kit says. 'You're not.'

I let that pass.

6

Charlie

'I hope you're not going to make a fool of yourself again tonight,' Rob snaps as he presses his fob and unlocks the car.

I glare at him over the roof. 'Give me a break. None of us were sober last weekend.'

'No one else had to crawl into the tent because they couldn't *walk*. For God's sake, Charlie. Kit works for you. What were you *thinking*?'

'Do we have to hash it out again now?' I hiss furiously.

I help Milly into her booster seat and buckle her in. We drive to Kit and Mia's in silence. I'm not exactly proud of my behaviour last weekend. I wasn't as drunk as Rob makes out, but those Wit's End cocktails of Kit's were stronger than they tasted. I'd already had a couple of glasses of wine before he even opened that huge thermos, and I'll admit I ended up drinking most of the contents. But it's not like I was waving my knickers over my head and singing 'Hi Ho Silver Lining'. All I did was climb in my sleeping bag and fall asleep. The worst sin that can be laid at my door is snoring.

The only reason Rob's using it as a stick to beat me with now is because I wouldn't have sex with him this morning. I don't normally turn him down, even if I'm not in the mood; I know how important sex is to him, both for the physical release and as a way to connect emotionally. But I was stuck at the school till late last night trying to find a way to move us forward without alienating Shelby still further, and then I came home and had to spend another three hours at my computer putting out fires before climbing into bed at midnight. So when Rob woke me up at 5.45 this morning by jabbing me in the back with his erection, yes, I was less than receptive.

'Can you go and put something sexy on?' he whispered in my ear.

'*Rob.*'

His hand skimmed my bare flank. 'Come on. Milly will be up soon.'

'Rob, I'm *sleeping.*'

'You said that yesterday morning.'

'And I was *sleeping* yesterday morning.'

'It's been days,' Rob said testily. 'I'm getting blue balls here.'

I pulled my pillow over my head. '*Two* days, that's all.'

'How would you like it if I didn't talk to you for two days?'

'I'm talking to you, Rob. I'm just not *fucking* you right now.'

'Fucking is *how* men talk. You stop fucking me, it's like you're sending me to Coventry.'

I glared at him. 'I'm supposed to take that comment seriously?'

'Most women would be *pleased* their husbands still fancy them after twenty years,' Rob said pettishly.

'Oh, I'm thrilled, Rob. Really I am.'

'It's not like I don't get other offers.'

'I'm sure you do.' Angrily, I threw off the bedcovers, lay back naked and opened my legs. 'Fine. Come on, then. Let's *talk*.'

'That doesn't exactly put me in the mood, you know.'

'Welcome to my world.'

Rob got up and stalked downstairs. I waited a few moments, debating whether to try and get back to sleep or go down after him and apologize. If I didn't smooth things over, I'd pay for it the rest of the weekend. I was on the point of capitulating, but something stopped me.

Ten years ago, even five, I'd have said we had a great love life. Neither of us had had much experience with the opposite sex when we'd first met, so we'd learned our way around the bedroom together. Rob was never particularly adventurous or quite as experimental as I'd like – more vanilla than tutti frutti, he was too fastidious to venture far off the beaten track – and once we found what worked for us, he settled into his groove and lost interest in trying anything new. But for a long time our sex life was perfectly satisfying; he was competent and attentive, and it used to be a matter of pride to him that I fell asleep content.

Things changed when we had Milly. Not because of me; once we'd got past the first few sleepless months, my libido returned to normal. But Rob started to act as if I *owed* him sex. As he put it during one particularly brutal row when Milly was about two, he'd given me a child he hadn't particularly wanted, much as he loves her now, and he expected payback in the bedroom. Which to his mind meant sex at least every other day, and it wasn't enough for me to lie back and think of England: he expected me to dress up in corsets and suspenders and high heels, and take what he called 'an active role' – for which read 'do all the work'.

I might have had more sympathy for his point of view if I'd been deceitful and sprung Milly on him, but she was very much a planned baby. We'd discussed the issue of children a year into our relationship, before we moved in together. I'd told him clearly I wanted a baby; not right then, but one day. When we were both ready. If he hadn't agreed that's what he wanted too, I'd have ended things then, while we still had our lives in front of us.

But when it came to it, 'one day' never seemed to arrive. I passed my thirtieth birthday, and then my thirty-fifth, and Rob seemed no nearer to 'ready' than when he was twenty-three. Our discussions on the subject had become tense. I would never have contemplated an 'accident' as some thirty-something women in my position do, but nor was I prepared to wait until it was too late. Reluctantly, Rob finally agreed to try for a baby, and two weeks later, far sooner than either of us had ever expected, I was pregnant.

I don't mind bedroom role-play and dressing up now and again. Like most men, Rob's very visual, and sometimes it's a turn-on for me too; we had a lot of fun one long-ago summer with a certain schoolgirl outfit. But it's not something I want to do all the time. Especially now I'm no longer a hard-bodied twenty-something. And not when it becomes less about me and more about the cheap thrill of a pair of crotchless panties or a cut-out bra.

We park outside Kit and Mia's house and walk up the driveway in rigid silence. Milly trails behind us, pale and subdued.

'Are you going to be like this all night?' I mutter as I press the doorbell.

'At least I'm not a frigid bitch,' he spits back as Mia opens the front door.

I reel at the unexpected viciousness. We haven't been getting on particularly well lately, but I've never known him turn on me with such spite. My hands are actually trembling as I take my coat off.

I practically inhale my first gin and tonic and, ignoring Rob's heavy stare, accept a second as we chat around the kitchen island, my nerves still jangling. Kit opens a wonderful Shiraz with dinner (the most delicious chicken cacciatore I've ever tasted) and I can feel Rob's eyes drilling into me every time I raise my glass to my lips. We have Eiswein digestifs afterwards, and I don't know if it's mixing my drinks, or simply the sheer quantity I imbibe, but the evening passes in a bit of a blur, which, given the poisonous marital zingers Rob lobs my way at regular intervals, is quite frankly welcome.

At some point, and I'm a little fuzzy on the details, we end up sitting in the living room, and Kit hands me one of his lethal Wit's End cocktails as he riffs on the subject of rock bands, groups that have stood the test of time. By the time I finish my drink, which Kit replenishes twice, I'm struggling hard to concentrate. Something about letting it be. Letting what be . . . oh, the Beatles! Got it!

I start to drift. Pretty shirt Mia's wearing. Crimson satin. Makes her boobs look great. Crimson. I like that word. I like words for red. Scarlet, vermilion, cardinal. Crimson's my favourite, though. *Crimson crimson crimson*. Funny how words go all weird on you when you repeat them, isn't it?

I think I'll have another glass of wine. Wine, anyone?

Kit and Mia are still banging on about rock classics as I lurch back from the kitchen, spilling my drink on my hand. Rob's fast asleep, snoring on the sofa. I've never been into music trivia, but I curl up in an armchair and knock back the wine, doing my best to follow the conversation. My eyes are a bit tired, though. Might rest them. I like the music Kit's playing, whatever it is. Peaceful . . .

. . . Crap. Fell asleep. Don't think anyone noticed, though. I've dropped my glass. Luckily it was empty. I quite like Lady Gaga, actually . . .

You're a music fascist, Kit. Anyone ever tell you that?

. . . I don't need any help upstairs . . . oops. Sorry. Let me help you pick them up . . .

Oh! I like your spare bedroom, Mia! Pretty wallpaper. Pretty like yo-o-u.

'God, Charlie, you're totally wasted. Come on, then. Let's get you into bed.'

I sit down obediently and hold my arms up like a child so she can pull my T-shirt over my head. My long earrings catch on the fabric, and I sit there patiently as Mia untangles me. She's got such pretty skin. I press my cheek against her neck. 'Pretty,' I purr, inhaling the coconut scent of her hair. 'Soft and pretty.'

'Get off, you twit. Come on, we need to get your jeans off.'

Giggling, I flop back on the bed. Mia tugs off my jeans and my knickers go with them. She helps me under the covers and then leans over to tuck me in. I wrap my arms round her neck and pull her down towards me, kissing her full on the mouth. Oooh, I'd forgotten how soft a girl's mouth can be. I like kissing her. It makes me feel all warm and tingly inside. Bit dizzy, too.

'I think I love you,' I warble as Mia gently disengages herself and pulls the duvet up to my chin.

'You are so going to regret this in the morning,' Mia scolds, laughing.

I close my eyes as she turns out the light and shuts the door behind her. To be honest, I'm beginning to regret it already. My stomach is churning, and my head is beginning to throb. I open my eyes and the room spins. Oh God. Not the whirlies. Vomit rises in my throat and I force it back down.

It's no good. I'm going to be sick. I leap out of bed, clap my hand over my mouth and run naked down the hall towards the bathroom

Straight into Kit, who's just coming up the stairs.

My hangover has faded by Monday morning. The humiliation, however, has not.

This isn't some drunken escapade I can chalk up to experience and forget. Kit *works* for me. As Rob has furiously pointed out more times than I care to remember over the past forty-eight hours, my irresponsible behaviour has put my job on the line. And with it, our home, Milly's school fees, the whole damn house of cards.

I press the heels of my hands against my eyes, willing the tears not to come. I know Kit won't say a word to anyone at school, but how can I expect him to respect me as his boss after this? At the very least, getting so drunk that I vomit and run around naked has to call my judgement into question. I'm a forty-two-year-old professional educator, not a teenager on holiday in Ibiza.

And what about Mia? Kit isn't one to gossip, but Mia writes a blog, for heaven's sake. I like her, I really do, but of all the people to witness my fall from grace . . .

I jump at the sound of the staffroom door opening. Kit's usually the first into work; I made a point of arriving early this morning so I can catch him before everyone else comes in. Through the glass wall between my office and the staffroom, I watch him go to the coffee machine in the corner and start spooning grounds into a paper filter. I pull myself together and open my door. 'Do you have a moment, Kit?'

He doesn't look up. 'I'll be right with you.'

I feel sick again. This is going to be even worse than I thought.

'I'm just going to say this once,' Kit says sternly, the moment my office door shuts behind us. 'I want you to listen very carefully, because I am not going to repeat it.'

I nod meekly.

'If you and I are going to be friends, we're going to do this my way. We're already on the brink of an all-out war with Shelby, and things are only going to get worse. I had a very interesting conversation with one of the trustees in the village pub last night. It seems the Sisters are considering financially withdrawing from the school, which is going to pull the rug out from under all of us.'

'What?'

'Wait. I'll get to that in a minute. We need to sort this out first.' He chooses his words with care. 'Look. We can't afford to give Shelby *any* ammunition. If she hears *one* whisper about our friendship outside these four walls, my support for you becomes worthless. We'll both lose credibility. Any friendship between us is only going to work if we agree to build a Chinese wall between work and our personal lives.'

'You won't find any argument from me there.'

'Here, at work, you're the boss. You're not my friend. And as my boss, you have my loyalty, and I have your back. Our friendship has no bearing on how we work together.'

'I'm so sorry about Saturday night,' I say, shame-faced. 'I should never have—'

Kit holds up his hand. 'Stop right there.'

'But I—'

'What happens outside these four walls *stays outside them.*'

I start to protest. I screwed up on Saturday, seriously screwed up, and I need to apologize and get it off my chest.

His expression softens. 'Look, Charlie. I already know you're sorry. And I'm telling you, there's no need to be. If you really want to discuss what happened on Saturday, fine. Next time you come over to our house, we can thrash it out and then put the matter to bed. But what we're not going to do is talk about it *here.* If we cross that line now, no matter how good our intentions, it's going to be hard to go back.'

'It's as simple as that?'

'As simple as that.'

'And Saturday?'

He shrugs. 'You think I was shocked?'

'No, but . . .'

'Stop overthinking it. You had too much to drink, you got sick, and you stayed over. The streak down the hall?' His mouth twitches. 'Entertaining though that was, I'm not a monk. I have seen it all before. Although,' he smiles openly now, 'perhaps not *quite* as well tended.'

My employee knows I have a shaved pussy. My humiliation is complete.

'Charlie,' Kit says, suddenly serious again. 'I told you, what happens outside school has nothing to do with work. My respect and loyalty to you is absolute. I'm not going to think any less of you. Let it go. We've got far more important things we need to deal with.'

'OK,' I say faintly.

'Are we good?'

I nod.

He opens the door. 'Let me get us that coffee, and then we can talk about how to handle this next trustee meeting before Shelby and Monica come in.'

My throat is suddenly tight. Men like Kit are thin on the ground. It'll still take me a while to put Saturday night behind me, but I suddenly feel lighter, as if a weight has been lifted off my shoulders. A line has been drawn, and we both know where we stand. It's going to make everything else going forward so much easier. I'm lucky to have Kit as an employee, but even luckier to have him as a friend. If only Rob could have been a fraction as supportive.

Quickly I banish the comparison.

That's a very dangerous road to go down.

7

Mia

Every time I picture Kit's face after Charlie careened down our hallway stark naked and ran full tilt into him, I get the giggles. Poor man, I've never seen him look so shaken. I'm only sorry I missed it myself; I was in our bedroom brushing my teeth when he burst in and shut the door behind him, leaning against it as if pursued by the hounds of hell.

'My boss has a shaved pussy!' Kit said in shocked tones.

Calmly I spat out my toothpaste and rinsed my mouth. 'I don't know why you're having such a maidenly fit of the vapours. Is it the fact that she's got a shaved pussy, or the fact that you know?'

'Mia! This isn't funny!'

'Oh, come on. It *so* is.'

'You're not helping. I have to face Charlie in the office on Monday morning.'

'Which bit of her?' I said, starting to giggle.

Kit's mouth twitched. 'She must have a very steady hand. That landing strip was perfect.'

'Good to know your powers of observation don't suffer in a crisis.'

'Seriously, though, Mia,' Kit said after we'd both stopped laughing. 'How am I going to deal with this? I don't want Charlie avoiding me. We've got too much going on at the office right now. She and I need to present a united front – oh, for heaven's sake, stop sniggering. You know what I mean.'

'How united do you want your fronts to be?' I giggled. 'I'm sure I can find you a razor.'

'*Mia.*'

'Come on, sweetheart,' I said, sliding into bed. 'It's not the end of the world. Charlie streaked down the corridor and you caught a glimpse of her well-manicured pussy. So what? She also threw up in the trash can and tried to kiss me. Stop getting so freaked out about the naked. She got drunk, is all. Just tell her Monday that work is work, and home is home, and leave it at that. What happens in Vegas stays in Vegas.'

Which is precisely what Kit says he told her when he saw her at school yesterday. I've got to say, I'm quite pleased with myself for taking such a sophisticated view of events. Not every woman would be happy her husband was on intimate terms with his (gorgeous, sexy, whip-smart) boss to the extent that he could describe her southern topiary. But I am a Woman Secure In Her Man's Love. I take such intimacies in my stride.

Until I talk to Lois, who doesn't admire my European *savoir faire* as much as I expect.

'Are you *nuts*?' she exclaims when I retell the story.

I shift the phone to my other ear, since the one Lois just yelled into is still ringing. 'Come on. *I* thought it was kinda funny—'

'Splitting my sides. Are you seriously telling me this doesn't raise any red flags for you?'

'Why would it?'

'Well, let me think about that,' Lois says sarcastically. 'Another woman getting naked with your husband, nope, doesn't cross any lines, we're good.'

I laugh. 'It's not like that. I told you, we're friends. Charlie's his *boss*. No way does she think of him that way. She doesn't need Kit; her own husband's a total hottie. And before you start, Kit's not into her either, I'm sure of it.'

'Don't give me that. I saw the picture of you and her on Facebook. Which, by the way, you should take down if you don't want the world to know your husband's boss is your new BFF.'

Hmm. She has a point. I'm so used to sharing everything with the world on my blog, I forget sometimes that discretion is the better part of valour.

'What's that photo got to do with it, anyways?'

'The woman looks *exactly* like you.'

'So?'

'So if Kit is into *you*, and we must suppose he is, given the poor bastard married you, he's likely into *her*.'

Sure, this thought has occurred to me too, at least fleetingly, but I don't believe for one second Kit would ever act on it. Not just because I know he loves me. It's simply not in his nature to cheat. He's honourable to the point of obsession. He'll drive ten miles out of his way to go back to a shop if the clerk gives him a penny too much change. He's like one of those honourable English officers who insisted on going over the top of their trenches first to set an example to their men.

But in all the years we've known each other, Lois has never steered me wrong.

'I know you're just looking out for me,' I say finally. 'But seriously, you're reading way too much into this. If you knew Charlie and Rob, you'd get it. C'mon, you know how rare it is once you're married to meet another couple and both of you to like both of them. Obviously it would be simpler if Kit and Charlie didn't work together, but you were *my* boss once upon a time, and we've been friends fifteen years.'

'I never ran naked down your hallway, Mia.'

'She just got drunk. We all did. Honestly, doll, you're blowing this way out of proportion. Sex doesn't even come into it.'

'Mia, sex *always* comes into it,' Lois says briskly. 'You've gotten real close to this couple real fast. Don't tell me sex isn't a factor. Of *course* it is.'

For the second time, I pause. She's right, of course. Sex *is* a factor. Not in the way she's implying – we're not about to swap husbands or pile into bed for an orgy – but Rob has clearly got the hots for me, and yes, OK, we both get off on a little light flirting. It's a long time since a man flirted with me. Normally, if a guy tried, I'd shut him down; but within the safety net of our four-way friendship, it feels safe. Even Charlie's slightly risqué teasing is kind of fun; sure, she kissed me when she was drunk, but I don't think for a second she really wants to get me into bed. We're all pushing the envelope a little, and what's wrong with that? A bit of flirting never hurt anyone. It's what makes the world go round, right?

'I'm not trying to piss on your parade,' Lois says into the hiss of transatlantic static. 'I'm glad you're having a good time. But you need to be careful, Mia. I've seen where this kind of thing ends. You get too intense too soon and it'll all blow up in your face. You've known these people – what? Six weeks?'

'Kit's worked with Charlie for nearly a year . . .'

'That's not what I mean, and you know it. Six weeks and you're acting like you're back at high school. Friendship takes *years* to build. This sounds more like infatuation to me.'

I'm beginning to feel a little pissy. Lois may have been around the block a time or two, but she's never lived anywhere but Manhattan her whole life. She's got no idea what it's like to be transplanted halfway round the world without friends, family or access to a decent cup of coffee. Friendship doesn't *have* to take years to build. Time's irrelevant. You can chat to a woman at the school gates every day for years, but that won't make her your friend, just an acquaintance you've known a long time. Or you can meet someone you click with instantly and become friends for life. We all accept romances can bloom and flourish in a few weeks, so why not a friendship? I don't know why Lois is being so negative. Anyone would think she was jealous.

No. That was mean-spirited; I take it back. Lois has always looked out for me. She just doesn't know Charlie and Rob, is all. She has no idea how lonely I've been, or how good it feels to look forward to weekends instead of wondering how to fill them.

I wind up the call and slide my phone into my back pocket. Lois is my oldest and dearest friend, but she's way off base this time.

Infatuation. The word still chaps my ass a week later. It's not like I doodle Charlie's name on my notebook, for God's sake. If my diary hadn't been such a sad wasteland before I met her, maybe she and Rob wouldn't be filling up so much of it now; but so what if they are? After all, they've lived in this village since year zero, they must know half the county, and *their* schedule is just as filled with *us*. Damn Lois. She's gotten me totally overthinking this.

On cue, the back door opens. 'We're here!' Charlie calls.

I go through into the kitchen, calling up the stairs for Kit on the way.

'We made mince pies!' Milly announces, thrusting a plastic container at me. Her freckled nose is still dusted with confectioner's sugar.

I lift the lid and peer into the box. 'Lovely!'

Charlie laughs as she unwinds a long cinnamon-coloured scarf and hangs it on a coat peg. 'You hate them, don't you?'

'Invention of the devil,' I agree. 'But Kit and Emmy love them.'

'They don't have real mince in them, you know,' Milly confides. 'They're just *called* that.'

Rob hands over a couple bottles of Sauvignon Blanc. 'These more to your liking?'

'Alcohol is a Christmas tradition I'm more than happy to uphold.'

'Love your dress, by the way,' Charlie says as the girls scamper away. 'Very festive.'

I glance down at the short red tunic I'm wearing over black pantyhose and high-heeled black suede boots. 'Boden. You converted me.'

'It'll be colour-block shift dresses and embroidered boho tops soon,' Charlie teases.

She's looking gorgeous herself, as usual, in an ankle-length navy tiered chiffon skirt and silvery cashmere turtleneck.

Rob's in a light grey shirt and jeans. 'Look at you, all matchy-matchy,' I smile, putting the wine in the fridge. 'You could be in a Christmas card photo.'

Rob glowers and I look to Charlie for enlightenment.

'We just got back from the studio,' she explains. 'He hates having his picture taken. I only did it for your mother,' she adds tightly to him. 'You know we'd never hear the end of it if we hadn't.'

'Kit thinks photography steals your soul,' I sigh. 'Didn't even smile in our wedding pictures. I think I've managed to get about three of him during our entire marriage. When I'm widowed, I'll have no proof he ever existed.'

My husband appears just in time to pour a round of eggnogs as the three of us pull stools up to the kitchen island. Rob takes a wary sip of his drink. 'What the hell *is* this stuff? It tastes like an alcoholic milkshake.'

'You've never had eggnog?'

'Eggs, milk, cream, sugar, nutmeg and brandy,' Kit lists off. 'When Mia makes it, a *lot* of brandy. You have been warned.'

The evening that follows is a riotous affair. The school semester ended this afternoon, so Kit and Charlie are buzzed. Emmy and Milly eat their pizza – OK, I know it's junk food, but neither of them was ever going to go for Kit's seafood *pot-au-feu* – in the playroom upstairs, meaning the four of us are free to get both tipsy and rowdy in the dining room without having to worry about keeping it down for the kids.

'We've run out of eggnog!' Rob wails as we clear the table and troop into the kitchen. 'I was just getting to like the stuff!'

'It's the Eggnog Riot all over again,' I giggle.

'I know I'm going to regret asking,' Charlie sighs. 'Eggnog Riot?'

'OK, so back in, like, 1820, a bunch of recruits smuggled whiskey into the barracks at the US Military Academy to make eggnog for their Christmas party. They got totally wasted, and about twenty of them ended up being court-martialled for smashing up the place. It's known as the Eggnog Riot.'

Rob opens the fridge and reaches for the wine. 'I don't blame them. Well, we're just going to have to slum it with the Sauvignon.'

None of us can walk a straight line by the time we finish loading the dishwasher and take the party through to the sitting room. I kill the overhead lamp and light half a dozen thick candles scattered around the room, then pull off my boots and curl my feet under me on the sofa next to Rob. Kit and Charlie take the other sofa, kitty-corner from us.

'Truth or dare?' Charlie says suddenly.

Rob sits up. 'Seriously? I haven't played this since I was at uni.'

'YOLO,' I tease.

'We need a bottle,' Charlie says, getting up to fetch an empty one from the dining room. She puts it on the coffee table between us and gives it a spin. 'OK, Kit, it's pointing at you. Truth or dare?'

He hesitates. I can see him weighing the options: his professional relationship with Charlie versus their friendship. How far is he willing to test the Chinese wall the two of them have built?

'Go on,' I prompt. 'I think we've all proved you're amongst friends.'

'OK, fine,' Kit says, succumbing. 'Dare.'

'Do a headstand,' she says.

'Christ. After all that wine?' Kit heaves himself to his feet. 'If I throw up, it's on you. And I mean that literally.'

To my delight, he grabs a pillow and stands on his head, bracing his feet against the bookcase as if he's done this a thousand times before. Go Kit! Who knew he had it in him? Clearly it just takes a few eggnogs to get that Brit poker out his ass. He doesn't even barf; the only casualty is a heinous purple china cat his mom gave him, and which I'm super happy to see broken into a hundred pieces.

'Your spin,' Charlie tells him once he's the right way up again.

Kit spins. This time the bottle ends up pointing towards me.

'Truth,' I say.

'Coward,' Charlie mocks. 'OK. Have you ever had sex with a woman?'

'Yes,' I say defiantly. 'My spin.'

Rob puts his hand on the bottle to still it. 'Hold on. We want details!'

'I was twenty-one, it was at college, I'd been to a party with an ex-boyfriend and his new girlfriend, and we all ended up in bed together,' I say. 'No biggie. My spin.'

Kit smirks knowingly at me. I've told him about the night in question, of course, and he knows the truth is I was actually passed out when my ex and his girlfriend got jiggy with it on the bed next to me. I didn't even kiss her. I silently will Kit to keep his mouth shut, not wanting to lose face in front of Charlie, who is evidently way cooler and more experienced than me.

It's my turn to lean forward and spin. This time, the bottle ends up pointing towards Charlie. 'Dare,' she says.

Rob sets down his glass on the table. 'I dare you to take Mia's tights off with your teeth.'

His eyes meet mine. They gleam, and I feel a frisson of excitement.

'You'd better not rip them,' I tell Charlie, standing up. The room sways slightly, and I have to hold on to the edge of the bookcase for balance.

'Hands behind your back,' Kit instructs as she kneels down in front of me. 'No cheating.'

'Hold up your dress,' Charlie says, her voice muffled by my tunic. 'I can't see what I'm doing.'

Rob and Kit snort with laughter as I comply. It takes her several attempts to catch the waistband of my pantyhose between her teeth, and I'm almost helpless with giggles by the time she manages to get them halfway down my thighs.

'Jesus, this is harder than it looks,' she pants, stopping to catch her breath. 'Thank God you weren't wearing jeans.'

I suddenly realize she's taken my panties along with the pantyhose by mistake. I don't want to be all prudish and freak out, so I lower my dress to preserve my decency and say nothing.

'Nice job,' Kit manages through his laughter. 'Your spin, Charlie.'

Charlie leans in close to me as she stands up again. 'You taste good,' she murmurs in my ear. 'Tangy.'

I freeze in shock. *Maybe not such a mistake after all.*

I take my place back on the sofa beside Rob, a nervous/excited tingle tickling my insides. I feel both aroused and exposed by my lack of underwear, even though I don't think anyone noticed, except Kit. He shoots me a hot look across the room, and I squirm lustfully. I can't wait to get him upstairs after Rob and Charlie have gone.

'It's your shout, Kit,' Rob says.

'Dare.'

Charlie smiles wickedly. 'I dare you,' she says, 'to go down on Mia.'

'Well?' Kit asks me.

8

Charlie

I'm not sure if Mia will agree to it. She may have travelled all over the world, and she can certainly talk the talk, but I don't think she's nearly as hard-boiled and streetwise as she'd have us believe.

Let's see if she can walk the walk.

'I dare you,' I challenge Kit, 'to go down on Mia.'

She looks taken aback and then quickly masks it with a nervous smile.

Kit raises an eyebrow at his wife. 'Well?'

She shrugs. 'It's your dare. How can I say no?'

'That makes a change,' Kit grins.

Until tonight, I'd assumed Kit would be the stumbling block to any colouring outside the lines, but I've changed my mind. Mia may have broadcast to millions on live television, but that doesn't make you a sophisticate. The innocence beneath the world-weary mask is part of her charm. With Kit, however, still waters run deep. I realize with a twinge of anticipation that this evening is only just beginning.

Kit kneels on the floor in front of Mia and gently pushes her bare legs apart on the sofa. 'Wriggle forward a little,' he murmurs.

Rob watches avidly. He can't take his eyes off Mia. I know he's had the hots for her since the day he met her; he couldn't have been more obvious if he'd unzipped his pants and got his dick out on the table. Physically, she's absolutely his type: long blonde hair, big boobs, and a style of dressing that's just this side of slutty, all high heels and short skirts and clingy T-shirts. My husband doesn't like anything being left to the imagination. If he had his way, I'd never step foot outside the door in anything but stripper heels and wipe-down PVC.

After twenty years, I know my husband. I understand what he wants. I haven't set Mia up. I've simply opened the door and waited to see if she'll step through.

The mood in the room has changed, the flirtatious banter giving way to a darker erotic charge. In the dim light of the flickering candles, I move around the coffee table, crouching down beside the sofa as Kit hitches up Mia's skirt. Her eyes are closed, her head tilted back against the sofa pillows; I don't know if it's from pleasure or embarrassment. I reach past Kit and slide my finger inside her. I don't think she even realizes it's me.

I put my finger in Rob's mouth so he can taste her. There's more than one way to keep a dog on the porch.

With a low groan, Rob pulls me onto his lap. He's rock-hard beneath his jeans. He pushes up my sweater, roughly scooping my breasts out of my bra. My head is inches away from Mia's. I lean across and kiss her, slipping my tongue between her lips as Kit eats her out beside me. She tastes of coffee and bourbon.

Rob shoves up my skirt and I break the kiss with Mia to tug my sweater off. I'm not wearing knickers; the elastic digs into the scar from my Caesarean, and anyway, Rob prefers it if I don't. Kit briefly catches my eye as he stands to take off his trousers. He has nice legs: lean and muscular. I glance away quickly before Rob notices me looking.

Kit sits down and lifts Mia onto his lap. She scissors her legs around his waist, taking him inside her as he pulls up her dress and yanks down her bra. I lean over and cup one breast with my hand, thumbing her nipples. She arches off the sofa, her eyes still closed as she cries out with pleasure; I have no idea if she even knows Rob and I are here. I want to kiss her again, but Rob is unzipping his jeans and thrusting inside me, his gaze locked on the live porn next to him as he grinds his hips against me.

My own orgasm gathers, a sweet tightening deep inside me. I grip Rob's shoulders, throwing my head back, riding him harder. Beside me, Mia moans loudly, her breath coming in short, sharp pants. Kit puts his hand gently across her mouth to quiet her. She writhes beneath him, shuddering as her orgasm breaks. Kit stands her up and bends her forward over the sofa. He thrusts his hand inside her, and she shrieks with little animal cries.

'Shhhh,' Kit laughs, his voice low. 'Mia, shhhh.'

His bare ass is inches away from me, his hard thighs tensing as he takes his wife again from behind. *He must work out*, I realize. He's got a great body. Much fitter than I'd have guessed.

Rob can't hold back any longer. The feel of him swelling inside me as he comes finally sends me spiralling into my own orgasm as Kit stiffens in climax next to me. The four of us collapse in a heap of naked skin and tangled clothing, our breathing slowly returning to normal.

Kit is the first to recover, easing his way free from the pile of sweating bodies. I hear the jangle of his belt buckle behind me, the sound of a zip.

'Can I get anyone a drink? More wine? Water?'

Mia holds out her hand and Kit helps her to her feet. She pulls down her tunic dress, smoothing it almost shyly over her bare thighs.

I slide sideways off Rob's lap. 'Coffee would be great,' I tell Kit as if we've just finished a nice game of Scrabble.

'I'll be back in a minute,' Mia says, disappearing with him.

Rob closes his eyes and rests his head against the sofa, tucking himself back in his jeans with one hand. 'Christ. *Christ.*'

'Happy?'

'What do you think?'

I pick up my sweater and bra from the floor and straighten my skirt. 'Then don't screw it up this time,' I say lightly, dropping a bland kiss on his forehead.

He likes to think of himself as a player now, but Rob didn't really discover women – or his effect on them – until the summer he travelled to Egypt for his first holiday without his parents. After his brother's death when Rob was thirteen, his over-protective parents had kept him on a tight rein. He hadn't even been allowed to get the bus to school; they'd insisted on dropping their precious remaining child off in person. He didn't learn to drive until he went to university, where he studied electronic engineering less than thirty miles from his parents' home, and commuted rather than living on campus. There had been one or two innocent romances, but nothing serious. How could there be when he was still living with his mother?

So he'd finally made the break a year after he graduated, quietly prompted by his father, who realized their son needed to live his own life or his brother's death would turn into a double tragedy.

Pretty girls fluttered around him in Egypt, attracted by his good looks, easy charm and the endearing self-deprecation born of his inexperience. I deliberately held back and played it cool. Gratified but slightly overwhelmed by all the female attention, Rob felt safe with me. I didn't chase or smother him, and, most importantly, never objected when he flirted with other women from the safety of our relationship. It didn't bother me. I knew I was the one he needed. With me, he could have his cake and eat it.

I realized Rob had a high libido, even if he hadn't yet worked it out. I didn't want him ever to feel he'd missed out by settling down so young. I trusted him not to have an affair, but I didn't want to tempt fate.

And the dive scene was like dangling a carrot right under his nose. There's a lot of adrenaline flowing when divers get together, a lot of sexual energy floating around, as there tends to be with dangerous sports. After a dive, we'd often smoke joints together, drop a few Es. Sometimes we'd end up back in someone's hotel room, or in their tent, and there'd be some fooling around. A couple would disappear for half an hour and come back flushed and rumpled. Sometimes they didn't disappear. Sometimes they stayed right there while the rest of us carried on drinking and smoking. Sometimes we watched. Sometimes we screwed our own brains out next to them, aroused by the sound and smell and sight of others having sex. And occasionally, just occasionally, those after-dive parties were a little more adventurous than that.

As a teenager, I'd experimented sexually. I was definitely attracted to boys: the raw sweat of them, the hardness of their bodies, the thrust of their strong cocks inside me. But I loved a girl's soft skin, too, the curve of her breast, the slickness between her thighs. I didn't believe in labels. It wasn't as simple as being straight or gay. Why does one person become your friend and not another? Sometimes you meet someone and you just click. For me, it was no different when it came to sex. But I knew I didn't want the alternative lifestyle forever. Ultimately, I wanted a conventional family life: children and a husband. But sometimes I wanted women too.

The chemistry with Rob was stronger than anything I'd felt for anyone before, man or woman. I fell in love with him and was happy to commit to him. But if we met the right woman at one of those parties – if we both felt the same attraction for her, if she was happy to go to bed with both of us, not just Rob, and if it was clear from the beginning that it would never be anything serious, never anything but fun – then yes. We went to bed with her. We had just one rule: whatever – and *who*ever – we did, we did together.

'It's not about the other women,' Rob said. 'I don't want them if you're not there. It's about *us*.'

One rule.

His affair was opportunistic rather than premeditated, which somehow made it even worse – the fact that he could carelessly *fall* into it as if he'd tripped and a woman had somehow landed on his prick. It was the year I had Milly. We'd planned a fortnight in Silfra in Iceland with a group of diving junkies, an incredible (if slightly chilly) dive in the only place you can swim between two continents, North America and Europe. From above it looks like a regular lake, but once you're submerged in the water, you're hovering in the gap where two tectonic plates meet. The chasm leads into a cave with off-the-chart visibility. It had taken months to put the trip together as we'd had to coordinate the schedules of a dozen people, and by the time we'd managed it, I was pregnant. Milly was only four months old when we were due to go, too young to leave with a babysitter, and anyway, I was still breastfeeding. We'd been looking forward to diving Silfra for years; there was no reason both of us should be disappointed.

So Rob went alone. But he didn't stay that way. He spent the fortnight screwing a woman I knew slightly and had never taken to; she took great delight in phoning me two days after they got back to 'apologize' for sleeping with my husband, hoping we could 'still be friends'.

His betrayal was lacerating. I could hardly bear to look at him. If it had happened four months before Milly was born, rather than four months after, I'd have left him. For years I'd given him far more leeway than most women would, facilitating his fantasies, sharing them with him. I'd let him have other women guilt-free, with none of the deceit and misery of an affair. And it still hadn't been enough.

'It was just *sex*,' he kept saying. 'It didn't *mean* anything. You didn't mind when I had sex with Hannah or Karyn—'

'I was *there* when you had sex with Hannah and Karyn! It was about *us*, something we *shared*. We agreed, Rob. We agreed this would never happen unless we both wanted it, unless we were *both* part of it.'

'I asked you to come with me,' Rob said defensively. '*You* were the one who insisted on staying with the baby. What was I supposed to do, live like a monk the entire fortnight?'

'Jesus, Rob! You couldn't just jerk off for two weeks?'

'Look, I'm sorry I didn't ask *permission*—'

'It's not about permission! You said you'd never *want* to sleep with another woman if I wasn't there. You told me it was seeing the two of us together that made it exciting. So how does screwing around behind my back fit into this, Rob? How was that about *us*?'

Our relationship barely survived. It wasn't just the affair; Rob simply refused to see he'd done anything wrong. All those years I'd been telling myself that sharing another woman with me was what excited him, when really he was just another unfaithful prick who couldn't keep it in his trousers. He only wanted me there to legitimize his affairs so he didn't have to feel guilty. If I'd offered him a truly open marriage and told him to go off and sleep with any woman he wanted, no questions asked, he'd have bitten my hand off.

After that, I closed the door on threesomes. *Not again, not ever.* I was done with enabling him to cheat on me quite literally under my nose. If I *was* the only one he loved, as he kept saying, if I was really the only woman he wanted, then going forward I'd be the only woman he had.

And he could prove his commitment to me the old-fashioned way: with a ring.

Marriage had never been important to me; I didn't think you needed a piece of paper to prove you loved each other.

To my mind, you couldn't be more committed than by having a child together. But Rob was raised a Catholic and had always believed in marriage. It really meant something to him, so of course he'd always laughed it off as irrelevant; even though we had Milly, I knew he still considered himself technically single. Which is why I now offered him a straightforward choice: marry me or move out. Not because marriage meant anything to me, but because it meant everything to him.

Our wedding marked a turning point for both of us. He'd been given his chance to walk away and had chosen not to. He'd chosen to commit to me, and only me, rather than lose me, and that was enough. I made the decision to trust him, refusing to let his affair define us. We put our relationship back together so well you could scarcely see the cracks.

Except in the bedroom.

The chemistry between us was as strong as ever, but it had become darker. A new undercurrent of tension existed between us. Rob never openly charged me with going back on a deal, but I knew that, deep down, it was how he felt. He'd only agreed to a child because no other woman would have let him have his cake and eat it the way I had. And now I'd put him on the same diet as every other married man. His response was to become less attentive in bed. More demanding. He expected me to dress up in sexy lingerie and slutty shoes, to do all the running, to be available for sex whenever he wanted whether I was in the mood or not. And I didn't protest because, in fairness, he was right. I *had* gone back on our understanding. God knows, I'd certainly had reason to, but that didn't change the facts.

I've tried to give him what he wants. But no matter what

I do, it never seems to be *quite* enough. If we have sex every day, he wants sex *and* dressing up. If we have sex and dressing up, he wants it twice on Sundays. Over the last few years, the tension has slowly seeped into other areas of our marriage. Increasingly we bicker and fight over everything and nothing. The more we argue, the less I feel like making love at all; the less we have sex, the more we row. Our marriage has become a Mexican stand-off, each of us waiting for the other to blink first.

I'm so *tired* of the fighting. It's not like I don't miss our more adventurous sex too. It's been seven years since I slept with another woman. Rob's affair forced me to be the one to police our relationship, but God knows, it's not out of choice.

Maybe it's time, I've found myself thinking more than once over the past year. *I trust him now, don't I? He's learned his lesson. It could work.*

But it has to be fair this time. And three isn't a fair number.

Perhaps four is.

9

Mia

I think I know what Lois is going to say.

'Jesus fucking H. Christ! Are you fucking *kidding* me?'

Yes. That pretty much covers it.

'Speak up,' I grumble. 'A few people in New Jersey didn't hear you.'

'For God's sake, Mia!' Lois exclaims. 'You dump an orgy on me and you expect me to pat you on the head and say well done?'

'It wasn't an orgy! We just had sex in the same room.'

'*Seriously?* Did you just *hear* yourself?'

I wince. I know exactly how it sounds; which is why I just shut the door of my study, even though I'm alone in the house. 'Look, I know how it seems, but it wasn't like that.'

'Were you all naked together?' Lois demands.

'Yes, but—'

'Was there touching?'

'We were next to each other on the sofa, if that's what you mean—'

Lois sighs impatiently. 'You know what I mean. Did you have sex with each other?'

'No! Not really . . .'

'Not *really*?'

I chew my thumbnail. Technically we didn't have sex with each other. Not actual, all-the-way sex. But that's splitting hairs. It was impossible to separate one act, one person from another, which is precisely why it was so erotic. Kit was the one inside of me, but Charlie was kissing me, and it was Rob's eyes locked on mine when I came.

'Oh, never mind,' Lois snaps. 'I don't know how ploughed you were, Mia, but you must've been out of your mind. What in hell's gotten into you lately?'

'It just happened,' I mumble, flushing. 'It was a one-off. You don't have to make such a big deal about it.'

'Grow up,' she says tersely. 'You're playing with fire and you know it. You've got a great marriage; why would you mess with it? And don't give me that "one-off" bullshit. These people are *grooming* you.'

'*Grooming* me? For God's sake, Lois. I'm not twelve!'

'Yeah? And you're way too old for "it just happened". What is this, high school? I'm telling you, Mia, this friendship is toxic. You think this is the first time Rob and Charlie have done this?'

'I wasn't calling to ask for permission,' I say tartly.

'Good. You wouldn't have gotten it.'

She hangs up. I sit at my desk and stare into space, more discomfited than I want to admit. I should never have told Lois; all she's done is stir up my own nagging doubts. On paper, there's nothing wrong with what happened with

Rob and Charlie last Friday; all four of us are consenting adults, and we went into it together, with our eyes open. Nobody went behind anyone's back, and anyway, we only had sex with our own spouses; there was no wife-swapping or swinging or whatever it's called these days. And I enjoyed it. I've been happily married to the same man for nearly ten years, and I have a seven-year-old child. To have my sex life take this kind of upswing when I'm nearly forty is unexpected, to say the least, and it's exciting for that reason alone. But no matter how many times I rationalize it, I still can't help feeling uneasy. *Am* I risking my marriage? Or does the fact that we even did it mean we're already in trouble?

I spend the rest of the day brooding about it, and when Kit comes home I raise the subject as soon as we're alone in bed.

'D'you think Rob and Charlie have had sex in front of other couples?' I ask baldly.

He shrugs. 'Who knows?'

'But you must have thought about it?'

'Why does it matter?'

Because I want us to be special. 'I don't know. Come on, what do you think? Did it seem to you like they'd done it before?'

'I wasn't really thinking about their sexual history at the time.'

'What *were* you thinking about?' I ask curiously.

He sighs. 'I wasn't.'

'But you must've been thinking *some*thing,' I press. 'Did you want it to happen?'

'I wouldn't have let it if I didn't.'

'No, I mean, did you fantasize about it? Did you ever think it might be on the cards?'

Kit takes off his glasses and puts them on his nightstand. 'Mia, do we have to talk about this right now? I've had a bloody knackering day with the trustees. Charlie and I are in the middle of a *coup d'état* and I've got more than enough on my plate without worrying about this.'

'Did she say anything about what happened?'

'Of course not,' he says sharply. 'We don't talk about anything personal at work, I've told you that.'

'But wasn't it weird, seeing her again after Friday?'

'No.'

'Come on. You can't do what we did and then waltz into the office and start talking about work like nothing happened,' I argue.

'Mia, that's *exactly* what we do.'

'I don't get why you won't talk about it,' I complain tetchily into the darkness. 'It's like you just want to sweep it under the rug. Are you sorry we did it?'

'I wasn't, but I'm beginning to change my mind.'

'We haven't even *discussed* it. Don't you think we should?'

Kit sighs heavily, then sits up, turns on the bedside light and puts his glasses back on. 'I can see I'm not going to get any sleep till we thrash this out. OK, Mia, have at it. What's on your mind?'

'I just think we should talk about something this big. Don't you?'

'Not really, no.'

'Why not?'

'Because the minute you start analysing it and taking it apart, you're going to kill it. Just leave it alone, Mia, and wait and see where it leads.'

Instantly I zero in. 'So you think it's going to lead somewhere, then?'

'Not if you keep worrying at it like a dog with a bone.'

'Please, Kit. *Talk* to me.'

He pulls me against him and gently strokes my hair. 'What is it, sweetheart? What's upsetting you? Are you regretting it? Is that what this is all about?'

'Do you think our marriage is in trouble?' I blurt out suddenly.

He laughs in surprise. 'Mia! Why on earth would I think that?'

'You don't think, if your marriage is strong, you shouldn't need other people?' I mumble.

'This is what you're so worried about?' He turns me in his arms so that he can see my face. 'Mia, our marriage is perfectly fine. We don't *need* anyone else, as you put it. That's not the point. What happened on Friday has nothing to do with how much we love each other.'

'So you think it's – you know – healthy? To experiment a bit?'

'I think it's no one's business but ours,' he says softly. 'And I think you need to stop listening to Lois. As long as you and I are both happy and open and honest about how we feel, then yes. Stop overthinking things, Mia.'

I pleat the sheet with my fingers. 'And you don't think it means our sex life is boring?'

'No, I don't think it means our sex life is boring,' he smiles. 'I think it means we've been married for nearly ten years, and maybe we've both got a bit stuck in a rut, but that's all. And before you go into a tailspin,' he adds dryly as my head jerks up, 'I think we have a *great* sex life. I love making love to you. There's no question of me wanting or needing anyone else. I'll be honest: Friday night was a huge turn-on for me. But that was mainly because it turned *you* on.'

'Lois thinks you must fancy Charlie.'

'I'm sure Lois does.' He stills my nervous fingers. 'Mia, Charlie is an attractive woman. And it was hot watching her kiss you, but that's because of how *you* reacted.'

My body tingles. Charlie's the first woman I've ever kissed. For the last three days, I've been replaying it in my head. I've never been remotely attracted to women before, just as I've never been attracted to red-headed men. No offence to the gingers out there: aesthetically, I can see Damian Lewis and Prince Harry are good-looking. They just don't do it for me. And neither did women before Friday night.

They still don't. The thought of kissing Lois, for example, gives me hives, and she's a gorgeous, smart woman and I love her to death. But the idea of kissing her . . . of going down on her . . . *no*. Really. *No*.

And yet when I think about Charlie, my insides turn to liquid.

'It's OK, Mia,' Kit says gently. 'Stop trying to label things and put them in boxes. Friday night turned you on, and that's OK. It doesn't mean our marriage is in trouble or you've turned into a lesbian. It was what it was. Stop trying to read more into it.'

The knot of tension in my belly eases. It's like receiving absolution. I trust Kit implicitly. More pertinently, I trust his judgement. Ever since we met, I've had a safety net, someone to protect me from making impulsive decisions without thinking things through. Nixing my sudden whim for a tattoo, for example. Or buying a houseboat when we moved to Oxford. He's proved himself right so many times on the small things, I've learned to trust him on the big ones. I know he'd never let anything happen to me; to *us*.

When I'm with him, I feel safe, grounded. It's one of the reasons I fell in love with him. So if he says Friday night was OK, it was OK.

'Are we good now?' Kit asks gently.

I nod, snuggling into his shoulder. 'Can I ask you something?'

'Go for it.'

'Have *you* ever done something like this before?'

'You really want to go into this now?'

'*Have* you?' I ask, startled. I never for one moment expected him to say *yes*.

'I've had threesomes before,' Kit says calmly.

For a moment, I'm rendered speechless. Kit, *my* Kit, sensible, conservative, back-seat Kit, getting up to – well, I'm not quite sure exactly. But something that clearly doesn't come under the heading *vanilla*.

'I did have a life before I met you,' he says, his mouth twitching. 'Come on, Mia. I *was* married, remember? As you'd say, this isn't my first rodeo.'

'Clearly.'

'I don't seem to recall you complaining about my experience before,' he says slyly.

'I'm not complaining! I'm just a bit – surprised. You've never mentioned it before.'

'My first wife was eleven years older than me, and she had eclectic tastes in bed. She decided she wanted us to have a threesome with her best friend. Unlike you and me, our marriage *was* in trouble by then, and we were throwing everything we could at it to save it.' He shrugs. 'It didn't work. But after we split, I moved in with the best friend. We had a pretty open relationship. It was fun, for a while. Then about two or three months later, I met you.'

'You were living with someone when we met? You never said!'

'It wasn't that kind of arrangement. She was heavily involved with a married man who wouldn't leave his wife. I was just someone to hang out with by that stage. Friends with benefits. We were both free to come and go as we pleased.'

I stare at my husband of nearly ten years in astonishment. How has this never come up before? Kit had three-somes? Friends with benefits? He lived with a woman who had a revolving door on her bedroom? Who knows what else he got up to? How did I not know any of this?

'You never asked,' Kit says, reading my mind.

'I didn't realize I had to!'

Kit's always been great in bed: one of those men who genuinely gets a kick out of turning a woman on, but without being all obsessive about it. (There's nothing more annoying than a man who needs to prove his sexual prowess by making you come five times before breakfast.) I'd figured it was because he'd been married to an older woman, but clearly there's a lot more to it. Not that I'm jealous. After all, it was a long time ago, and I'm the beneficiary of all that practice anyways. It's kind of hot, picturing Kit at the centre of some kind of orgiastic love-in.

Really hot, actually.

'You look a little flushed,' Kit says, taking off his glasses again.

'I feel a little flushed,' I say, sliding my hand between his legs. He's rock hard beneath his boxers, and I quiver in response.

Kit fumbles with the bottom of my T-shirt, and I help him pull it over my head. He quickly strips off his own tee and boxers and kneels astride me. I reach for him, but he bats my hands away and dips his head to one breast, tweaking the spare nipple between his fingers. I open my legs to accommodate him, a wave of pleasure rippling through my body. *He is good at this*, I think blissfully as he slides lower, deftly thumbing my nipples while his mouth seeks out my clitoris. I don't care if it was his ex-wife or his mistress or the entire female population of the Western Delta who taught him this. I'm just glad he was such a good study.

I'm not normally quick off the mark when it comes to the Big O. As a rule, I need a full twenty minutes' warm-up and fine-tuning before getting down to business, and even then, there's no guarantee. As Kit says, you can't get a coconut every time. But tonight we've barely gotten started and already I can feel my orgasm building. Maybe it's the idea of Kit as some kind of Don Juan cavorting on a king-size bed with hordes of naked women. Or the fact that I've thought about nothing but sex for the past three days. But I come so hard and fast, Kit has to clamp his hand over my mouth to quiet me.

Moments later, he comes himself, powering into me with long, shuddering thrusts. He eases out of me and we both lie there, breathless but satisfied. Finally, Kit leans up on one elbow and drops a soft kiss on my lips.

'I told you our marriage was strong,' he says.

10

Charlie

'So who is this woman, anyway?' my friend Gail asks.

I open the oven and bend down to put in the tray of devils on horseback. 'I told you. She's the wife of one of the teachers at school. She used to be a reporter for CNN, but she writes a column for one of the big papers in the US now. It's on her blog, *Across the Pond*—'

'She's American?'

I laugh. 'You don't have to say it like you're sucking lemons. Come on, Gail, give her a chance. She's lived here for ten years – she's quite civilized. You might even like her.'

Gail neatly sips her tea, investing the action with a wealth of meaning I don't have to be a mind reader to work out. Ever since we met Kit and Mia, Gail and her husband Dave have slipped off our radar, and I feel horribly guilty about it. Hence my attempt to bring both couples together at our party tonight for New Year's Eve, though I suspect my efforts are already doomed. I invited Gail to come early to 'help out' to give her home-court advantage when Mia arrives.

'I hear Mia Allen's quite pretty,' Gail says, casting out bait.

I don't rise to it. 'Attractive, I'd have said, rather than pretty. She's got a certain energy about her. And bags of sex appeal, of course.'

'That doesn't worry you?'

'Should it?'

'Well, you know Rob,' she laughs, attempting to sound offhand. 'Always had an eye for a pretty girl.'

'Just because you're on a diet, it doesn't mean you can't look at the menu,' I say lightly.

Gail straightens a pile of red paper napkins. 'Dave would never look at another woman,' she says firmly. 'He never has, not in twenty-seven years.'

I should be charmed by the fact that Gail and Dave are childhood sweethearts, happily married for almost three decades. They have four teenage daughters – nineteen, fifteen, and thirteen-year-old twins – and for the last ten years have run a hair and beauty salon together in Oxford, with Gail expertly managing it and Dave . . . I've never quite worked out what Dave does. Other than take credit for his wife's hard work. But by any normal measure, theirs is a successful marriage. It's just all a little too cloying for my taste. I suspect Gail's frequent over-the-top Hallmark proclamations of marital happiness are made more to convince herself than me.

The kitchen door opens, sending a blast of icy air into the room. 'My ears burning?' Dave asks jovially, as he and Rob come in. His smile doesn't reach his eyes.

'We were just talking about Kit and Mia Allen,' I say.

'I'm surprised you haven't met them before, actually. They live at your end of the village.'

'Over the bridge,' Dave says dismissively. 'We wouldn't mix in the same circles.'

As far as Dave's concerned, 'over the bridge' is a slum tenement eschewed by anyone with 'real' money. In reality, it's the oldest and most charming part of the village. Most of the homes are converted from three- and four-hundred-year-old mews and labourers' cottages. They're small and impractical but quirky and full of character, with inglenook fireplaces and low oak beams and ancient flint walls. I'd swap our efficient minimalist Sixties rabbit hutch for Mia and Kit's warm, cosy home in a heartbeat, but Rob would hate it.

Thanks to a generous legacy from Gail's parents, the Conants live on the 'right' side of the bridge, in a vast, custom-built McMansion. A combination of at least six architectural styles, including Gothic, Italian Renaissance and Hideous Monstrosity, it sprawls across a plot of several acres and incorporates a mirrored gym, private eighteen-seat cinema and pink-tiled underground swimming pool. Quite how they got planning permission is beyond me. Our next-door neighbours replaced the disintegrating slate on their Grade II-listed building two years ago with slate tiles sourced at huge expense from the original quarry, and were forced to rip them off and start again – at a cost of nearly eighty thousand pounds – when council planners discovered the new tiles were half an inch wider than the originals.

In fairness to Gail, she's not a snob, and I suspect she'd be much happier living in the thick of the village with the rest of us. Trapped alone in her huge house on its lonely hill, her children spreading their wings and starting to leave the nest, she must be terribly lonely.

'I think something's burning,' she says suddenly, nudging my arm.

'Oh shit.' I grab a tea towel and whip out the tray of devils on horseback. The bacon sizzles and spits at me. 'Nick of time. Crispy but not cremated.'

Gail reaches for one, then glances at Dave for approval. He shakes his head curtly, and she drops her hand. I suppress the urge to slam the hot tray on his head. Gail is a rail-thin size eight, having spent much of her adult life on a permanent diet. When I first met her twenty years ago, she was a size twelve, with a voluptuous hourglass figure I'd have killed for. Now her clothes hang from her skeletal frame, and she looks haggard and a decade older than she is. Over the years, Dave has literally worn her down to a shadow of her former self.

'What time's everyone arriving?' Rob asks through a mouthful of hot bacon and prune.

'Seven.' *As I've told you at least half a dozen times today.* 'If you and Dave can man the bar, Gail and I have got everything else covered.'

Thanks to Gail, I actually have time for a shower before getting dressed for the party. I'm about to put on the pretty grey jersey wrap dress I've laid out on the bed but something makes me hesitate. Knowing Mia, she'll be wearing something hot and sexy that has Rob drooling with lust. I can't compete with her Jessica Rabbit curves, but this *is* my party. We're pretty much the same age and size; if she can do it, so can I.

On impulse, I throw open my wardrobe and rummage through the hangers looking for an LBD I haven't worn since before I had Milly. It's a bit Eighties bodycon, with a stretchy Lycra miniskirt and see-through lace panels over the bodice, but to my surprise and pleasure, it still fits perfectly. I team it with black seamed hold-ups and a pair of high-heeled stilettos I normally only wear inside the bedroom.

'Christ!' Rob says when I teeter precariously down the stairs to find him alone in the kitchen. 'Who are you, and what have you done with my wife?'

I strike a pose. 'Like it?'

'Are you kidding? You look amazing. Turn round.'

I oblige, laughing as Rob bends me over the kitchen counter. I can feel his heartfelt appreciation in the small of my back. 'Rob! People will be coming any minute!'

'So will I,' Rob groans.

'Charlie?' Gail calls down the hall. 'Charlie, are you downstairs yet? A car just arrived. I think it's Dominic and Patsy.'

Rob fumbles under my skirt. 'Come upstairs for a minute. I promise it won't take long.'

'We have guests,' I say primly, wriggling out of his grasp.

Dave wanders into the kitchen clutching a bottle of beer against his belly. 'Not sure *I'd* let my wife go out dressed like that,' he says with false bonhomie.

'Your loss,' Rob says, reminding me exactly why I love him.

I throw open the back door. Other than political canvassers, I don't think anyone's ever come to the front door of our house since we first moved in.

'Dominic! Love the new beard!' I exclaim as he comes up the garden path. 'Patsy, you look beautiful!'

'Liar,' Patsy says good-naturedly. 'It's the same bloody tent I wear every Christmas. Makes me look like a bloody sofa.'

'A *beautiful* sofa,' I smile, kissing her cheek.

Everyone suddenly arrives at once, and for the next thirty minutes Rob is frantically fielding drinks and I'm passing around trays of canapés, while the kitchen heats up with the press of bodies and the hum of wine-soaked laughter. Rob throws open the French doors to the terrace, and the social lepers are soon huddled together by the old stone wall near the outdoor jacuzzi, plumes of cigarette smoke mingling with their breath on the crisp night air. The hot tub was put in by the previous owners; when we moved here four years ago, I wanted to have it taken out, terrified Milly would somehow end up floating face down in the water, but Rob was adamant we keep it. We compromised by putting a sturdy lock on the cover. As always, I'm the willow in this relationship, Rob the oak.

'Good Lord,' Paul, my next-door neighbour, says suddenly. 'Who's *that*?'

Mia looks sensational, of course. Tiny black sequinned hot pants and high heels, a sexy peephole sweater that reveals a matching black sequinned bra, and a wicked slash of starlet-red lipstick. I know I look good, all things considered. Mia, on the other hand, throws every consideration out of the window.

Gail catches me by the arm. 'He's very good-looking, isn't he? You didn't tell me *that*.'

It takes a moment for me to twig. 'Kit?'

'He looks like Brad Pitt.' She giggles girlishly. 'No wonder you keep working late.'

Actually, she's right: Kit does look rather hot tonight. He's ditched the rumpled-professor corduroy jacket and trousers for a fine-knit grey sweater that defines his well-muscled shoulders and a pair of worn jeans that make his long legs look endless. He's a good half-head taller than all the other men here, including Rob. I feel an unexpected flash of desire.

Why so unexpected, Charlie? Of course you want him. You have done since the moment you met him.

Rob materializes next to me out of the throng. 'Where's the bourbon?'

'What d'you need bourbon for?'

'Mia wants some. Come on, have you seen it?'

'Mia doesn't like bourbon,' I say, surprised.

'Well, she asked me to get some in specially, so I did. Oh, forget it. I'll find it myself.'

'Those two seem thick as thieves,' Gail observes as Mia and Rob huddle together over the drinks table on the far side of the kitchen.

For a second I don't respond, my gaze still on Kit. He catches my eye and raises a sardonic eyebrow. I smile back.

'Brewing up trouble, no doubt,' I say, returning my attention to Gail. 'Why don't I introduce you? Maybe you can keep the pair of them out of mischief.'

Rob slings his arm casually around Mia's waist, and her blonde hair tangles on his shoulder as she leans into him to open the bourbon. She really does look gorgeous in her peek-a-boo sweater. Her creamy breasts swell against the top of her sparkly bra, and I flashback to the image of her naked that night. From the bulge in Rob's jeans, he's clearly thinking the same thing.

They smile and subtly separate as I drag Gail over. 'We're doing a blind taste test,' Mia says. 'Your husband here bets he can make a better Dark and Stormy than Kit. Want to take him up on it?'

'What's the forfeit?' I ask.

She throws an inviting look my way. 'I'm open to ideas.'

'So I've heard.'

You could cut the sexual tension between us with a knife. Gail coughs awkwardly. 'What's a Dark and Stormy?'

'It's a cocktail,' Mia explains as Kit joins us. 'Kit's speciality. I don't recommend them if you've got to work the next day.'

'You really think you can take me on?' Kit asks Rob.

'Blind taste, remember,' he warns.

The two of them start mixing and pouring amid laughter and noisy heckling from those standing nearby. Volunteers are lined up for the testing, and before long most of the room is involved. Mia takes centre stage between the two men, organizing and adjudicating. I can see how she did so well on television. She has a natural magnetism, a presence. Every eye in the room is on her, and she seems perfectly at home under the spotlight. I don't envy her in the slightest. The limelight is the last place I'd ever want to be.

By the time midnight strikes, we've collectively worked our way through blind taste tests for Slippery Nipples, Mai Tais, Manhattans and Long Island Iced Teas, and we're all blind drunk.

Rob has carefully positioned himself next to Mia to welcome in the New Year. As everyone cheers and blows whistles and slurs the first few lines of 'Auld Lang Syne', I see them turn to each other and kiss, and then I'm engulfed by Dave in an unwelcome slobbery snog. By the time I prise him off, Mia has her arms wreathed around Kit's neck, and Rob's nowhere to be seen. I watch Kit and Mia kiss for a few moments, trying to remember the last time Rob and I kissed like that. We have sex, yes, some of it still good, especially since the Allens came into our lives; but we never kiss. Perhaps we've just known each other too long.

The party starts to break up. No one's in any fit state to drive home, but since nearly everyone lives within walking distance, it doesn't matter. Patsy and Dominic call the only cab available in a twenty-mile radius, while Gail phones her eldest daughter, who's promised to pick them up on the way back from her own party in return for use of the car.

Dave pours himself a double whisky and settles into the sofa in the sitting room. 'How about a quick dip in the jacuzzi while we're waiting for Chloe, Rob?'

'I'm sure Rob and Charlie would rather get off to bed,' Gail says quickly.

'No, it would be nice to watch the fireworks from the jacuzzi,' Rob says. 'They usually have some in Oxford you can see from here. It's a clear evening. Kit? Mia?'

'Sure,' Kit says.

Dave is already standing up and stripping off his clothes. 'You coming, Gail?'

'I think I'll just put the kettle on,' his wife says hastily, disappearing into the kitchen. 'It's not really big enough for six, anyway.'

Rob opens the hot tub and swings the cover into its cradle, while I turn the lights down inside the house and dig out some towels. Steam rises from the hot water as if from the primordial soup. Dave is in the water first, naked, as always. Kit follows suit, but to my surprise, Mia primly keeps her bra and knickers on.

'It's OK,' I say, shimmying out of my clothes. 'We're not overlooked.'

'What about Milly?'

'She's staying with Rob's mother tonight.'

'It's not about you,' Mia murmurs, glancing pointedly towards the tub.

I understand her reticence. Dave is gawping openly at us; any minute now, his erection will break the water like a surface-to-air missile. 'Ignore him. He's harmless. If you ever gave him the slightest sign of encouragement, he'd run in the opposite direction like a little girl.'

'Do girls always run away?' Mia says archly.

Before I can reply, she's unhooked her bra and stepped out of her knickers and into the jacuzzi. Rob is naturally right behind her, which means I get to be last man in.

'You're such a gentleman,' I tell my husband crossly as water slops over the side.

'Not such a fan of Archimedes, then,' Kit quips.

There's a crack in the distance, and we all look up as fireworks explode into the sky. Rob's right: it's a wonderfully clear night, and the pyrotechnic rain of gold stars against the black velvet sky brings out the child in all of us. My husband's hand finds mine in the warm water, and I lean against him, relaxed and content. Things have been so much better between us since that night with Kit and Mia. He got what he wanted, and he's happy again. Which means I'm happy. All he ever has to do is pay me some attention and I melt like an ice cube in the sun. He can drive me to the edge of reason, and then haul me back with one lazy smile.

Gail appears on the terrace just as the fireworks end. 'Dave, Chloe is here.'

Reluctantly, Dave heaves his bulk from the jacuzzi. I wait until he's safely wrapped a towel around his fleshy waist and gone inside and then climb out myself. 'Better see them off and lock up.'

The hot water has addled what few sober brain cells Dave may have had left. He loses his towel and staggers round the house looking for his clothes, naked but for the blazer he found in the hall, his penis a pale pink worm curled in a nest of grey hair. His poor daughter doesn't know where to look.

Gail grabs his arm. 'I've a good mind to leave you here to sleep it off,' she hisses furiously, buttoning up the blazer. 'But if you think you're getting out of lunch with Mum and Dad tomorrow, you've another thing coming.'

Somehow, she and Chloe bundle him into the back of the car, and they finally leave. I pick up my own discarded clothes, hooking my finger through the straps of my heels, and go upstairs to throw on a T-shirt.

At the turn of the landing, I glance down into the garden. There are only two people left in the jacuzzi. I watch my husband lean towards Mia, cup her face in his hands and give her the kind of kiss he no longer gives me.

'Everything OK?'

I jump, dropping my shoes. Kit retrieves them for me, one hand securing the towel at his waist. 'Here.'

'Thanks.' Awkwardly, I adjust my own towel. 'Did you have a good time tonight?'

'So far.'

It's hard to read the expression on his face in the half-darkness. My heart thuds in my chest and there's an answering echo in the beat between my thighs.

'So far?' I say.

11

Mia

Kit climbs out of the tub and grabs a towel, following Charlie indoors and leaving Rob and me alone. We carefully avoid looking at each other. I lean back against the padded head-rest, my breasts just breaking the surface of the water. The fireworks have finished now, and the night sky is inky, speckled with stars.

Rob floats opposite me. His foot brushes against my knee, and I pull it across my thigh, working my thumbs into the sole of his foot from heel to toes.

'Jesus,' Rob groans. 'Where'd you learn to do that?'

'If I tell you, I'll have to kill you.'

'Fine. Just don't stop.'

I straighten up slightly so his foot is resting lightly between my thighs. A breeze whistles round my shoulders and ripples the surface of the water. I'm acutely aware of our nakedness in the warm darkness, the pressure of his bare calf against my skin. We've been caught up in this dance all evening, ebbing and flowing round each other.

Drifting in our slipstream, eddying round us, are Charlie and Kit. There may have been thirty people at this party, but it was only ever about four.

God, I must be wasted. I don't normally wax this lyrical.

'Mia, I swear to God I can feel that in my jaw,' Rob gasps as I reach the ball of his foot. 'You're giving me a fucking hard-on.'

I smile complacently and switch to his other foot, this time nestling it provocatively in the space between my breasts. My nipples peak in the chill air. Rob throws his head back in abandon, his arms outstretched along the sides of the tub. I see his erection surface in the moonlight.

Suddenly he snaps open his eyes, sits up and yanks my ankles so I slide off the seat towards him. Laughing, I snake my legs round his waist, and the two of us abruptly stop moving, floating there in the water, skin to skin, my breasts grazing his chest, the tip of his erection nuzzling my stomach.

'This is getting dangerous,' Rob says hoarsely.

I nod. Neither of us moves. He looks down at my breasts and then roughly cups them. His thumbs find my erect nipples, and a bolt of electricity shoots straight to my groin. I'm shocked by how much I want him. *We should stop doing this before it gets out of hand.* But neither of us moves.

'Mia,' he rasps. 'If you don't stop me, I'm going to have to fuck you.'

The water splashes against us, ruffled by the gathering breeze. Rob grips my face with his hands and kisses me hard. It's different from Kit's kisses: harsher, more insistent. He pushes me toward the side of the tub, his erection probing fiercely between my legs, and I'm suddenly aware we're careering toward the point of no return like a runaway truck.

I break away, my heart a hummingbird in my chest. 'We should get out. Kit and Charlie will think we've drowned.'

For a moment his eyes darken, and I almost wonder if it's too late to stop him.

He smiles suddenly. 'You go in.' He glances ruefully down at his erection. 'I need a moment.'

I laugh and the tension between us dissipates. 'I'll see you inside.'

Suddenly shy, I wrap a towel modestly round myself and go into the house. I should have gotten out the tub when Kit did. What if he'd seen us? I can't deny I'm attracted to Rob, but I love my husband. I enjoy flirting, but I don't actually want an affair. It wasn't fair of me to let things go so far with Rob, when I have no intention of following through.

I don't know if it's the alcohol or the hot tub or the sudden change in temperature, but as I enter the kitchen I feel suddenly giddy. I lean against the sink and turn on the faucet, pouring myself a cool glass of water and holding it against my forehead. Where is Kit, anyways? He's been gone a long time. Charlie too. Not that they'd do anything behind my back, I'm sure. Unless they thought it *wasn't* behind my back, of course. Maybe they consider it part of the game. Maybe it *is*. Goddammit. I feel like I'm flying blind. Is that why Kit got out of the tub and left me alone with Rob? Did he think that's what I wanted?

A hand touches my shoulder and I leap six feet in the air.

'Kit! Jesus Christ! Don't sneak up on me like that!'

'I didn't sneak up on you. You were miles away.' He takes the glass from my hand and puts it on the counter, looking at me with concern. 'Too much heat?'

'Something like that.'

'Are you OK?'

'I felt dizzy for a minute. Too long in the tub. I'm fine now.'

He glances over my shoulder. 'Where's Rob?'

Trying to get his dick back in his pants. 'Sorting out the hot tub.'

'You sure you're OK?'

'Why shouldn't I be?'

He hesitates. 'I left you alone together for a reason, Mia.'

Damnation! I knew it! Has everyone but me read some secret English orgy playbook?

'What on earth for?' I demand. 'Is this some kind of test?'

'Of course not! I'm just giving you some space, that's all.'

'Space to do *what*?'

'I told you. If you want to have some fun, that's OK . . .'

'Look, he kissed me, that's all.'

'I don't mind if it was more than a kiss. It's OK. If it's what you want.' He pauses, his eyes locked on mine. 'Is it?'

I'm waiting for the other shoe to drop. What kind of down-the-rabbit-hole *Twilight Zone* is this? Why is my husband, who I *know* loves me, telling me it's OK to 'have fun' with another man? A horrible worm of doubt niggles away at me again. Maybe Lois is right. Maybe he's setting me up with Rob so he can get to Charlie. But if he really wanted to sleep with her, surely it would be easier for him to have an affair with her behind my back than to set up some kind of crazy wife-swapping thing? And I know Kit. He wouldn't cheat on me. He just wouldn't.

'What about you?' I ask, lobbing the ball back in his court. 'What do *you* want?'

'Mia, there's no hidden agenda,' Kit says, accurately reading my mind. 'What excites *you*, excites *me*. Your libido has gone through the roof since we met Charlie and Rob. I want to see where that goes.' He gives me a long, level look. 'Don't get me wrong: I'm not writing you a blank cheque. You can have fun with Rob, or Charlie for that matter, but don't make a fool out of me.'

We both turn as the French doors open. 'You two are staying the night, right?' Rob asks, coming inside and locking the terrace doors behind him. 'You'll never get a cab now. Charlie's already made up the bed in the spare room.'

Of course we're staying over. My toothbrush is in my purse. We've paid our excitable Polish babysitter the price of a small car to take care of Emmy till tomorrow lunchtime. I've shaved my legs, painted my toenails, and suffered the ritual pain and humiliation of a Brazilian wax. None of these things did I do for the benefit of a cab driver.

'I think Charlie's in the sitting room,' Rob says. 'Why don't you go through? I'll fix us all a nightcap.'

'I know the way you mix drinks,' Kit says firmly. 'I'm staying right here to keep an eye.'

'Pot, meet kettle,' I giggle, leaving them to it.

I find Charlie slotting her iPod into its dock in the other room. She's swapped her towel for a plain white T-shirt that doesn't quite cover her butt. As Melissa Etheridge fills the room, she curls up in the corner of one deep red velvet sofa, her long bare legs tucked under her. She looks about seventeen.

'Can I ask you something?' she says as I sit in the other corner of the sofa, still wrapped in my own towel.

'Go for it.'

'Do you two have any rules?'

Instantly I know she's not talking table manners. I hesitate, not sure how to answer. Kit and I haven't exactly sat down and drawn up a manual of extra-marital sexual etiquette: *thou shalt not kiss thy husband's boss on school property.*

I tuck my towel tighter around my chest. 'I'm not sure what you mean.'

'Let's stop tiptoeing around the elephant in the room,' Charlie smiles. 'We haven't talked about what happened before Christmas, but I'm assuming from the fact you're here now that you and Kit were OK with it. But none of us want to cross a line by mistake and end up jeopardizing our friendship.'

Wow. Call a spade a spade, why don't you? I'll never get used to the way the Brits talk so frankly about sex, like it was the weather or something.

'You mean, like kissing is a big a no-no for hookers?' I mumble, blushing furiously.

'A little *Pretty Woman*, but yes. That was the general thrust of my question. Forgive the pun.'

I can't even look her in the eye. This is way beyond my comfort zone. I'd have been happy to keep ignoring our friendly neighbourhood elephant till he died of old age.

'Look, Kit and I have never done anything like this before,' I blurt out suddenly. 'We're not swingers, if that's what you think. We don't have an open marriage. We love each other.'

'I took that as read,' she says dryly. 'If I thought for a second you didn't have a great marriage, I wouldn't let you within a mile of my husband. You think I'd dangle a sexy blonde in front of him if I didn't know you were madly in love with your own husband? Only a really strong marriage can take something like this. If it's in trouble, bringing other people into the relationship would blow it out of the water.'

Kit made exactly this point about his first marriage. 'Well, what about you?' I ask curiously. 'I take it this isn't your first rodeo?'

'By which I assume you're asking, in your sweet American fashion, have we done this before?' Charlie deadpans. 'No. Nothing like this. I think we're all feeling our way here. Which is why I'm asking now, before we go any further, if there's anything that's off limits for the two of you.'

Oh, the hell with it. If she can be all cool and European about it, so can I.

'I don't mind fooling around, but I don't want to go all the way with Rob,' I say suddenly. 'And I don't want you to go all the way with Kit. I know it seems like splitting hairs, but—'

'It's fine. No going all the way. But the rest?'

'That's OK,' I say quickly before she gets too specific. 'You?'

'I'm not going to lay down rules about what we do anatomically. But it has to be the four of us together. Not just you and Rob. For example,' she adds evenly.

We sit silently for a moment, digesting the conversation. I'm relieved we've finally put our cards on the table and cleared the air; and also nervous that I've inadvertently entered into some kind of pact without reading the small print. I thought things would just . . . *happen*. Or not. And now I think I've agreed to something, and I'm not entirely sure what.

She smiles, and I smile back nervously, tensing as she leans in and kisses me, my mouth moving awkwardly with hers. Suppose I don't like it after all? I've never been to bed with a woman. The reality may be ways away from my sapphic fantasies. What if I can't bring myself to go through with it? How am I going to back out now without looking like an idiotic prude? How in hell will we stay friends?

But then her tongue slips between my lips, and I find myself responding. Desire washes over me as she pulls open my towel and cups my breast, kissing her way down my neck, soft, butterfly kisses, finding that sensitive sweet spot in the hollow of my collarbone. Her face is soft against my skin. She smells so good: mangoes and honey and the fresh clean scent of soap. She pulls at my nipple, peaking it between her fingers, and I moan with pleasure.

Tentatively I reach for the hem of her T-shirt and tug it over her head. I cup her breast in the same way she just did with me, wondering how hard to thumb her nipple. *This must be what it's like to be a teenage boy*, I think wryly, *trying to figure out how a woman's body works*. I may have earned a black belt with men, but I'm a total novice here. It's like trying snowboarding for the first time after years as an expert alpine skier. The two may seem similar, but none of the same rules apply.

Charlie slithers down my body, her long hair swishing silkily against my skin, and drops to her knees between my legs. She parts my thighs and I tense again. Does this mean I've got to go down on her in return? How does it work, two women together? Do you take it in turns or is one of you—

Ohhhhhh.

Suddenly I can't think. All I can do is feel. Her tongue flicks over my clit, feathery touches that hit the mark every time. I twine my hands in her hair, dizzy with arousal, and push back against her, so the two of us fall in a tangle onto the thick striped rug on the floor. We're kissing again, our bodies pressed against each other, our legs interleaved. Then she wriggles free and flips me onto my back, dipping between my legs again. I lose myself in the pure pleasure of it, with none of the usual anxiety: *am I taking too long? Is he waiting for me to come so we can get to the headline act?* She makes me feel we have all the time in the world.

Gaining in confidence, I turn on the rug so we're head to tail. She tastes sweet, far sweeter than I expected. I've tasted myself before, on Kit's lips, but this is completely different. I don't know how hard or fast I should do this, what works for her, if I should be using my fingers, but as I kneel over her she starts tonguing me again, and for the first time ever I appreciate the exquisite pleasure of a sixty-nine. Suddenly I'm not sure where I end and she begins.

I'm only aware Rob and Kit have joined us in the room when I feel a firm hand on my ass, and a moment later two thick fingers – Kit? Rob? – plunge inside me. More hands find my breasts as I kneel on all fours over Charlie, and it's unbelievably intense, more erotic than anything I've fanta-sized about these past few weeks. I come with a sudden cry, wet and liquid. And then we're all moving again in a cat's cradle of legs and arms and breasts and cocks, the four of us forming a circle of pleasure. Rob locks eyes with me over Charlie's head, coming in her mouth without breaking our gaze, and it's the hottest, most intimate thing I've ever experienced.

Kit eases me away from the group and covers my body with his, slipping easily between my wet thighs. I hook my legs round his waist, gripping his shoulders as he pumps into me. He comes in three or four hard thrusts, his climax so intense he lifts me off the ground with him.

He gropes for a blanket on the arm of the sofa, and pulls it over us. For a long time we lie curled into each other, sweating and exhausted. Finally I raise my head and realize we're alone.

'Where are Charlie and Rob?'

'They left a while ago,' Kit murmurs.

'Why?'

He shrugs briefly. 'Shhhh. I don't know. Go to sleep.'

'We can't sleep here.' I sit up and shake him. 'Come on. I'm freezing. We need to get to bed.'

We tiptoe through the silent house to the guest room. Outside, the light is already grey; it'll be dawn soon. We climb into bed and Kit pulls me into the crook of his shoulder, and I stay there, even though we're not the kind of couple who usually spoon together at night.

'Did you get what you want?' he asks quietly.

I smile into the darkness. 'So far,' I say.

12

Charlie

I'm so used to Rob's bad behaviour, I almost don't notice it any more. But an ambush the moment I get home after an incredibly long and taxing day at work gets even my distracted attention.

'Where do you *think* I've been?' I retort.

'It's nearly nine o'clock at night,' Rob snaps. 'You work at a bloody *school*. So what have you been doing since three thirty?'

Wearily, I drape my jacket over the back of a kitchen chair. 'Take a wild guess, Rob. I've been putting out fires in one damn meeting after another, that's what. We've just been told the Sisters of Calvary *are* withdrawing their financial support from the school, which means we either close or find some way of running it independently. Shelby wants—'

'I don't want to hear about work,' Rob says, holding his palm up like a traffic cop an inch from my face.

I swat his hand away. 'Would you *stop*?'

'I can't hear you when you raise your voice.'

'I'm *not* raising my voice,' I say through gritted teeth.

'It's your tone.'

'Rob, I really don't need this,' I sigh, opening the fridge. There's nothing in it but wilted lettuce and a hard lump of cheese. 'I assume you and Milly have already eaten?'

'Pizza. There's none left,' he adds gratuitously.

'Fine. I'll make myself a cheese sandwich.'

'Was Kit there?'

'Was Kit where?'

'At your meetings.'

I put down the breadknife. 'Yes, of course he was. He's on the FP team, you know that.'

'How convenient. Especially with his wife away.'

'Don't even go there. If you want to project, I can't stop you. But I have no intention of getting caught up in your fucking paranoia.'

'Don't swear at me.'

'I wasn't swearing *at* you.'

'If you can't have a civil conversation, there's no point even discussing this.'

'Fine by me.'

We're not having a genuine conversation anyway. As usual, we're having a conversation about how *to have a conversation.*

'You were the one making a big song and dance about Mia after New Year's Eve,' Rob says snidely. 'One rule for you and another for me, is that it?'

'I did *not* make a big song and dance about you and Mia,' I sigh. 'I just asked what went on between you two in the jacuzzi, that's all. I want everything to be transparent and out in the open. If I'd had a problem with it, do you think I'd have gone ahead with what happened afterwards?'

'For that matter, I'd still like to know what really went on with you and Kit when *you* were alone.'

'Fine. Ask. *Again*. And I'll tell you nothing. *Again*.'

'Nothing went on, or you'll tell me nothing?'

I pinch the bridge of my nose. 'Believe what I tell you, Rob, or don't. It's up to you.'

'You do realize you've put your job on the line with all this?' Rob says, changing tack abruptly. 'If anyone ever found out, your reputation would be shot.'

'So let's stop it now. Never see them again. Works for me.'

Rob's eyes narrow as he tries to work out if I'm serious. I wait him out. I'm not bluffing. I had fun on New Year's Eve, of course – I've never enjoyed another woman as much as Mia – but my family has to come first. If opening the door on this scene again is going to drive a wedge between Rob and me, what's the point?

Fifteen, twenty years ago, when we first went down this road, I was almost as enthusiastic as Rob. I enjoyed sleeping with other women; sharing the experience with him was incredibly erotic. But this time round, I'm doing it for the sake of our marriage, because I can't see any other way forward. Because I know that if I don't, sooner or later he'll have an affair I *can't* control. Sooner or later, there'll be a woman who'll steal him from me, destroy my family and break my daughter's heart. If I thought for one second that woman might be Mia, I'd walk away in an instant. But she's never going to climb over Kit to get at Rob; I know it, even if my husband doesn't. The flirting and teasing are just a power trip for her, validation that she's still got it. Kit knows that too, which is why he gives her so much freedom.

Rob's the one I'm married to. Rob's the one who made

the commitment to me: forsaking all others, till death us do part. The irony that I'm reliant on another woman being in love with *her* husband to keep mine on the straight and narrow isn't lost on me.

In my darker moments, I feel like Rob's pimp. I've effectively procured Mia for him and stood back and watched him trail after her like a dog on heat. He was all over her like a cheap suit on New Year's Eve; Gail wasn't the only one to take me aside and warn me, as if I didn't have eyes in my own head. And I let it happen because I have my eye on the bigger picture. He may not seem worth it to anyone else, but he's worth it to me. God help me, I love my husband. I'd do anything for us. But when I look at myself in the mirror, there are times I don't like what I see.

I need to rewrite the terms of our marriage, or we're not going to make it. Rob has to learn to give, as well as take. For twenty years, he's had the controlling interest in our relationship. If he didn't like my friends, I stopped seeing them. If he wanted to share them in bed, I shared them. If he used all his holiday entitlement diving, so there was no time for a family break, I took Milly to visit my parents on my own. He has no idea how to even *spell* the word compromise. But the more I give, the more Rob demands. Even my patience isn't inexhaustible. I've enabled his behaviour for two decades, but no more. I've changed. Grown up. I'm not the tolerant, insecure twenty-two-year-old I was when we first met.

I facilitated this foursome for Rob, but now I need to get something out of it too. My husband had access to other women until he ruined it with his affair, but I've never once so much as looked at another man. Even if Rob could have got past his possessiveness, I didn't want anyone else. But there's something about Kit Allen that makes me think again.

There was a moment on New Year's Eve, standing on the landing in the moonlight with Kit, when I wanted him more than I've wanted any man in a very long time. I literally ached for him to fuck me, a naked, punishing hunger that gnawed at my insides. For all his professorial bookishness, there's a raw masculinity about Kit that makes me long for him to grab me by the hair, throw me onto his bed and give me a good seeing-to. Rob may be controlling, but his refusal to take responsibility puts everything on my shoulders. It's hard to then set that aside and yield when he wants me to. With Kit, the impulse is unbearably tempting.

But I know it's one I can never give in to. Kit works for me, which puts him forever off limits. Sleeping together would compromise *us*, who we are. We can go so far, but no further. And I accept that. But Rob has to let me have *some* freedom. I'm not asking to go all the way with Kit, as Mia quaintly puts it. But Rob has to give me some latitude. Otherwise this whole thing will be entirely on his terms, yet again, and I'll find myself back in the same place I was eight years ago.

My resolve hardens when I see the file of New Year's Eve photos Rob has downloaded from his iPhone to the computer. More than half are pictures of Mia. I'm as sure as I can be that she won't betray either Kit or me, but I have an uneasy sense my husband is becoming obsessed with her. For a brief moment, I debate severing the friendship altogether, but apart from the problems that would cause me at work, I actually like Mia a lot. I don't want to lose her as a friend. And if I remove Mia from his orbit, who's to say he won't find someone else?

We don't get together with the Allens for nearly six weeks after New Year's Eve because Mia is in Florida visiting her sick father. Appropriately enough, it's Valentine's Day before we see them again. She and Kit invite us over for dinner to celebrate her return.

Rob is like a cat on a hot tin roof getting ready to go over to their place. He changes his shirt three times before we finally leave, and I nearly suffocate in the car from the aftershave fumes coming off him. *I was right to be worried,* I think. *And right to make sure I'm the one in control of this relationship. Who knows where this would have ended if I hadn't made sure I was part of it?*

Mia opens the door wearing a pair of sheer palazzo trousers and a shimmery grey translucent top. Every time she moves you see a hint of nakedness beneath.

'Welcome back!' I exclaim, hugging her. 'How was Florida? And how's your dad?'

'Warm, and warm,' Mia laughs, kissing my cheek and giving Rob a hug. 'Come on through. Dad's doing pretty well, all things considered. The chemo seems to be holding things at bay.'

'Well, we missed you.'

'Nice tan,' Rob comments as we follow her down the hall to the kitchen.

Kit is mixing up cocktails by the sink. 'No abstentions,' he warns as we pull out stools and gather round the island. 'After the week we've just had at work, this comes under the heading medicinal.'

'Seconded,' I sigh.

Shelby has known about the Sisters' decision to withdraw from the school for over a year, but instead of telling us so we could all decide the best way forward together, she's been plotting behind the scenes like Lady Macbeth. Her plan is for St Alphonsus to merge with Berwicks, an independent school three miles away, which will effectively destroy the character and essence of our school. Berwicks is concerned only with money and influence; its pupils are the cream (thick-but-rich) of Oxfordshire, and there are no scholarship places. St Alphonsus has always been about community, giving back, providing opportunities to youngsters who'd otherwise never have a chance in life. If Kit and I are to have any hope of prevailing against Shelby, we need to work together more closely than ever. Rob *has* to trust me.

There's a little of the second-date nerves about us all as we go through to the dining room to eat. I know we're all thinking the same thing: after what happened last time, how is this evening going to end? Rob and I have chewed it over endlessly, and I'm sure Kit and Mia have done the same, but we've never sat down and talked about it, all four of us. I'm guessing from the way Mia's dressed, from the flirty nature of her tone, the sideways glances she keeps giving Rob, that she and Kit want to take things further as much as we do. But I *am* only guessing. How do we segue into it? New Year's Eve was easy. The jacuzzi did most of the work; so much easier to fall into bed – or onto the rug – when you're already naked.

I realize I've lost track of the conversation and pull myself back to the here and now with an effort.

'No, tell the truth,' Mia is saying to Kit, leaning across the dining table so that I catch a glimpse of her breasts beneath that diaphanous shirt. 'You hate my blog. You think it's beneath me.'

'I do not hate your blog,' Kit says reasonably.

'So why do you keep going on at me to write the Great American Novel?'

'Nor do I keep going on at you to write the Great American Novel,' he adds tolerantly. 'I simply said that you *could*.'

Mia shrugs. 'I don't want to. There's no money in it, for a kick-off.'

'You wouldn't be doing it for the money.'

'The kudos, then? You think there's more prestige in writing a novel than a trashy newspaper column?'

He laughs. 'Mia. I'm not rising to it.'

'Look, you can just *say* . . .'

'What's it to be, Kit?' Rob teases. 'Truth or dare?'

Ahhh. We have our segue.

Neither of our daughters is here tonight. Milly's staying with Rob's parents, and Emmy is on a play date. Which means the four of us are free to play games of our own.

My body pulses with a fizz of desire as Kit puts an empty wine bottle in the centre of the table. Whatever my misgivings about the extent of Rob's interest in Mia, there's no doubt I want this too. I fancy Kit; it may sound hopelessly juvenile, but there's no other word for it. And I'm attracted to Mia almost as much as to the situation itself. Its inherent danger just turns me on all the more.

We know the form now: we spin and drink, spin and drink, ratcheting up the sexual tension as we move from *what's your worst sexual experience?* (answered by Rob, who lies, because there's no way he's letting Mia know he's jailbait to a certain type of older man) to *take off your bra without removing your top* (his dare to Mia, until she points out she's not wearing one). We unzip jeans with teeth, pass ice cubes from mouth to mouth, submit to and perform low-level sexual favours. The game may be a teenage cliché, but it's effective.

Kit's turn to spin, and the bottle points towards Rob. 'I dare you to identify your wife's pussy blindfold,' he says. 'And you only get one feel.'

'*Shit*. Did you shave this week?' Rob asks me.

'If you can't remember, I'm not telling you,' I retort crossly.

Kit ties a scarf over Rob's eyes. Swaying slightly from all the alcohol we've consumed, Mia slips off her palazzo pants, and I lift the hem of my skirt. Neither of us is wearing underwear.

I shiver with arousal as Rob gently probes between my legs, only too aware of Kit's eyes on me. Fortunately for my husband, he guesses correctly. If he couldn't pick me out of a line-up of two after twenty years together, he'd have been going home minus a crucial appendage.

'Why don't we take this upstairs?' Kit murmurs, his timing and tone pitch-perfect.

Without speaking, the four of us go up the steep, narrow staircase, the air thick with erotic tension. This is very different from New Year's Eve. This is premeditated. We've all been thinking about it for six weeks, and the sense of anticipation is intense. *We're really doing this. We're crossing another line, eyes wide open.*

It's the first time I've seen their bedroom. Unexpectedly self-conscious, I glance around. The ceiling has been raised beyond the exposed wooden rafters, the red herringbone brick walls partially covered with exotic Persian silk carpets, presumably picked up on Mia's travels. The wide-planked oak floor has been worn smooth by centuries of bare feet. There's no room for any furniture other than a huge king-size bed – the American influence – which must have been built *in situ*, since there's no way it could possibly have been manoeuvred up the winding staircase. Covered in a thick midnight-blue velvet bedspread, it dominates the room. The overall effect of the décor is seductive and inviting.

Kit has put on some music, and Mia and I turn to face each other, nervous and excited at the same time. I sense that she's waiting for me to take the lead again, and so I take the hem of her gauzy top and lift it over her head. It's all she's wearing, other than jewellery and her signature scent: Chanel No. 5 – very Marilyn Monroe. Tentatively she helps me unbutton my silk shirt and unzip my skirt. Taking her hand, I move towards the bed. She's more submissive in bed than I'd expected, given the strength of her personality outside the bedroom. I feel suddenly protective of her as we both lie down on the bed opposite each other, the velvet bedspread sensuous against my bare skin. I run my hand gently over her skin, following the contours from her rounded shoulder into the dip of her waist, up again over the curve of her hip. No wonder Rob is so hypnotized by her.

He joins us on the bed now, behind Mia, so that she's between us. The mattress dips with Kit's weight as he spoons behind me. Rob glances nervously over my head, and I know exactly what he's thinking: *I'm naked in bed with another man! The fact that there are two naked women between us doesn't change the fact that I'm naked in bed with another man!*

And then Kit starts to caress my buttocks from waist to

thigh with slow, measured, excruciatingly soft strokes, and I lose track of the players in the game. Everything becomes a soft-focus blur of sensation and taste and touch and smell as first Kit kisses me . . . then Mia . . . and then Rob. We move together on the bed like dancers following an un-written choreography, changing partners and position as if we've done this a thousand times before. I come again and again, and eventually find myself in a sweaty, tangled heap with Mia, our legs interleaved, the two of us breath-less and spent. I have no idea where Kit has gone.

Over her shoulder, Rob catches my eye. I know what he wants.

And I spread Mia's legs with my knee and give it to him.

Her eyes flick open. I see the surprise in her face as she registers it's Rob, and not Kit, who's inside her, and feel a flash of guilt. We've just broken her rule; this isn't what she wanted. But she's starting to enjoy it now, I can see it, her hips are moving in sync with his thrusts, and she's moaning with pleasure. Besides, aren't we a bit old for high school rules? We tore up that playbook the moment we came upstairs together. And this is what Rob wanted, it's what he's been panting for since day one. I know perhaps I'm a bad friend, but I'm a good wife. *I'm a good wife.*

I also know he isn't worth it.

13

Mia

Kit's not the kind of guy to yell or lose his shit. It's just not his style. He doesn't often get mad at all; mostly, when he's upset, he turns all serious and disappointed, which is so much harder to deal with. Especially when he does it early in the morning, when you're barely conscious and your defences are down.

I know I'm in trouble when he sets my coffee on the nightstand and sits on the bed next to me instead of tiptoeing back downstairs like he usually does at weekends.

'How's your head?' he asks as I struggle into a semi-seated position.

Feels like a jazz band is warming up inside. 'I've been better.'

'I can imagine. You certainly put it away last night.'

I sip the scalding coffee. 'What time is it?'

'I let you sleep till eleven.'

'Eleven! Why didn't you wake me before?'

'I tried. You weren't having any of it.'

I do dimly remember an attempt to shake me awake, now I think about it. 'Where are Charlie and Rob?'

'They left about an hour ago.'

'They left without waking me? Everything OK?'

'With them? As far as I could tell.'

He waits. I close my eyes. Talking is Kit's thing, but it *so* isn't mine, especially when I have a raging hangover and feel like I'm about to throw up.

'Drink your coffee.'

'It's too hot.'

'Drink it. You need it.'

I sip. He waits. I sip. Hey, I can keep this up all day.

'All right,' Kit sighs, 'have it your way. As usual. I'll be the one to go first. We need to talk about last night.'

'I thought talking about it was off limits,' I mutter. 'When I wanted to talk, you said that would kill everything. You told me not to overthink things.'

He ignores me. 'I don't have a problem with you fooling around with Charlie or Rob. I didn't set you any limits, or tell you what you could or couldn't do. The only thing I asked for was that you be honest with me, and that we do this together.'

'I *have* been honest,' I say, genuinely puzzled.

'Last night, I might as well not have been in the room.'

'I don't know what you mean.'

'You made it clear you wanted to be with Rob, not me,' Kit says firmly. 'You actually pushed me off you. You didn't even notice when I got out of bed and left the room.'

I want to protest, but I've never known Kit exaggerate for effect. He's as straight as an arrow. The thing is, I really *don't* remember pushing him away. But if he says that's what happened, it must have done. I remember Kit kissing me and pulling me towards his side of the bed . . . and yes, I did move back to Charlie, not to exclude him, of course, but to *in*clude her – and then it all gets a big confused. One minute I was kissing her, and the next Rob was suddenly on top of me. Inside of me. Had Kit left the room by then? He's right, I didn't notice. But I hope so. I know he says he's OK with whatever I choose to do, but how would he feel for real, watching another man having sex with his wife?

I *told* Charlie that was off limits. My one rule. I know I didn't object at the time, but I was caught up in the moment. It had already happened by the time I realized what was going on. And – if I'm totally honest with myself – deep down, I wanted it to happen. I fancy Rob, I just haven't wanted to admit it, or take responsibility for it. I could have stopped it, and I didn't. Does that count as infidelity?

'Look,' Kit sighs. 'I meant it when I said I wanted you to have fun. I'm not upset about what went on between you and Rob, whatever that was.' He holds up a hand. 'And I don't want you to tell me, either. It doesn't matter. I don't need chapter and verse. But you made me feel like a third wheel last night, and I'm not happy with that.'

'I didn't mean to push you away,' I apologize, flushing. 'If it came across like that, I'm sorry.'

'Mia, I'm not jealous. Really. But this has to be fun for me too, or else I might as well just leave the three of you to get on with it without me. Charlie and I are never going to have the same freedom as you and Rob. I don't have a problem with that, and neither does she. We've reached our own understanding. But I expect *some* give and take from

Rob. A little respect, at least. All the liberties I let him take with you, and he gets twitchy if I so much as touch Charlie?'

I know it's totally unfair, but I'm glad Kit and Charlie have work coming between them. Kit may not be jealous, but *I* am. I don't mind sharing him – up to a certain point. The thought of my husband making love to another woman, even someone I like as much as Charlie, makes me feel sick. Hypocritical, I know. I'm having my cake and eating it. I don't blame Kit for being pissed.

'Kit, did Rob actually tell you to stay away from Charlie?' I ask.

'He didn't have to. Every time Charlie comes anywhere near me, he gets edgy. He's constantly watching us, checking up on what we're doing. It kind of kills it for me.'

I look up in alarm. 'Are you saying you want to stop?'

'I don't know,' he sighs. 'I don't want to spoil your fun. But if Rob is going to be like this, it's not going to work. It all boils down to trust. I have to work with Charlie. We're going to that education conference on Wednesday for two days. I can't have Rob ringing every five minutes wanting to know what we're getting up to while we're away.'

I don't want to stop. For the first time, I realize how much I want things to continue. I've discovered a side to myself I never knew existed. The idea of a threesome, or sleeping with a woman, would have had me running for the hills not so long ago; now just thinking about it turns me on. Sex with Kit has always been good; he's considerate, patient and adventurous. But everyone gets a bit stuck in a rut after a decade together, don't they? We all miss the thrill of the chase. I love Kit, and I'd never want to hurt him by cheating behind his back. Rob's sexy and a little bit dangerous, but he's half the man my husband is. This way, I get all the frisson and excitement of an affair without any of the risks. I can't bear the thought of having to give that up yet.

Somehow, I have to find a way to keep Rob on board.

February in England sucks. I adore my adopted country most of the year, but right now it's grey, damp, cold and miserable. At least back home in Boston there's snow. It may be twenty below, but it looks way prettier than the wet, dismal view outside my kitchen window right now.

I schlep into the sitting room, pulling my bobbly wool cardigan tighter round my shoulders. I've been rattling around the house all afternoon, bored and lonely. Emmy has a sleepover with a school friend tonight, and Kit's at the conference in Birmingham with Charlie. This is where having my best friend and husband working at the same place is a bad idea. I don't even get a Girls' Night Out as consolation when my man's out of town.

My phone pings. A text from Rob:

Fancy dinner here tonight? St Alphonsus widows unite!

I smile. Don't tell me. Pizza?

I'm hurt. I do other takeaways too.

I hesitate. It would certainly beat sitting at home feeling sorry for myself all night. And I enjoy Rob; I'd be lying if I said I didn't get off a little on the fact that he obviously fancies me. But we've never got together on our own, and I don't know if it's a good idea. The rule book got torn up on Valentine's Night, and now I'm not sure where we are.

My fingers move rapidly over the screen.

Charlie cool w me coming over while she's away?

Her idea.

That changes things. Maybe if Rob and I are hanging out together, he won't be so paranoid about Charlie and Kit being away together. Which is probably why she suggested it – smart girl. I tap away at the screen again.

OK. Y not. What time?

7? U bringing Emmy?

At sleepover, I text. Just me. OK?

C u in an hour. And wear the kinky boots!

For pizza??

You're right, bad idea. The house would spontaneously combust if you walked in wearing them . . . so would I . . .

I laugh. I'm almost tempted. Wd wake up this dull village.

You know me. I like a good bang.

I'm still laughing as I go upstairs to change. Rob has a serious shoe fetish; anything high and spiky works. I pull out the chocolate-brown suede knee boots he loves, pairing them with a denim miniskirt I've had since forever and a zip-up cashmere hoodie. The four-inch heels are crippling to walk in, but I can just about scoot to and from the car without tripping. And it'll give him a cheap thrill, so why not?

I knock on his back door a little after seven, and Milly opens it. She's dressed as Spiderman; I'm escorted to the kitchen by a human arachnid leaping from dresser to bookcase with glorious disregard for property.

'Damn it, Milly! Stop climbing on the – oh, Mia! Sorry about this. Milly, get down! If your mother saw you on her desk, she'd have kittens!'

'I take it the princess phase is over?' I ask wryly.

'Never thought I'd miss pink boas.'

'Don't knock it. You'll be longing for Spidey when she goes all Goth on you.'

'Not a chance. She'll have been sent to a Romanian convent long before then. So, what can I get you to drink?'

'White wine would be great.'

I slide onto a kitchen stool, demurely crossing my legs. From my perch, I can see through into the dining room, which is formally laid for two with napkins and crystal and fat candles. I smile inwardly at his rather touching need to impress. 'You expecting company?' I tease.

'Milly ate with the babysitter before I got in from work, so I thought you and I could sit down in peace and quiet and enjoy our meal,' Rob says, handing me my wine. 'Salmon work for you?'

'You're cooking?'

'I realize it won't be up to Kit's standard,' Rob says, slightly miffed, 'but I *can* cook.'

'Salmon would be great,' I enthuse. 'Can I do anything to help?'

'Just cross and uncross your legs like that a few more times. God, I love those boots.'

He puts a pan on the stove and starts sautéing some garlic. 'So, how was Florida? I never really got to ask the other night.'

'As I recall, we were otherwise occupied,' I say slyly. 'Florida was great. It was good to visit with my dad again; it's been a while. He seems to be doing well, despite the chemo. I think moving south from Boston has been good for him. He goes jogging every morning by the ocean, and he's looking happier than I've seen him in a while. And it was great to get some sun.'

'I bet. I'm surprised you came back.'

'Ditto,' I sigh, only half joking.

He tosses the salmon into the pan. 'D'you miss the States?'

'Some days more than others. I miss Dad. And it's nice knowing what people are talking about without having to ask. Like the other night, when Kit and I were at the pub with some of his friends, they all started quoting *Fawlty Towers* and I had no idea what was going on. Sometimes it can just get a little old, being the only Yank in the village.'

'I can imagine. If Dave mimicked my accent every time I opened my mouth, I'd get a little fed up, too.'

'Oh, he never fails to entertain.'

Rob makes a Caesar salad from scratch, grinding up anchovies while I grate some parmesan. I'm a little surprised: Charlie doesn't exactly talk up his domestic skills. As soon as the salmon's done, he plates it up and carries everything through to the dining room. I follow with the wine.

'Wow! This is seriously good,' I say appreciatively through a perfectly cooked mouthful of fish. 'Who knew?'

'Contrary to rumour, I can find my way around a kitchen,' Rob says dryly. 'I know it suits Charlie to present me as some kind of Neanderthal, but I pull my weight.'

'More than I do,' I say ruefully. 'I am the world's least domestic goddess.'

'With a body like yours, who cares?'

I laugh. 'You wouldn't say that if you were married to me.'

Rob proves surprisingly good company over dinner. We haven't spent much time alone until now; on the few occasions when we have, we haven't been talking. I can't deny it's been fun, but I'm enjoying the fact that tonight we've got the opportunity to relax and just be friends. He's certainly making an effort. Not only with the food; he's going out of his way to entertain, topping up my glass and making me laugh. It's almost like a first date, but without the nerves. As long as he doesn't get the wrong idea. A little light flirting is fun, but there's nothing else on the menu as far as I'm concerned.

Milly climbs onto my lap as we finish a delicious raspberry sorbet. 'Will you read me a story?'

'Go on,' Rob says. 'I'll clear up here and put on some coffee.'

Three chapters of *Little House on the Prairie* later – 'I've been saving it for you,' Milly says earnestly. 'You're the only one with the right accent' – she's spark out, her favourite stuffed tortoise clutched in her arms.

I go back downstairs and join Rob in the sitting room. 'You're a brick for doing that,' he says gratefully. 'I know this makes me a terrible father, but I hate reading bedtime stories.'

'It's better than having them read something *to* you. That takes *hours*. You sit there trying not to scream while they spend six minutes sounding out a single word. Kids shouldn't be allowed to read till they're good at it.'

Rob snorts. 'I take it you're not home-schooling Emmy any time soon?'

'Are you kidding?' I sit on the sofa beside him and put my legs over his lap. 'One or other of us would end up dead by the end of the first day. Can I take the boots off now? My feet are killing me.'

'Let me.'

He grasps the heels and tugs them off. I drape my stockinged feet back over his knees and lean sideways against his shoulder. Van Morrison is playing on the iPod, and the lights are turned down low. I feel relaxed and mellow and slightly drunk. When Rob kisses the top of my head, I smile and snuggle comfortably into him.

He kisses me again, turning my face towards him. I don't think I've kissed him before. He tastes minty: he must have brushed his teeth while I was upstairs.

'Rob . . .'

'You are so damn sexy,' Rob says huskily. 'I'm at halfmast just sitting here with you.'

He is, too. His erection is digging into my hip as I lean across his lap. 'Maybe I should be going,' I say softly.

'You've had nearly a bottle of wine. You'd better give yourself a chance to sober up,' he says. 'Here, why don't you let me rub your shoulders while you finish your coffee?'

I do feel a bit light-headed. I must have drunk more than I thought. I dip my neck obediently and Rob starts to knead my shoulders. The pressure is soothing, and when his hands dip a little lower in front, skimming the contours of my breasts, I barely notice. Gently, he unzips my sweater, his fingers slipping inside the lace trim of my bra. I should stop him, really, and I will in a minute. It's just so nice, that's all. And it's not like we haven't done this before.

He eases me back on the sofa, his body half covering mine as he kisses me. Somehow, he's unhooked my bra, freeing my breasts, and is sliding my sweater down my arms.

'Rob,' I breathe, pushing lightly against his chest. 'Rob, I'm not sure this is a good idea.'

'Charlie said she didn't mind,' he whispers. His mouth is on my throat, and I feel a liquid beat between my thighs.

'No, but . . .'

'Kit said it was OK, didn't he? He didn't mind the other night.'

I'm finding it hard to think. I've had too much to drink and Rob has his hand up my skirt, inside my panties, and he's stroking me with firm, rhythmic, intoxicating strokes, and his mouth is on my breast, sending hot sparks of desire zinging through me. He stops for a moment to unzip his jeans and I sit up abruptly. 'I don't think we should, Rob. I'm sorry.'

'Come on. You know you want to. Last time was amazing, wasn't it?'

I pull my skirt down and look around for my sweater. 'It just doesn't feel right, not without Kit and Charlie.'

'What d'you think they're doing right now?'

'I'm sure they're not doing anything like this,' I manage as Rob pushes me back down on the sofa again. He's naked now, and my body flames beneath his touch. He is incredibly attractive. Oh God. I'm not sure how much longer I can keep saying no.

'Let me just taste you,' he pants. 'We can stop then. Just let me taste you.'

He's already between my legs, teasing me with expert flicks of his tongue. It feels good; beyond good. Kit told me to go with what I wanted, to have fun. He wouldn't mind. That's assuming he ever finds out . . .

No. If I'm afraid of telling him, then it can't be right.

'Please, Rob,' I say, pulling hard at his shoulders. 'We have to stop.'

He raises his head. Man, he's good-looking. He has this

raw, animal sexuality that just turns me inside out. The expression in his eyes tells me he knows exactly what he's doing to me.

Without breaking our gaze, he pushes his fingers inside me. I can't help it, I'm coming. I claw at the sofa as my orgasm breaks over me. 'Jesus, Rob. Oh God, stop. Please, we have to stop.'

'You don't mean that,' Rob gasps.

With a huge effort of will, I scissor my legs, forcing his fingers out of me, scrabbling to sit up. 'I do. I'm sorry, we can't.'

'You're going to leave me like this?' Rob says, half laughing.

I slide to my knees and take him in my mouth. I don't really want to, but I should have stopped this earlier. I have to give him something now.

He pushes back against my shoulders. 'No. I want to fuck you.'

'I can't. I'm sorry, I can't. Not like this. It feels all wrong.'

'Isn't that why you came over?'

'No!' I force a smile, groping around on the floor for my clothes. 'No. Come on, Rob. Don't spoil the evening. I should just finish my coffee and go home.'

'You're just going to leave me high and dry?'

Suddenly the mood has changed. He's not laughing now – his expression is dark and unsmiling. I'm acutely aware I'm half-naked, my breasts exposed and my skirt rucked up around my waist. I don't even know what happened to my panties. I grab a cushion and hold it against myself.

'Rob, I said *no*,' I repeat firmly. 'Let's just leave it.'

'Now? You're saying no *now*?'

'Please, Rob. Don't be like this . . .'

'You can't come over and tease me all night and then say no!' he exclaims. 'For fuck's sake, Mia! This isn't a game!'

I stand up. 'I'm going home.'

He moves so fast I don't see it coming. One minute I'm turning towards the door, and the next Rob has me bent over the arm of the sofa, his knee between my thighs, forcing my legs apart. Suddenly he's inside me, thrusting hard and angrily. He yanks my hair, snapping my head back, his other hand gripping my arm so tightly I cry out in pain. I'm dry with fear. It feels like he's scraping out my insides with sandpaper. I'm shocked how much it hurts.

He pumps into me one final time, then stiffens, shudders and abruptly pulls out. I slump against the sofa, too stunned to move. *I can't believe what just happened. I can't believe he just did that to me.*

He zips up his jeans behind me. 'Let me get you that coffee.'

Slowly I turn my head. I stare at him in disbelief. He doesn't quite meet my eyes. Does he think we're just going to go back to normal? To pretend this *never happened*?

I push myself upright and back away, my boots and clothes in my arms. I can feel his cum trickling coldly down the inside of my thigh.

'Mia, wait . . .'

'Don't you dare touch me!'

The gravel is cold and sharp against my bare feet. My hand shakes as I open the car door. I throw my clothes onto the passenger seat as I clamber in, lock all the doors and rest my head against the steering wheel, trembling from head to foot. *I can never tell Kit about this. He'd kill Rob. No one can ever know.*

How did this happen? How did I let this happen?

I press the heels of my hands against my eyes and sit up. I pull on my sweater, fighting to get my shaking arms into the sleeves. I feel starkly, unnervingly sober. I drive home carefully, sticking to the speed limit, stopping at every light. I want to cry with relief when I finally pull into my own driveway, but somehow I hold back the tears.

I run into the safety of my home, pausing only to open the trash can and throw in the boots.

14

Charlie

No one ever lost money by underestimating the self-control of a man left alone with an attractive woman. It's entirely my fault for believing my husband has a conscience, let alone a single shred of self-restraint.

'Just because you *could* didn't mean you *had* to!' I cry tearfully.

'Then why the hell did you tell me it was OK?'

'Jesus, Rob! Are you really that stupid, or just that fucking selfish?'

He stiffens. 'I refuse to have a discussion with you if you can't be civil.'

'You lost any right to complain about my language when you screwed my best friend!'

He pushes his face into mine, his eyes flat and hard. 'You stood right here in the kitchen and told me you didn't have a problem with it. Now you want to crush my balls because I took you at your word?'

'I said it might be nice if you and Mia took the girls out for pizza!'

'That's not all you said, and you know it.'

We square off furiously, neither of us giving an inch. 'OK, I also asked you if you wanted to sleep with her, yes!' I concede angrily. 'How does asking the question qualify as *permission*?'

'That's not the way I remember it,' he snaps.

'Go on, tell me. How, exactly, *do* you remember it?'

'You told me if I really wanted to sleep with her, I should go ahead.'

'And you took that as a green light?' I demand.

'How else was I supposed to take it?'

He knows damn well I was being sarcastic. I can't believe he's being this manipulative and disingenuous. 'You were supposed to take it the way it was meant,' I say bitterly.

'So this was another one of your little tests, was it?'

'Of course not!'

He laughs shortly. 'Would you like to get a mirror and look yourself in the eye when you say that?'

Suddenly I'm not so sure. I know how strong the sexual attraction is between them. *Was* I testing him? Did a part of me want to push him and see if he was capable of spending an evening in her company without trying to screw her?

'So why *did* you tell me to ask her over?' Rob demands now, scenting blood in the water. 'What did you think was going to happen?'

'I thought you'd have a pizza!'

'You asked me if I wanted to fuck her, and I told you yes. And you told me to go ahead.'

'You know I didn't mean it! I was just . . .'

'What? Setting me up? Playing another one of your mind games?'

'For God's sake, Rob! So what if I was! You couldn't have proved me wrong, for once? You couldn't have turned her down?'

'You started this whole thing with Mia and Kit!' Rob exclaims angrily. *'You're* the one with the agenda. Where do you get off, turning on me for doing exactly what you set me up to do! You helped me *fuck* her, for God's sake!'

I've got no answer to that. He's right. And I still feel guilty about it. 'It wasn't enough for you, though, was it?'

'I can't win with you, can I? You *wanted* me to fail your stupid bloody test so you could take the moral high ground and hold it over me for another five years. Well, you got what you wanted. Happy now?'

'You're the one who cheated! How dare you turn it back on me!'

'I did not cheat! You asked me if I wanted to fuck her, and I was honest and said yes. You came home and asked me what happened, and I told you the truth. So how did I cheat? Yes, we had sex. Yes, it was good. Yes, I enjoyed it. Do you want to know what position we did it in? How many times I came?'

'Why *did* you tell me, Rob? Because you wanted to rub my nose in it? Or because you were scared Mia would tell me first?'

'What d'you want from me, Charlie? Blood?'

'I want to know I'm enough for you!' I burst out. 'Whatever I give you, it's never enough, is it? You always want more!'

'I can't deal with this.' He grabs his keys and wallet

from the kitchen table. 'You create this whole little manufactured world, and then you piss on me for doing exactly what you expect me to. I need some air.'

The back door slams behind him. I collapse at the table, my head in my hands. I don't know how he does it. He screwed around with my best friend, and I'm the one left feeling I'm in the wrong. As always, he's managed to turn the tables and come out on top. And this time, I only have myself to blame.

I want to crawl into bed and pull the duvet over my head, never mind that it's Saturday morning and I've hardly seen Milly all week; but it's her seventh birthday tomorrow and we're having a party for a dozen little girls, including Emmy, at our house. So while she's next door playing with the neighbour's daughter, I transform our sitting room into a fairy grotto, stringing Christmas lights around the walls, draping swathes of pink satin at the windows and looping pink netting across the ceiling. I've ordered a three-tiered princess cake from the bakery in Oxford and bought Cinderella-themed paper plates and cups. The effect is nauseatingly Disney and the antithesis of every feminist instinct, but it's what Milly wanted when we discussed her party last month, so I'm not going to pass judgement. I hope if she'd been a boy with princess dreams, I'd be as sanguine.

When she gets home, Milly takes one look at the wonderland I've created and bursts into tears.

Rob's just back and is pulling off his coat. 'It's been Spiderman and superheroes for weeks,' he hisses as Milly storms upstairs to her room, declaring her life ruined. 'How could you not *know*?'

'She never said!'

'Perhaps if you worried about your own child more often, instead of everyone else's at that school of yours, you'd have noticed without being told.'

How is this fair? I take Milly to dental appointments and parties, cheer on her football team from the sideline in the freezing rain and entertain her every weekend while Rob goes diving, but I make one mistake, and he's now the Parent Who Cares, while I'm the neglectful, career-obsessed working mother.

'I don't have the energy to fight you,' I say tiredly. 'It's our daughter's birthday tomorrow, and she's upstairs sobbing her heart out. D'you think we could put our own issues aside just for today and work together?'

For a moment I think he's going to slap me down, but then he shoots me an equally weary smile. 'OK. I've got some netting in the shed,' he sighs. 'I used it last year to keep the birds off the tomatoes. We can take down the pink stuff and use that instead?'

'We could put bats and spiders in the netting from the Hallowe'en box, but it's not really superhero stuff, is it?'

'Gotham City,' Rob exclaims, inspired. 'You sort out the cake and the kitchen. Leave the sitting room to me.'

I get on the phone to the bakery, which comes up trumps, offering to re-ice the cake overnight in Wonder Woman colours and add as many plastic superheroes as they can find. By the time I come back from an emergency run for superhero plates and cups, Rob has taken down the pink netting and transformed Cinderella's castle into Gotham City. When Milly comes back downstairs, she bursts into tears again – but this time they're happy ones.

He bails on Sunday before the party starts, of course,

but I expected that. He's done more to help than usual, and anyway I'm not sure I'm ready to see him and Mia together in the same room. I want to concentrate on Milly, and I know I won't be able to do that if I'm watching to see how Rob and Mia behave together. Frankly, I wish she wasn't coming; I need to get my head round what's happened first. I realize I don't have the right to feel either jealous or angry, given the fact that I opened this door, but I'm only human. And she *did* sleep with my husband.

At three o'clock precisely, the house is overrun by a dozen small, over-excited Spidergirls, Catwomen and stubborn princesses who have no intention of swapping their glittery tiaras for silly capes and face masks. I pour fortifying glasses of wine for the mothers and one father foolish enough to brave a little girls' party, and then chivvy the children outside to wear themselves out under the watchful eye of Gail's thirteen-year-old twins, who I'm paying a king's ransom to babysit. Mia and I barely get a chance to say hello in all the furore.

Gail corners me in the hallway as I hang up coats. 'What's this about St Alphonsus closing?' she demands. 'Is it true?'

'Where did you hear that?' I exclaim.

'Never mind. Is it true?'

'No. Well, not exactly.' I hesitate. 'Gail, if I tell you, it can't go any further.'

'So it *is* true?'

'The Sisters of Calvary are withdrawing from the school, yes, but it absolutely isn't going to close—'

'*Withdrawing*? Why?'

I drag her down the hall, out of earshot of the kitchen. 'Shhh! Look, they don't *want* to. The school itself is doing really well, but the Sisters are getting old. There simply aren't the vocations any more. They've got a huge pension shortfall, and they can't afford to keep the school on. They need to sell up so they can access the money tied up in the land.'

'So what's going to happen?'

I sigh. 'That's the million-dollar question. There's talk of a merger with Berwicks—'

'You can't do that! It'll ruin St Alphonsus!'

'Gail, *please*. Keep your voice down. I can't have this getting out, or there'll be a mass exodus of pupils. Who did you hear it from, anyway?'

'One of the trustees told Dave in confidence. He knows our girls go there and wanted to give us a heads-up. If you're not going to merge, what *is* going to happen?'

'We're trying to figure out a way to run it as an independent. If we can put a financial plan together and get backing from the banks, we may be able to make it work.'

'You should talk to George Wyatt. He's one of the trustees, too, isn't he? He hates Berwicks. He'll pull out all the stops to make sure a merger doesn't happen.'

'Thanks, Gail. I'll do that.' I pin a bright smile on my face and we return to the kitchen. 'So. Can I help anyone to more wine?'

Tact may not be Gail's strongest suit, but as the mother of four teenage girls, she's a hardened professional when it comes to little girls' parties. She successfully oversees pass the parcel, musical chairs, dead fish, karaoke and our own unique version of *Britain's Got Talent*, ruthlessly dealing with any number of catfights and tantrums along the way. I leave her in charge and slope outside for a moment's peace and quiet. I must have been mad to organize a party at home. There's something about the pitch of a dozen girlish seven-year-old voices that sets my teeth on edge. I could never have taught at a primary school. Give me hormones and teenage drama any day.

I suddenly notice Mia sitting on the low wall near the jacuzzi staring into space. She jumps guiltily when she sees me, concealing something behind her back.

'What are you doing out here, Mia? You must be freezing.'

She produces a smouldering cigarette with an embarrassed smile. 'Sneaking a cig. Didn't want the kids to see.'

'I didn't know you smoked.'

'I don't.' She shrugs. 'Well, not often.'

'Kids' parties not your thing?'

'Oh no, it's fine. I've just been kinda stressed lately.'

She doesn't look herself, I have to admit. It's only been a week since I last saw her, but beneath the fading Florida tan she looks tired and drawn. 'Everything OK?'

'Sure. I'm OK, really. Just a lot on my mind.'

I sit on the wall next to her. Slightly to my surprise, now I'm with her I don't actually feel jealous or angry. Aside from the fact that I'm as much to blame for the situation as she is, she's my friend, and something's obviously wrong. I wonder if there are problems at home. Maybe Kit hasn't been quite as indifferent to her sleeping with Rob as he's made out.

'Look, Mia,' I say carefully. 'I'm sorry about what happened on Valentine's Day. I know it went further than you wanted, and I'm sorry for my part in that.'

She looks at me blankly. 'Valentine's Day?'

'I pushed you further than you felt comfortable with Rob. I shouldn't have done that, it wasn't fair.'

'Oh. That. No, it's fine,' she says distantly.

There's something about her affect that's off. I can't quite put my finger on it. It's not like her to be so distracted and subdued. 'So you're OK with it, then?'

'Is Milly enjoying her birthday?'

The abrupt change of subject takes me by surprise. 'Milly? Oh, yes, she's having a great time.' I hesitate. 'Mia, if you're worried about what happened with Rob when Kit and I were out of town, don't be. I'm not upset with you. He and I have a few personal issues to sort out, but none of it has anything to do with you and me.'

'He told you?'

'Yesterday, as soon as I got home. Look, it's OK. I know you guys fooled around. But I don't have a problem with—'

'He said we fooled around?'

I don't know why she's making me labour the point. 'He admitted you slept together,' I say uncomfortably. 'He didn't try to hide anything. Like I said, he and I have to work through a few things, but that's not for you to worry about. I'll be honest, I wouldn't want it happening every week,' I add, smiling to take the sting from my words, 'but as long as everything is kept out in the open, I can work with that. Please, I don't want it to affect our friendship.'

Mia looks directly at me for the first time. I have absolutely no idea what's going on in her head. She laughs coolly and stubs out her cigarette on the wall. 'I promise you. It won't happen again.'

I watch as she gets up and walks back into the house, feeling distinctly uneasy. There's something she's not telling me, something to do with Rob. And I know instinctively I'm not going to like it.

15

Mia

It's my fault. I should never have gotten myself into such a dumb situation. What was I *thinking*? Going over to his place wearing a short skirt and those stupid high-heeled boots when his wife was out of town. Sitting there at dinner drinking and flirting with him, then snuggling up to him all cosy on the sofa. No wonder he got the wrong message. Obviously I tried to call a halt when he got a bit too hands-on, but evidently I didn't try hard enough. I know I left it a bit late, but I did say no, several times. I said no very clearly. I tried to push him off and get dressed, I *told* him I didn't want to, but I guess he couldn't help himself. He was all revved up by then. Which is as much my fault as his. I can hardly blame him for getting carried away in the heat of the moment . . .

Fucking bastard fucking bastard fucking bastard fucking bastard.

I drain my wine glass and reach for my mascara. I need to get over this. There's no point being mad at Rob. What happened happened. It's not like I was dragged into a back alley and raped by a stranger. You can't call what happened to me *rape*. I've been around the block enough times to know things are rarely that black and white. Someone jumps you in an alley, holds a knife to your throat, no one's going to question what that is, no matter what you're wearing. But if you're on a date and you've both been drinking and you go back to his place and make out and you allow him to get to second base . . . maybe you say no at first, but then he kisses you and strokes you and turns you on and you change your mind, you let him put his hand in your panties . . . which means that when he tries to move to third base and you say no again, even though you think you really *mean* it this time, naturally he'll assume that a bit more kissing, a bit more stroking and you'll change your mind again, and of course often that's exactly what happens.

We'd had sex before, after all. Just a few days earlier, right in front of his wife. I hadn't planned on that, either. I'd told Charlie it was my personal no-go area. But when it came to it, I didn't object, did I? I was far too carried away myself by then, and if I'm honest, deep down I wanted to do it too. Rob and I have had this chemistry since the very beginning. I didn't want to take the responsibility of saying yes, but when it happened, I went along with it. I enjoyed it. So can I really say I didn't want it when Rob forced himself on me over the back of the sofa? How is it any different?

I *didn't* want it. I really didn't. Not just physically. I *told* Rob, I said it didn't feel right, not without Kit and Charlie. I said I wanted to stop, didn't I? I said it more than once.

But he put his fingers inside me and I came, so how can I not have wanted it?

He should have stopped. I asked him to stop. He called me a tease and did it anyway.

Bastard bastard bastard bastard bastard.

I refuse to see it as rape. It was . . . non-consensual sex. A misunderstanding, a situation that got out of hand. We're all grown-ups here, we all know the difference. I'm not a *victim*. I won't be a victim. If it *were* rape, then that would make me vulnerable, my whole world fragile. It would mean Rob had gotten the upper hand. It would mean the death of my friendship with Charlie, because how could I be friends with the wife of a man who raped me and not tell her? How could I look her in the eye? But if it was just a misunderstanding, a mistake, that's different. I can draw a line under it and put it down to experience. I don't have bruises. No one attacked me. I'd willingly had sex with Rob before, I've admitted I fancied him, and even if I didn't want it this time – even if I *really* didn't want it – does that make him a rapist? Or just someone who got the wrong end of the stick?

We've all been playing with fire for months with our sex games and foursomes. Where there are flames, someone's bound to get burned. I need to put it behind me and move on. It's been six weeks now. I can't keep stewing about it.

'Mia!' Kit calls up the stairs. 'Are you ready? They'll be here any minute!'

I open my bedroom door. 'Five minutes! I'll be right there!'

I square up to my reflection in the mirror and pick out my hottest red lipstick. I've managed to avoid Rob since it happened, scheduling my dates with Charlie for when I know he's going to be elsewhere. Not that I've seen much of her recently either; she and Kit have been holed up at work trying to put together some Hail Mary plan to save the school. I'm hoping enough time's elapsed for me to draw a line under everything. Though it would be good to maybe hear a *sorry* from him. But apart from that one night, we've always gotten on so well. And I adore Charlie. *Time to look at the bigger picture, Mia. Suck it up and grow a pair. It's not like you haven't had bad sex before. That's all that night was. Bad sex. No need to make a drama out of it.*

I blot my lipstick and tug down my very short, very tight black dress. No way am I letting what happened with Rob dictate what I wear.

Kit looks startled when I appear in the kitchen. 'Mia. That's a bit much, isn't it?'

'Don't you like it?'

'It's not a question of whether I like it or not. It's just dinner. You don't think that dress is a bit OTT?'

'You think I'm too old for it?'

He sighs. 'Why do you always do this?'

'Do what?'

'Make it personal.'

'How is telling me I'm too old to wear a short skirt *not* personal?'

'I did *not* say you were too old. Don't put words in my mouth.'

'So what's wrong with it then?'

He attempts to put his arm around me, but I shrug him off and go to the fridge to refill my wine glass. 'Mia, please. Why are you trying to pick a fight with me?'

'You just said you don't like my dress. I'd like to know why, that's all.'

'You really want to know?'

'I really want to know.'

'Fine,' he sighs. 'I think you look better in elegant clothes that flatter your figure, not dresses that reveal everything you had for breakfast. You're an incredibly sexy woman, and you don't need to wear cheap, obvious clothes to prove it.'

I'm shocked by a sudden rush of tears. I turn away, furious with myself. I'm sick of being such an emotional train wreck. I'm not a crier, never have been. What in hell is *wrong* with me?

'Mia . . .'

'It's none of your business what I wear,' I snap defiantly. 'Who says you get to judge?'

'I'm not judging—'

'You never wear the clothes *I* like,' I add irrelevantly. 'And I keep asking you to grow your hair longer, but you never do.'

'Mia, I have a job to hold down,' Kit says tiredly. 'I can't turn up to work looking like a leftover from the Seventies.'

'So quit bitching when I wear a dress you don't like.'

'I didn't say I don't like it. I just said—'

The back door opens. 'Hey, guys!' Charlie calls.

Kit touches my hand and smiles, an olive branch. *Please, let's stop fighting*, his smile says. *Let's just enjoy this evening with our friends.*

I snatch my hand away. I can't help it. I don't want to fight either, but everything seems to rub me the wrong way these days. I can't bear to be touched; I can't stand being left alone. I'm constantly exhausted, but I can't sleep. I haven't had an orgasm since . . . *since*. It's like I've gotten some kind of mental block. I keep thinking I've worked through all the crap, and then it comes back and bites me in the ass. But I shouldn't be taking it out on Kit. It's not his fault he wasn't there that night. He doesn't know what happened, and obviously I haven't told him.

With a quiet sigh, Kit turns from me and takes the proffered bottle of wine from Charlie's hand. 'Happy birthday,' he says warmly, kissing her cheek.

'This is so sweet of you,' she says. 'Sundays are a rotten night to have a birthday. Everywhere decent is closed.'

'Café Allen is always open to you.'

'Wow! That's some outfit!' she exclaims in surprise as she comes into the kitchen and catches sight of me. 'You certain you didn't get the wrong venue?'

'Just felt like pushing the boat out,' I shrug. 'Not every day your best friend turns twenty-nine.'

'Happens more often than you'd think,' Charlie says wryly.

'Great dress,' Rob says, hovering behind his wife.

I don't look at him. 'Thanks.'

'What can I get you to drink?' Kit asks. 'Cocktail? Wine? Champagne?'

'White wine would be great. What are you cooking? My mouth's watering already.'

'That's just the stock for the lobster.'

'Lobster? My God, Kit, that's so extravagant! You shouldn't have.'

He laughs. 'Blame Mia. She had me scour the countryside for Maine lobster, which are apparently the only ones worth eating.'

Rob lifts the lid off the pot and sniffs. I watch him, waiting for some kind of covert signal to me, an acknowledgement that he owes me an apology. A remorseful smile, a look that tells me he knows he screwed up and is sorry for it. But he's just carrying on smiling and chatting as if nothing's wrong. My anger, never far away these days, starts to bubble up. How dare he tell Charlie we *slept* together? As if I was complicit in it! And I can't set the record straight without telling her what really happened. Which means the bastard's going to get away with it.

I put on my game face and do my best to get in the mood for Charlie's sake, but I feel sick every time I look at Rob. Kit serves a delicious starter of seared foie gras, and then the lobster with clarified butter, but I'm too tense and angry to eat more than a few mouthfuls. I sit at the dining table knocking back wine, feeling like I'm watching the proceedings from a thousand miles away.

'A toast,' Kit says as the last clean-picked lobster claw is thrown into the dish in the centre of the table. 'To Charlie.'

I hand her a small wrapped package. 'Happy birthday. It's from all of us.'

'Oh, Mia,' Charlie says. 'You didn't need to do that.'

'What is it?' Kit asks me.

'Kit,' I groan. 'You kind of just killed the "from all of us" tag.'

'If Kit had a hand in picking it, it would be a remastered edition of a black-and-white classic film, or an esoteric edition of Twain essays,' Charlie grins.

Sometimes I think she knows my husband better than I do.

She opens her present. A pair of elegant silver Dinny Hall hoop earrings. The kind I'd love to own myself. And isn't that the definition of a perfect gift?

'Oh, Mia,' she murmurs softly. 'They are *so* beautiful. You really shouldn't have.'

'Of course I should,' I say, reaching for the wine bottle.

'So, what did your lovely husband get you for your birthday?'

'I haven't given it to her yet,' Rob says quickly.

'We don't really do birthday presents,' Charlie adds.

'C'mon. Seriously? You haven't bought her anything?'

'Mia,' Kit says warningly.

I'm a little tired of people saying *Mia* like that. I'm neither an unexploded bomb nor a child. 'You *did* buy her a gift, right?' I demand. 'I mean, who doesn't buy their wife a present on her birthday? Are you embarrassed about it? Is it a vacuum cleaner? A fax machine?'

'No, of course not.'

'So why can't you tell us?'

'It's probably a surprise, Mia,' Kit says, exasperated. 'None of our business.'

'Oh, it's a surprise?' I drawl. 'Something lovely and romantic? Diamonds? A trip to the Caribbean? I can totally see why you'd want to keep that secret.'

'Like Charlie said, we don't really do birthday presents,' Rob mutters.

But I'm on a roll now, fuelled by the best part of a bottle of Pinot Grigio. 'So you didn't get her *anything*?' I press. 'Nothing at all? You just don't bother with all that kind of stuff these days? Well, you have been together much longer than we have. Kit got me a beautiful sea glass necklace last year. It didn't cost that much, but the *thought* that went into it . . .'

'Rob's not that big on gifts,' Charlie says, her smile a little tight. 'We work it out as we go along. I see something I like, he owes me a birthday present . . .'

'That's not entirely fair,' Rob protests. 'I told you I'd take you shopping at the weekend.'

She tops up her wine. 'Like I haven't heard *that* before.'

'Like you haven't spent a month's salary on a bloody necklace before.'

'Not *your* salary,' she says sharply. 'That wouldn't buy me a pair of earrings.'

Kit spreads his arms. 'Hey. I think we're getting off the point here. It's Charlie's birthday, so let's all—'

'Fuck that!' Rob says, pushing back from the table. 'You have a problem with what I do for you, Charlie, why don't you tell me?'

'I didn't say that . . .'

'Fuck you didn't.'

'Rob—'

I shove back my own chair and stand up. 'Leave her alone.'

'Stay out of this,' Rob snaps.

'I don't think so. You're in *my* house. Charlie is *my* guest!'

'*Mia*,' Kit says. 'Stay out of this.'

'Stay out of this?' I shout, suddenly incandescent. 'After everything he's done?'

Kit looks bewildered. 'What's going on? This has nothing to do with you.'

'I think we need to leave,' Charlie says, edging back her chair.

'No, please,' I beg, suddenly realizing things are getting out of hand. 'Don't let's spoil your birthday.'

'I think you've already done that,' Rob sneers.

I want to kill him. *I want to kill him*. This isn't some abstract it-would-be-nice-if-he-was-dead fantasy. I want to physically tear him limb from limb, I want to gouge his eyes out, I want to see him bleed, I want to see his dick served on a plate before me . . .

I want him to be sorry.

'We had a great evening,' Charlie says, clearly close to tears. 'Thank you so much.'

'There's no need to go,' Kit says calmly. 'Let's all sit down and have dessert. It would be a shame to spoil a good evening and end on a sour note. Come on, Rob, Mia. Sit down.'

Charlie hesitates. 'We can stay for dessert,' she says to Rob. 'Since they've gone to so much trouble.'

'We're leaving,' he snaps.

'Come on. If Kit's gone to all the trouble—'

'I said *we're leaving*. What part of that don't you understand?'

'Don't talk to her like that,' I say suddenly.

'Keep out of this,' Rob snaps.

'No! You can't talk to her like that!'

'Honestly, it's OK,' Charlie says. 'It's time we were going anyway.'

'Where d'you get off, talking to your wife like that?' I demand, swaying slightly. 'Who in hell d'you think you are?'

'Goodnight, Kit,' Rob says, ignoring me. 'Thanks for a great dinner.'

'Charlie,' I say. '*Charlie.*'

'I have to go,' Charlie says hastily. 'We'll see you next weekend.'

Rob throws me a look. A look laced with triumph and satisfaction – and menace. A look I remember only too well. A look that says, *I win and there's nothing you can do about it.*

Kit shows them out. I run upstairs to my office and lock the door, leaning against it as if someone is trying to batter their way in. He's right. There's nothing I can do. It's just my word against his. Why should anyone believe me? He's gotten away with it. He's gotten everything he wants.

Except . . .

Except I happen to have access to a world far bigger than Rob imagines. I have an audience. A following. In this world of Twitter and Instagram and Facebook, I have friends.

Did no one ever tell him the pen is mightier than the sword?

16

Charlie

The morning after my birthday is not a good one. There's nothing good about birthdays once you've hit forty at the best of times. And yesterday was decidedly *not* the best of times. Rob and I rowed bitterly all the way home from Kit and Mia's, and I ended up spending the night in the spare room. My back aches from the unfamiliar mattress, and my head from too much wine. And Rob and I have resolved nothing.

I put on the kettle and stare blankly out of the kitchen window. What on earth happened last night? Rob was stroppy before we even left home, complaining that he didn't want to go out, he was tired, it was a Sunday night and he had to get up in the morning. He made us late getting there, which is unforgivably rude when someone is cooking you dinner. Then Mia spent the whole evening hissing and spitting like a cat at Rob, and he was utterly obnoxious back. You'd have thought if anyone had the right to be upset, it would be Kit and me. I think it's fair to say we're the injured parties here, given what the two of them got up to while we were away. If we can deal with it, why can't they?

Suddenly chilled, I fold my hands around my tea. I know I haven't heard the full story about that night. Rob only gets aggressive when he's in the wrong. I assumed at the time it was because he felt guilty for sleeping with her, but maybe there's more to it. Mia's been off with me ever since it happened; in fact, I've hardly seen her, and when I have, she's been edgy and distracted. I've been putting it down to her annoyance over the long hours Kit and I have been putting in at work while we try to come up with a rescue plan for the school. I thought she might be jealous of me, even. But maybe I've been getting it all backwards. Perhaps *I'm* the one who should be jealous. Was their fight last night a row – or a lover's tiff?

I wouldn't put it past Rob to have an affair. It wouldn't be the first time, after all. But Mia? Would she really do that to Kit or to me?

There's a sudden roar of anger from the direction of Rob's study, and I jump, scalding my hand with hot tea. I'm running it under the cold tap as the kitchen door flies open, slamming into the wall so hard the cups on the dresser rattle.

'Rob! What on earth's the matter?'

'Did you know about this?' he shouts furiously.

'Did I know about what?'

'Mia! Have you seen what that bitch has done?'

I stare at him, completely nonplussed. 'I have no idea what you're talking about.'

'It's all over the fucking Internet! I've had half a dozen people text me already and it's not even eight o'clock in the morning! What the fuck does she think she's playing at! This is my fucking *career* we're talking about!'

'*What's* all over the Internet? What are you talking about?'

'Her blog! Her fucking *blog*!'

He shoves his iPad across the counter. I dry my hands and scroll down the page, speed-reading Mia's blog entry from last night. She has a beautiful knack for capturing the British psyche in all its awkward, self-deprecating, apologetic self-consciousness, but for once I don't have time to appreciate her epistolary skill. I get to the bottom of the post, and blanch.

> And so to my own experience last night. Oh dear, Rob Brady, star employee of Black Rock IT. Shouting at your wife in front of the neighbors? How very ungentlemanly, especially when someone's gone to all the trouble of cooking you dinner. Back home to Mother, please, to learn some manners.

I look up at Rob in shock. I could kill Mia. Not because of what she's written, which isn't particularly vicious, but because she's just handed him a moral victory, regardless of whether or not he was in the wrong. She might see it as just taking him down a peg or two, and maybe in her self-regarding, virtual world of journalists and bloggers and the Twitterati this is just par for the course; but back in the real world, it doesn't work like that. It's bad enough she's used his full name, but by naming his employers too, she's taken this to a whole new level. Like so many companies these days, Black Rock is automatically alerted to every online mention; there's no way they'll miss a blog by a professional journalist with a syndicated US newspaper column. It could even cost him his job. If Mia wanted his attention, she's got it.

'It's everywhere!' Rob yells, red-faced with fury. 'Who the fuck does she think she is?'

'Have you asked her to take it down?'

'She's not answering her fucking phone!'

'Let me try ringing Kit—'

'I'll sue her for every penny she has!' he shouts. 'She won't have a pot to piss in by the time I'm finished with her!'

'Calm down,' I snap. 'No one's suing anyone. I don't suppose anyone's even seen it yet. Just ask her to take it down—'

'I'm not grovelling to her! *She's* the one who owes *me* an apology! I'll fucking get her *deported* . . .'

I shush him as Kit picks up. 'Sorry to call you so early, but—'

'I've seen it,' Kit says tersely. 'I had five texts from Gail and Dave about it before breakfast.'

Shit. 'Can you get her to take it down?'

'I've tried. She's not having any of it.'

'What do you mean she's not having any of it? Doesn't she realize the damage this could cause?'

Behind me Rob slams his fist on the counter. 'I'll have her fucking job for this! You tell him!'

'Would you back off?' I hiss, retreating into my study and shutting the door. 'Look, Kit, she *has* to take it down. Rob's boss is going to have a fit when he see this. Rob's job is on the line.'

'Believe me, I know. I've told her. But she's refusing to delete it, and unfortunately I can't make her.'

'Why? We both know this has nothing to do with freedom of speech.'

'Of course it doesn't. She's pissed off with him, and this is what she does. It's the world she lives in.'

'It's not the world *we* live in,' I say sharply.

Kit sighs heavily. 'Look, Charlie. The more I push her, the more she digs her heels in. I don't know what her problem is with Rob; she won't talk to me about it. Maybe you can get to the bottom of it. Hold on.'

I hear the sound of Kit's feet on the stairs, then snatches of a whispered conversation.

Tell her I'm asleep.

This is your mess, Mia. You clean it up.

I can't talk to her.

Mia, she's your best friend. You owe her an explanation, at least.

'Charlie,' Mia says suddenly in my ear. 'I'm not taking it down.'

'You have to,' I plead. 'Please, Mia. If anyone at Black Rock sees it, Rob could lose his job.'

'Bullshit.'

'Mia, Black Rock is an American company from the Midwest. I don't have to tell you what that means. He has to be squeaky clean. He had to sign an affidavit swearing he'd never smoked a cigarette before they'd even give him a job, for God's sake. And you're airing his dirty linen in public and naming them in print!'

'He should've thought about that before he started shooting his mouth off,' Mia retorts.

'Last night? That had nothing to do with you!' I protest. '*I'm* the one he was angry with. He behaved like a prat, and he was rude and obnoxious after Kit had gone to so much trouble, and believe me, I've told him as much. But you've gone way too far!'

'It's just a blog. I don't know why everyone's making such a big deal. Maybe next time he won't be so damn ungrateful when someone invites him to dinner.'

'It's not just a blog and you know it! Mia, please. Just take it down.'

There's a pause.

'Tell Rob I'll take it down if he apologizes,' she says suddenly.

'Apologizes for what?'

'Ask him.'

She hangs up on me. I go back into the kitchen, the phone clenched in my hand. The queasy feeling in my stomach intensifies. *Ask him*. But I've read enough courtroom thrillers to know no lawyer ever asks a question he doesn't know the answer to.

'You shouldn't have come,' Mia says, but she steps back from the door and lets me in.

'You didn't give me much choice.'

'I told you. All Rob has to do is apologize and I'll take it down.' She shrugs. 'Though I think everyone's getting their panties in a bunch over nothing. It's not like I called him a kiddy-fiddler.'

'That's not the point, Mia, and you know it. It almost doesn't matter *what* you said. It's the fact you said anything at all.'

She folds her arms, not budging from the hall, her expression stony. She has the same look of nervy defiance I see on the faces of kids at school when they know they've pushed things too far. I suppress the urge to shake some sense into her. I've learned the worst thing to do is back someone into a corner. It's all about saving face.

'Mia, why are you doing this?' I say reasonably. 'You're risking our friendship over one stupid row. It's not worth it.'

'Someone needs to teach him a lesson. He can't go around treating people like shit and expect to get away with it. There are *consequences*.'

Consequences? Does she truly not realize the implications of what she's done? Even if I buy into the idea that to her this really is no big deal, she must realize by now that to us it's a very big deal indeed.

'I know Rob can be difficult sometimes, and he was totally out of order last night, but this isn't the answer,' I say. 'If he's fired, we could lose everything – our house, Milly's school, all of it. Please, take that post down before it causes any more damage.'

She glares stubbornly at me from behind the barricade of her folded arms. 'If he's going to dish it out, he needs to learn to take it.'

'Well, he doesn't see it that way, and frankly, neither do I,' I snap, finally losing patience. 'I don't know what's going on with the two of you, but if you have an issue with him, you should have come and discussed it privately, not started a public slanging match. We're supposed to be *friends*.'

'Because he's been *such* a great friend to me.'

I gaze at her helplessly. Her body is rigid with anger, but her eyes tell a very different story. 'Mia, please,' I beg. 'Tell me what the problem is. I'm your friend. Help me make this right.'

For a moment I think I've reached her. Her expression

softens and I can sense how close she is to giving in. And then she shuts down again, her face hardening. 'Rob's the one who needs to make things right, not you.'

My own anger flares back into life. 'Fine. If you want to throw our friendship away over nothing, I can't stop you. I hope you think it's worth it,' I add bitterly. 'You're ruining things for Milly and Emmy, too. Not to mention making it almost impossible for Kit and me at work. But as long as *you* feel vindicated, that's all that matters.' I hesitate, waiting for Mia to say something in protest, but she doesn't even bother to look up. 'If that's the way you want it. I'll see myself out.'

By the time Rob gets home from work, my grief and hurt have congealed into cold, hard resentment. In just a few short months, Mia had become my closest friend. I *trusted* her. I shared my husband with her, for God's sake! Whatever her grievance is with him now, I don't deserve to be treated like this. I haven't done anything wrong. At the very least, she owes me some kind of explanation.

'How did things go at work?' I ask warily.

He throws his coat over the back of a chair, ignoring it when it slides onto the floor. 'The bitch took it down before the West Coast woke up, so fingers crossed it'll stay under the radar. I took some shit at the office here, but I think it's going to be OK.'

Despite my anger with Mia, I flinch at the insult. 'She took it down?'

'Sometime this morning. Obviously thought better of—'

'When?'

He shrugs and opens the fridge for a beer. 'How should I know? What does it matter? Before ten, anyway. I checked before I went into a conference call with Germany. Didn't want to get bloody ambushed.'

I didn't see Mia until eleven. She'd already removed the post before I reached her house! Why didn't she tell me? Why let me argue my case and plead with her if she'd already taken it down? Pride? Sheer stubbornness? It's almost as if she was looking for a fight.

Well, I guess that makes me Idiot of the Week.

Fine. I know when I'm not wanted. Maybe this whole *friendship* was just a game to her. Fodder for her bloody blog. Confessional journalism, isn't that what they call it? Clearly she needed raw material, and Rob and I provided it. God knows what she has up her sleeve for next week, though she'd better be very careful she doesn't reveal too many secrets.

I sink onto a kitchen stool, suddenly very tired. Mia must have known how incendiary that post was. She lit the blue touchpaper, and then stood and watched us burn.

'Are you OK?' Rob asks.

'It's been a long day.'

Unexpectedly he comes over and puts his arms around me. 'It's OK. I get it. She was your friend. I'm sorry it had to end like this.'

'How could she do this, Rob?' I mumble into his shoulder. Suddenly his arms seem like the safest place in the world. 'What did we ever do to her?'

'She's a journalist. They live by different rules. They don't give a damn about the rest of us.'

'Mia wasn't like that.'

'Well. Clearly she was.'

I want to argue, but I have no fight left. 'Did *you* see this coming?'

The briefest hesitation. 'No.' He sighs. 'I really thought Mia was one of us.'

'But you two always got on so well.'

'I made an effort. Because of you.'

I know that's not entirely true. How many times in the past have I begged Rob to be nicer to my friends for my sake? How many have I lost because he treated them so badly? But there's no point arguing about it now. 'I had no idea,' I say weakly.

'Poor darling. You always think the best of everyone.'

'Maybe if we just give it some time. Let all this blow over . . .'

'I don't think so,' Rob says sharply. 'Best to move on.'

I'm about to protest, but the words die on my lips. The bitter truth is, no one forced Mia to write that blog. Even if she didn't fully comprehend the ramifications of what she was doing, which I find unlikely, she still refused to back down even when she knew how upset we were. She seemed almost brazen about it. I don't need or want someone so destructive in my life.

At least with Rob I know where I am. He might be selfish and thoughtless sometimes, but he's never set out to hurt me on purpose. We have twenty years of shared history. Meanwhile, I've been putting my friendship with Mia ahead of my marriage, stupidly letting her come between us. Last night I took her side against him when she was the one who caused the argument in the first place. But given the way she's behaved in the past twenty-four hours, she clearly doesn't have my best interests at heart. I'm lucky Rob is prepared to overlook how disloyal I've been. He may not be perfect, but we love each other. If Mia was trying to break us apart, it's backfired on her spectacularly; she's only pushed us closer together. However angry I might have been with my husband's behaviour last night, she's wiped the slate clean for him.

Rob slides his hand up my skirt now, his fingers pushing inside my knickers. I'm not in the mood, but this isn't about sex, it's about reconciliation. Starting over.

I've made my choice.

17

Mia

Hands up who thinks there should be breathalysers on computer keyboards to stop you hitting *send* when you're trashed?

Goddammit. I can't believe I was so *stupid*. Kit's right: it doesn't matter how badly Rob behaved last night, venting online simply made me look like a vengeful press whore and ceded Rob the moral high ground. Nor can I explain to anyone *why* I flipped out. If I tell Kit or Charlie what happened now, they'll think I'm making it up just to get even. I've boxed myself into one hell of a corner.

Hand on black journalistic heart, I still don't think what I wrote was *that* bad. I knew it would piss Rob off, sure – that was the whole idea; but I just wanted to make a point. I wasn't out to get him fired. Which I point out to Kit – again – when he gets home from work on Monday evening still fizzing with anger.

'Mia, you're an intelligent woman,' he retorts. 'You've

been a journalist long enough to know what kind of storm a few well-placed words can whip up.'

'Come on. Rob's just a little bent out of shape . . .'

'I don't blame him! I know you think it was only a clever put-down, but you could have cost Rob his job. As it is, you've probably cost us all our friendship. Charlie was so upset she didn't even come in to work today. She's my boss, Mia. You've just made my life ten times more difficult than it needs to be.'

'It'll blow over,' I shrug with more bravado than I feel. 'Everyone says things they regret in the heat of the moment. It can't have been much of a friendship if one little fight—'

'It's not a "little fight", and you didn't *say* it, you posted it online for the entire world to see! You turned a simple argument into World War Three. I don't understand you, Mia. I really don't.'

Kit hardly ever gets mad. He's always the one who lowers the emotional temperature, restores calm. No matter what I throw at him, he takes it in his stride. But I don't think I've ever seen him this angry. As if I don't feel bad enough already. I never meant to upset him – or Charlie, for that matter; I was just trying to bring Rob down a peg or two. I didn't mean to cause this much trouble. I swear to God, if I could take back that post I would. I knew as soon as I sobered up this morning that I'd gone too far and I should have removed it then. But I was still pissy, and hungover, and just too damn stubborn to back down.

'Look, I deleted it, didn't I?' I mumble.

'If you'd removed it this morning when I asked you to, Rob might never even have seen it. Instead you got on your high horse and refused to listen to me.' He holds up his hand to still my protest. 'Wait. I haven't finished. You keep saying you didn't know it was going to cause so much trouble, and OK, let's suppose for a moment that I buy that. Maybe in your world it *isn't* a big deal, though in mine it's not the way friends treat each other. But then Charlie phoned and asked you, in fact she *begged* you, to remove it, and you *still* didn't take it down. Out of respect for your friendship, if nothing else, you should have done as she asked.'

'I did! After I spoke to her on the phone I took the whole entry down. I killed all the links to the other sites, too, so there's no record of it anywhere online.'

'So why didn't you tell her that when she came round to see you this morning?' Kit demands. 'What the hell were you trying to achieve? All you did was make a bad situation even worse!'

I have no answer to that. I should have just apologized to Charlie and got it over with, but that would have meant showing a bit of emotion, and if I'd dared to let myself do that, I might have broken down completely and told her everything. I know she probably thinks I'm a cold-hearted bitch now, but better that than have her know the truth about her husband.

'Everyone was making out like I was the bad guy, and I just got mad,' I say finally. 'You yelled at me, then Charlie yelled at me on the phone, and then she came round in person and yelled some more. It just got my back up.'

'You *were* the bad guy!' Kit exclaims. 'And Charlie didn't yell at you. She asked you nicely, and then she pleaded with you. Frankly, she was a lot nicer to you than I'd have been in her place. What the hell is wrong with you, Mia? I thought she was supposed to be your friend?'

'She *is*! *I* was the one trying to defend her last night . . .'

'She didn't need you to defend her, and certainly not

like this! Rob was behaving like an arsehole yesterday, but it had nothing to do with you. He's *her* husband. No man takes kindly to having a strip torn off him in public by a woman, least of all someone like Rob. All you did was tip things over the edge.'

He's right on every count. I had kept my feelings on a tight leash after that night with Rob, but then I blew it all by getting wasted. I screwed up. Big time.

'I'm sorry,' I say suddenly. 'You're right, I shouldn't have interfered. And I'm sorry if I've made things tricky at work. I didn't mean to.'

He sighs. 'I know you didn't. But try looking at it from Charlie's point of view for a change. You know very well she has enough to deal with where Rob's concerned without you piling in and getting involved. You've just aggravated the situation between them for no good reason. Not to mention creating a major headache for both of us when it comes to working together. I've already got enough stress without this. And honestly . . . I thought you were better than this. You *are* better than this.'

I bite my lip, thoroughly ashamed. There's nothing more painful and humiliating than someone you love being disappointed in you.

'What d'you want me to do?' I ask penitently. 'How can I fix things?'

'I'm not sure you can. But you could start by apologizing to Charlie. And Rob, of course.'

I'd rather walk over hot coals than apologize to that asshole.

'Rob's the one you offended,' Kit says, reading my mind. 'Your apology to Charlie is a waste of time if you don't apologize to him.'

Fine. *Fine.*

'What if no one will talk to me?'

'You keep trying.'

I press the heels of my hands into my eyes as Kit stalks upstairs, willing myself not to cry. The anger that's sustained me for weeks has suddenly evaporated just when I need it most. Rob hurt me at the deepest level, striking where a woman feels most vulnerable, and I hit back the only way I know how, eviscerating him with words. I feel as if at some strange karmic level we're even now. I can never excuse what he did, even though I can't deny my part in what happened that night. I sent out confusing signals – I accept that. I take responsibility for putting myself across ambivalently. All I want is for him to acknowledge his part. I want him to admit that what he did was wrong, and say sorry. Surely he must know why I retaliated in print? He must get it?

But I really didn't want to hurt Charlie. That's the last thing I ever meant to happen. Somehow, I have to make things right with her. And if that means apologizing to Rob too, then I'm just going to have to suck it up.

Given our last encounter, I'm surprised Charlie even lets me in the door when I turn up at her house the following afternoon, much less invites me into the kitchen and offers me a cup of tea. Not that I should read anything into it: if an alien invasion force arrived on a British doorstep having wiped out half the population en route, they'd probably get much the same response.

She doesn't ask me to sit down. 'I got your email.'

'I wasn't sure you'd read it.'

'We wouldn't be having this conversation if I hadn't.'

'I'm so sorry,' I blurt. 'I didn't mean to upset you. It wasn't you I was mad at.'

'You hurt me,' Charlie says painfully. 'I thought you were my friend. I know Rob behaved badly on Sunday, but if you had a problem with him, about that or anything else, you should have talked to him about it. Failing that, you could have talked to me. There was no need for you to air our dirty laundry in public and attack him like that.'

'I know, and I'm *so* sorry—'

She cuts me off. 'Whatever has gone on between you two is a matter for you to sort out among yourselves. I have to support him – he's my husband. But beyond that, it was none of my business. You *made* it my business when you wouldn't even do me the courtesy of respecting our friendship and hearing me out.'

'I know,' I say again desperately. 'I was just so *pissed* at him.'

'Why?'

A simple enough question; one I was hoping to avoid. There's no plausible reason for me being so angry – other than a truth I can't share. 'It was your birthday,' I say weakly. 'I didn't think he should get away with talking to you like that.'

She looks at me disbelievingly.

'I just wanted to teach him a lesson, that's all,' I add, aware how hollow it sounds. 'He can't go around treating women like that. Someone needs to stand up to him.'

'That wasn't the way to do it, Mia. Trust me, I know he can be a royal pain in the arse, but I can hold my own with my own husband.'

'I realize that now . . .'

'It's not just the post. When I came round to see you,

177

you completely blanked me. You threw up a wall and acted as if you didn't care about me or our friendship or anything else. I didn't deserve that.'

'I wasn't blanking you, Charlie, I swear to God. I didn't mean to shut you out. I was just so tense and wound up, and when I'm like that, I close down. I can't help it.' Tears clog my throat. 'I never meant to upset you, I swear. I was trying to defend you, and I completely messed up. But please don't think it's because I don't care. If anything, I care too much.'

The kettle boils and she makes us each a mug of tea, then silently hands me one. For a long moment she stares into her cup as if reading the leaves.

'I don't understand you,' she says finally. 'One minute you're jumping in with both feet to defend me whether I need it or not, and the next you're cutting me dead. I don't know how you normally do friendship, Mia, but this isn't my idea of it.'

'I don't blame you for being angry . . .'

'I'm not angry. I'm sad. And disappointed.'

I wince. That word again. 'Can't we put this behind us and move on?' I plead. 'You know how sorry I am. I don't know what more I can do.'

'As far as Rob's concerned, our friendship is already over.'

'What about you?'

'He's my husband. If I have to choose between you, he's always going to win.'

'But you and I can still be friends . . .'

'Whether I want to or not, I can't be your friend if it's going to cause me problems at home. Things are difficult enough already. And Rob doesn't forgive and forget easily.

When someone rubs him up the wrong way, he washes his hands of them and moves on.'

'Is that it, then?' I ask bleakly. 'You're washing your hands of me?'

'You didn't seem that bothered about our friendship yesterday,' Charlie says coolly.

Six months ago, I'd have said the only things that mattered to me were my family and my job. Now I can't imagine life without Charlie's friendship. I don't want to be the outsider any more. I want to connect, to belong. My friendship with Charlie means everything to me. 'I wouldn't be here if I didn't care,' I say quietly.

'It's going to take time to build trust again, Mia. I thought our relationship was rock solid, and you lit a bonfire under it. It'll take a while for things to heal. You're going to have to be patient and give me some space.'

'Of course . . .'

She quells me with a glance. 'But it's only going to work if you can fix things with Rob. I'm not going to put my marriage in jeopardy for you. I hope you can understand that. If he refuses . . .'

'It's OK,' I say. 'You don't have to spell it out.'

I pull my jacket over my head and run through the rain to Rob's car, which is waiting at the end of our driveway. I hesitate, my hand on the door handle – I haven't been alone with him since that night. A wave of nausea rises in the back of my throat. I can feel him shoving me down across the sofa, forcing my legs apart. Forcing himself inside me, *hurting* me.

He's not going to do anything. It's broad daylight. He wouldn't dare.

I yank open the door before I can change my mind. Rob has refused to come into the house, so we sit here, in his car – his private bubble and my own personal tenth circle of hell.

I grit my teeth and stare out the windshield. If I want to be friends with Charlie, I have to make things right with Rob. I brought this on myself. Taking our drama public was my mistake, no one else's. I screwed up big time. If I'd left well alone, he'd be the one having to apologize to me. I've got no one but myself to blame for this particular mouthful of excrement.

'Well?' he says.

'I'm sorry,' I grind out.

'If you wanted my attention, you've got it,' he snarls.

'I don't give a shit about your attention,' I snap before I can stop myself.

'Then what the fuck is this about?'

I dig my nails into my palms. *Don't look at him, don't think, just spit it out.* 'Look. I wanted to say sorry in person. I should never have written about you on my blog.' I force a note of conciliation into my voice. 'But let's take a breath here, Rob. We've both screwed up at one point or another. Can't we just put it behind us and move on?'

'Damn right you screwed up!'

'I know, and again, I'm sorry.'

'What the *fuck* were you playing at, Mia? I don't know how it works in America, but in England we don't go around libelling friends and wrecking their careers! Jesus. What the hell is wrong with you?'

I lean my cheek wearily against the cool glass. 'Take a wild guess, Rob.'

'I'm not playing your fucked-up games.'

'Come on. Don't make me spell it out.'

'Spell *what* out? I haven't done anything! I didn't attack you in print, or put your job on the line. I haven't even retaliated after that blog of yours, and trust me, I could've made your life bloody difficult. You're not the only one who can play dirty. I'd like to know how in hell *I'm* to blame for anything here.'

I turn my head. 'Think back a month or two.'

He meets my gaze head on. Either he's a damn good actor, or he really does have no idea what I'm talking about. There's absolutely no flicker of recognition or guilt in his eyes.

I just want him to say sorry. I want him to acknowledge that what he did was wrong.

'You raped me,' I say quietly.

He recoils as if I've sucker-punched him. 'I did *what*?'

'I told you no,' I tell him, forcing my voice to sound steady, 'and you did it anyway.'

He snorts incredulously. 'You're in a snit because we *slept* together? Christ! This is all because we fucked and I didn't call you afterwards?'

My anger returns in full force. I went too far with that post, I get that, but I'm not the only one in the wrong here. Rob raped me. I may have behaved like an idiot, I may have sent out the wrong signals and left it late to change my mind, but *he raped me*. I can just about live with what he did; it's his refusal to acknowledge it was wrong that chaps my ass.

'We didn't *sleep* together!' I explode. 'I told you to stop and you did it anyway!'

'Are you saying I *forced* you?'

'What would you call it?'

He slams his fist on the steering wheel. 'I've never forced a woman in my life! You can tell yourself I *raped* you if it helps you sleep at night, but the truth is you wanted it as much as I did! You turned up at my house dressed like a hooker, you got your kit off in double-quick time. You said no, then you said yes. Now you've got buyer's remorse and you want to blame me. Well, sorry, love, but no go. What happened happened. Live with it.'

'That's really how you see it?'

'That's really how I see it.'

We stare at one another, neither of us willing to blink first. His expression is cold and implacable. Either he's mentally revised our encounter as some kind of *Fifty Shades* mutual passion, or he really does think what he did was acceptable.

I never expected him to prostrate himself and beg for my forgiveness, but I thought that if I got him alone, he might acknowledge his guilt – to me if no one else. That's all I want. All he has to do is say sorry, and it's over. I'm not going to hold it against him. I know I was giving out confusing signals; I can't deny the truth of anything he just said. However, I'm not the only one who made a bad call that night. But he won't admit that, even to himself. He's certainly not going to admit it to me. Either I accept that and let it go, or I walk and never look back.

I walk.

18

Charlie

Four down. Eight to go.

I extend my hand. 'Thank you, George. We really appreciate the support. As soon as we have anything more to tell you, one of us will be in touch.'

'Not a problem,' George Wyatt replies gruffly. 'St Alphonsus means a lot to me. The Sisters gave me my start in life. And taught me to give something back, I might add. I don't want to see the school swallowed by that bloody Oxbridge hothouse down the road. Enough over-privileged clods getting a free ride as it is. Need to keep the playing field level.'

Inwardly I send up a quick prayer of thanks to Gail for suggesting I speak to George. Of the twelve trustees on the school board, he's the most respected, and therefore influential. He epitomizes everything St Alphonsus stands for. His appearance suggests precisely the elitist Oxbridge background he decries: the bespoke Savile Row suit, the neatly barbered silver hair, the handmade brogues. But when he speaks he gives away his origins. Born sixty-three years ago in the bombed-out rubble of the East End, he was abandoned on the steps of a convent when he was just a few days old. Thanks to the Sisters of Calvary, he received a first-class education and went on to build a significant fortune from Wyatt Travel – a fortune that will now underwrite St Alphonsus to the tune of several million pounds.

'With George on board, we should find it easier with the other trustees,' Kit says as we get into my car.

'Not necessarily. His financial support is crucial, of course, but it's not just about the money. We need votes.'

'With him, we already have four.'

'So does Shelby. Plus she has voting rights herself, of course, so that puts her just two votes short of an overall majority.' I pull out onto the Woodstock Road and head back into Oxford. 'I suspect Miller will vote with her. He doesn't like her personally, but he's been pushing for expansion for years, and the merger with Berwicks would certainly do that.'

'What about Sarah?'

'She hasn't committed yet, but I think she'll side with us. She likes Shelby, but she really believes in the school's mission. She won't want to dilute it with a merger.' I tap my thumbs thoughtfully on the steering wheel. 'Yeates and Bristow are the wild cards. Both of them have only been on the board a couple of years, and Bristow's youngest is already in his final year. Whether he'll have the stomach for the fight once his son graduates is up for debate.'

'Neither of them has given you any indication which way they're leaning?'

'No. They're both still keeping their cards very close to their chests.'

Kit runs his hand through his hair. Longer than ever, I notice. It suits him. 'Shit. The announcement is in a fortnight. This is going to go right down to the wire.'

'I have a meeting set up with Sister Judy on Friday. If I can persuade her to postpone going public until we've spoken again to the other eight trustees, we may be able to pull this thing together. Otherwise . . .' I shrug despondently. I'm aware I should be setting a positive example to my employee, especially given how hard he's been working, but I've simply run out of energy. What with Rob on my case at home and Shelby hounding me at work, and unable to turn to Mia for support, I feel besieged and defeated. Usually I'll fight tooth and nail when my back is against the wall, but right now I just want to rest my head on the steering wheel and howl.

'Hey,' Kit says kindly. 'Chin up. We've got the financing in place, which is little short of a miracle. Think how much stronger our position is now than it was just a couple of weeks ago. Now isn't the time to give up.'

'You're right. I'm sorry to be so negative. It's – I'm just . . .' I hesitate, my voice cracking. 'I'm just a little tired of fighting a war on all fronts, that's all.'

The pink elephant crammed in the rear of the car suddenly kicks us both hard in the back: *Rob and Mia*.

My husband not only still refuses to speak to Kit's wife, but he has forbidden me from doing so either. I've complied because he *is* my husband and I have a child to consider, and you don't throw away twenty years for a friend, however dear a friend she may be. But it's driving a wedge between us. I'm doing what he's asked, but I respect and like him a great deal less for asking me. We've barely spoken for weeks. Our silences are barren wastelands filled with the rotting baggage of our marital history, which has been brought to the surface by the proscriptive way he's treating Mia.

For the past month, Kit and I have valiantly being doing our best to maintain a Chinese wall between our professional and personal lives, but it has been almost impossible. Whether we like it or not, for the last seven months the fulcrum of our relationship has been not work but the four-way friendship we created together with our spouses. It's impossible to revert to a purely professional relationship now. Like it or not, Mia and Rob are shadowing us every step of the way.

But Rob refuses point-blank to see how difficult he's making things. He claims he's putting his foot down for *us*, because having Mia in our life is toxic, but actually he doesn't give a damn how I feel. If he did, he'd let it go. I've already forgiven her. I forgave her the moment she came to me and apologized. The truth is, I can't help feeling a sneaking admiration for the way she stood up to Rob. Not many people take him on, including me. And she apologized to him, even though she must have choked on the words. That meant more to me than anything she could have said. Rob let her grovel, and then refused to forgive her anyway. I know my husband. He'll have taken particular pleasure in that. His gracelessness has left a bitter taste in my mouth.

'Do you fancy a drink?' Kit asks as we sit gridlocked in traffic. 'I don't know about you, but I could use one. It's almost four; not much point going back to the school now.'

I smile gratefully. 'A drink is *exactly* what I need.'

The gods are clearly with us: a car vacates a space just

as we pass the Royal Oak, and I dive into it, mouthing apologies to a cyclist who only narrowly avoids becoming roadkill. I seat myself at a table in the beer garden as Kit goes in to get our drinks, shedding my suit jacket and savouring the warm May sunshine. In the distance, a clock chimes four times. I close my eyes, absorbing the gentle murmur of voices at nearby tables, the rough wood of the picnic bench against the back of my knees, the distant thrum of traffic. I can't remember the last time I simply stopped and smelled the coffee, as Mia would say.

I miss her. Every day that goes past without seeing her, I miss her more. The wound left by her absence is as raw as ever.

'How is she, actually?' I ask impulsively as Kit returns with our drinks.

He doesn't need to ask who I mean. I'm breaking the unofficial terms of our agreement by even mentioning her, the first time I've done so in a month, but all of a sudden the rules don't seem to matter.

He sits down opposite me. 'She misses you,' he says simply.

I nod. I don't need to say any more.

The two of us sit in companionable silence for a while. I feel soothed in a way I can't quite explain. Unlike Rob's silences, Kit's are benevolent, akin to being swaddled in a warm blanket on a cold night and held until you're ready to speak.

'If you want to talk,' he says quietly, 'I'm here.'

I look up, my gaze a little blurred at the edges. He's such a *nice* man. You don't meet many men like him these days. Honourable. Decent. The kind of man who opens a door for you and stands when you leave a table – not to show off how well-mannered he is, how well brought up, but because he respects you. How many men these days truly respect women? Fear them, perhaps, especially when the woman in question is in charge. Resent them, certainly. Desire, disdain, require, dislike. But respect?

Rob has never respected me. A man who respects you doesn't ask you to share him with another woman. He doesn't belittle your career, undermine your achievements, or abdicate all parental and domestic responsibility. He cares what you think. He troubles to please you. He *notices* you.

Mia doesn't know how lucky she is to have Kit, I think wistfully. He's not just a good man, he's a great cook, and he's attractive, too. Surreptitiously I take in the broad shoulders beneath his neat blue linen shirt, the muscular outline of his thighs in their plain khaki trousers. Rob's bad-boy magnetism is more overt – with his dark come-to-bed eyes and that fallen-angel smile, he's still the sexiest man I've ever met. But I'm starting to become immune to his charms. Kit's quiet self-deprecation may be easier to overlook, but his dependable strength is increasingly appealing. The more time I spend with him, the more I appreciate his company. And he really does have the most amazing blue eyes. When he looks at me like that—

Stop. You're married. He's your best friend's husband. You're married.

He reaches across the table now and sympathetically squeezes my hand. With an effort, I quench my less-than-neutral response. *We're friends. Colleagues. Nothing more than that.*

Abruptly he pulls his hand away. I glance up, surprised. He's staring at me as if he's never seen me before.

'Kit? Is something wrong?'

Hastily he pushes back from the table. 'We should be going. I promised Mia I wouldn't be late.'

He feels it too.

I drop Kit off outside his house, then collect Milly from her after-school martial arts class and drive home. My heart sinks when I see Rob's car already parked in the driveway. I'd been hoping for a few moments to myself before he got in from work. I need to get my head around what just happened between Kit and me. I know I didn't imagine it. I also know nothing can come of it. But it happened. It was real. For the first time in God knows how long, a man *noticed* me.

Come to think of it, my heart sinks when I come home most evenings these days.

Milly runs upstairs to do her homework, and I go through to the kitchen, where Rob's waiting for me. 'Did you do this?'

'Did I do what?'

'*This!*' He brandishes a shirt. 'You put it in the dryer, didn't you?'

'I don't know,' I say distractedly, dumping Milly's backpack on the counter. 'Yes, I should think so. I am the only one who does the laundry, after all.'

He shoves the shirt into my face. 'You didn't hang it up! Look at the creases in it!'

'Why do you care?' I demand, slapping the shirt away. 'I'm the one who has to iron it.'

'You'll never get creases like this out. I've told you, you need to hang up my shirts when they're three-quarters dry.'

'I washed twenty of your shirts this morning,' I retort.

'I counted them. *Twenty*. Then, while you were having a nice hot shower, I woke Milly up, gave her breakfast, fed the cat, put on your coffee, fielded a dozen emails and cleaned up the cat sick. I did all this while I waited for your precious bloody shirts to be *three-quarters dry*. After which I took them out and put them on hangers so they wouldn't crease, before getting into the car to go and do a full day's work. Forgive me if I missed one and left it in the dryer with the rest of the laundry. Sorry about that. *One out of twenty*. It's not ruined. Just put it back in the laundry basket and I'll do it again tomorrow.'

'I need it now,' Rob snaps. '*This* shirt. I have an important meeting first thing. I want to wear my grey Zegna suit. And I need this shirt. Not the blue one. Not the green one or the striped one. *This* one.'

'Fine. I'll iron it.'

'It's not about ironing it! I want you to launder it properly in the first place!' He throws the shirt into the kitchen sink, where it slowly subsides onto this morning's dirty breakfast dishes, which are still sitting unwashed in the greasy water. 'You don't give a shit about how I look, do you? It's all about you. *Your* job. *Your* problems. You don't listen to anything I say. I'm at the bottom of your list of priorities.'

'Are you serious?' I exclaim. 'I got up at six to wash *your* shirts! Jesus Christ! How many other wives, working or otherwise, do you know who do that?'

He folds his arms. 'I can't hear you when you talk to me in that tone.'

'When was the last time you washed *my* shirts? When was the last time you loaded the bloody dishwasher, for that matter?'

'All I hear is blah, blah, blah.'

I want to hit him. 'This marriage is supposed to be a partnership,' I say, forcing myself to stay calm. 'We're in it together. The fact that I do your laundry at all is a *favour*. It's not a fucking human right.'

'If you can't conduct a civilized conversation without swearing, there's no point talking.'

'I do not *owe* you laundry. I choose to do it *because we are a team*. I'm sorry one shirt slipped through the net—'

'My *favourite* shirt!'

'The one you just threw in the sink?'

'It's not just the shirt. It's the way you treat me. The shirt's part and parcel of everything else.'

'What's that supposed to mean?'

'Don't interrupt me. You do that all the time, cutting across me when I'm talking. You never *listen* to me. You're incredibly rude.'

Pointedly, I say nothing and wait.

'So now you're just going to ignore me?' Rob demands.

'I wanted to be sure you'd finished this time, so that I didn't interrupt.'

'I'm glad you think this is funny.'

'Oh, I don't think it's funny at all.'

He glares at me. 'You're sarcastic, you're rude, you interrupt me. You don't listen to me. It's impossible to have a conversation with you.'

'In that case, please don't bother.'

He throws me another filthy look and stalks out of the kitchen. Moments later, I hear his study door slam. He'll be on his computer now for hours, surfing online, chatting with his diving buddies. I'll be lucky if he speaks three words to me for the rest of the evening. And then when we go to bed, he'll be all over me, wanting to get laid. *Expecting* to get laid. Failure to comply will mean another Cold War of intermittent tantrums and the silent treatment. If I sell my body for a quiet life, what does that make me?

I cook dinner, and then call Milly downstairs, sending her off to wash her hands while I dish up. Chicken breast and salad; uninspired, I know, but right now it's the best I can do.

I'm tempted to leave Rob to stew, but there's no point upping the ante. It's already been a long day; I just want to eat my dinner and go to bed. It's a beautiful evening, so I set three places on the patio outside and call Rob.

'Did you make salad dressing?' Rob demands when he comes into the kitchen.

'Just olive oil and balsamic.'

'I wanted Caesar.'

I grit my teeth. 'Fine. You can make some Caesar dressing,' I say, as I take my plate and Milly's outside. 'There's a tin of anchovies in the cupboard.'

'I can't find them!' Rob yells from inside the kitchen.

'Cupboard above the sink!' I call back. 'Milly, you go ahead and eat. Daddy will be out in a minute.'

I sip my wine, picturing Kit's evening. He probably cooked dinner himself, and is even now chatting convivially to Mia across the dining table, talking about his day and asking her about hers. Maybe even discussing the new play he wants to see at the Oxford Playhouse. Including Emmy in the conversation, occasionally ruffling her hair, making his daughter feel cherished and loved. I wonder again if Mia has any idea how *lucky* she is.

Ten minutes later, Rob finally come out and joins us. He's made just enough dressing for himself, I notice, as he slams his plate on the table.

'You started without me,' he snaps.

'I didn't know how long you'd be, and Milly was starving.'

'Shame on you, Amelia. Where are your manners? You're being unbelievably rude.'

Milly's eyes fill with tears. She ducks her head, trying not to let him see.

I sigh. 'Rob, I said she could go ahead and start.'

'She should have known better than to listen to you.'

'Please. Just sit down and eat.'

'Not until she's apologized for her rudeness.'

I'm seized by a sudden surge of white-hot rage. He's deliberately being unkind to Milly to get back at me. 'Leave her alone! I'm the one you have a problem with. Don't take it out on her.'

'One of us has to show our daughter some discipline. You seem completely incapable of it, so I guess it's down to me.'

'This conversation is totally inappropriate,' I hiss. 'If you have something to say to me, let's go inside.'

'No. Milly needs to know there are consequences when you behave badly. And take your elbows off the table, Amelia. Use your serviette.'

'*Napkin*,' I snap.

'What?'

'Napkin, not serviette. If we're going to get all Emily Post about it.'

Rob reddens with anger. 'Are you *correcting* me?'

Milly is openly sobbing now. I pull her onto my lap,

stroking her hair as I glare at him over her head. 'Does it make you feel big to reduce a seven-year-old to tears?' I demand furiously. 'What is your problem, Rob? All this drama because I dried one of your shirts the wrong way?'

'You know damn well this is about more than laundry!'

'What I *know* is that it has nothing to do with Milly!'

'Don't try and set her against me,' he warns. 'She's my daughter too.'

Milly covers her ears. 'Please stop fighting,' she begs. 'I don't want you to get divorced!'

The air is instantly sucked out of my lungs. Remorse sweeps over me. Milly shouldn't have to see or hear this. 'No one's getting divorced,' I soothe, forcing myself to smile at Rob. 'Mummy and Daddy are just having a little quarrel, that's all. Like you and Emmy do sometimes. It's OK. It doesn't mean we don't love each other.'

'Could have fooled me,' Rob snaps.

'Of *course* we love each other,' I say, holding my hand out to him. 'And we love you, too. I tell you what, Milly. Let's all make friends and have some ice cream. Does that sound good? Ice cream, and it's not even the weekend!'

Rob shakes me off. 'You can't buy your way out of this with ice cream.'

My arms tighten around Milly as he marches into the house. I don't know how he can do this to her. It's one thing attacking me; I'm old enough to handle it. But there's no excuse for taking it out on our daughter. *None*.

Rob has always been selfish and controlling, but when it was just at my expense, I could live with it. He's an only child, after all; to some extent, he can't help it. Before we had Milly, I didn't mind that he dictated everything we did. For the first ten years we were together, our lives revolved around diving, which suited me too. But after Milly was born, things changed for me. She became the centre of my life. No wonder Rob didn't want to change: for him, things were perfect just the way they were. Why would he want to fix what wasn't broken? It's my own fault: I should have stood up to him a long time ago. I've allowed him to get away with all sorts of bad behaviour unchallenged for far too long. Even now, I'd probably put up with the status quo if it was just about me. But I refuse to let him treat Milly the same way. More importantly, I don't want Milly to grow up and marry a man like her father. I want better for her.

I want her to be as lucky as Mia.

19

Mia

'I feel like we're having an affair,' I grin as Charlie glances furtively round the café before pulling out the chair opposite me and sitting down.

'We might as well be.'

'Be still my beating heart. Your place or mine?'

'Mia . . .' Charlie warns.

I lift my hands. 'What? We can't laugh about this? We're two grown women, and here we are, sneaking around, sending each other coded texts and hiding out in tea rooms so your husband doesn't find out we're still friends. That isn't ridiculous?'

'Of course it is,' Charlie sighs. 'But it's this or nothing. He hasn't changed his mind, and he's not going to. He told me not to see you . . .'

'How old are you, five?'

She frowns. 'Mia, I'm here, aren't I? Rob isn't getting the final say in this. But my marriage is in enough trouble.

I don't need to open up a new battlefront every time I have a cup of tea with you.'

Instantly I'm contrite. She's right; she didn't have to go out on a limb for me like this. I certainly didn't expect her to. Two months ago, when Rob made it clear he wasn't going to forgive me, Charlie told me she couldn't see me any more. It felt like someone had carved a piece of my heart out with a spoon. The fact that Kit still got to see her at work was salt in the wound. I quizzed him every day the moment he got home – 'How did she seem this morning? Does she look like she's missing me? Who's she been having lunch with instead of me?' – until he'd finally had enough and refused to talk about her at all. I drove past her house at weekends just to see if her car was parked in the drive. I stalked her on Facebook. I wrote email after email that I didn't send. I sobbed down the phone to Lois (surprisingly sympathetic) at four in the morning. In other words, I acted like a crazy woman.

Eventually, I started to pull myself together. Without telling Kit, I began putting out feelers to some of the US networks about coming back. He'd be able to get a job teaching in the States, no problem. With his accent? They'd be biting his hand off. Emmy was plenty young enough to switch schools. And I'd had enough of this damp, unfriendly island. I was so over defending my country, my politics, my goddamn *vocabulary*, for God's sake. I wanted to go home.

And then Charlie called. For about half a minute, I was tempted to hang up. I'd only just managed to surface; I didn't want to slide right back down the chute. But who was I kidding? I'd have walked over hot coals for this woman. Forty minutes later, the two of us were crying in each other's arms over a nice cup of Earl Grey in a discreet little teashop off the Broad. In the month since then, we've met up two or three times a week, for lunch or coffee. But it's not the same. It's not enough.

I'm grateful she's sticking her neck out for me, I really am. I know I should accept the situation gracefully and not keep asking for more. It just drives me crazy we can't see each other openly. I hate all this sneaking around as if we've got something to be ashamed of. It was kind of fun in the beginning, like we were getting one over on Rob, but now it just feels underhand and sleazy.

Crap. This really *is* like a freaking affair.

'Does he have any idea you're seeing me again?' I ask.

'No. He hasn't asked. I don't know what I'd say if he did. I can't lie to him.' She turns to the waitress hovering tactfully near our table. 'English Breakfast, and a scone with cream and jam, please.'

I order the same. 'It's been two months. He's bound to get over it sooner or later.'

'Rob doesn't get over things like this, I told you. If a friendship takes effort, he just walks away. He doesn't work at relationships,' she adds bitterly. 'As far as he's concerned, if someone has a problem with him, *they're* the one at fault.'

She isn't talking about me any more. 'Charlie, what's going on with the two of you?' I venture. 'You can tell me to butt out if you want, but things obviously aren't getting any better between you. Is it because of what I—'

'It has nothing to do with you,' she says firmly. 'This is about Rob and me. We're working through a lot of baggage right now. We have been for a while. Our problems started long before you came on the scene.'

'Want to talk about it?'

She hesitates. 'I can't break a marital confidence,' she says finally.

'I'm sorry. I didn't mean to pry.'

'You're not. But Rob and I have an agreement. It's not my story to share.'

I reach for the milk pitcher. I may not like everything about this benighted country, but I've learned to appreciate the restorative benefits of a nice hot cup of tea.

'Look, you didn't come here to talk about me and Rob,' Charlie says briskly. 'I don't want to inflict my problems on you. How are things with you and Kit? I'm sorry I've stolen him away from you for the past few weeks, but he's been doing an amazing job . . .'

I'm not even listening. I know I should keep out of her business, but she's in pain and I can't help myself. Mom used to say to friends going through a bad patch: *if you can remember the first time you met and still smile, there's hope.* Maybe that's what Charlie needs. To reboot and go back to the beginning.

'If you met Rob for the first time now,' I interrupt, 'what would attract you to him?'

She looks taken aback. 'You mean physically?'

'Anything you like,' I shrug. 'Imagine you're at a party. You meet him for the first time. What do you find attractive about him?'

'We're both single?'

'Yes. Everything else is as it is now – you're the people you are today. But you're single, and meeting for the first time.'

'Well, I still fancy him,' she says, after a long minute.

'There's always been great chemistry between us. So there's that.'

'OK. What else?'

'He's a fantastic diver. I mean, it's not just a hobby with him. He's brilliant at it. He's broken dozens of records for solo dives. I know it sounds a bit weird, but when someone's really good at something, it's incredibly sexy, don't you think?'

'Sexy, diving. Got it.'

I wait. Charlie makes a great production of spreading strawberry jelly and cream on her scone.

'Look, it's hard to put aside our history and come to it fresh,' she says defensively.

'Fine. So tell me what you found attractive when you actually first met him, then.'

'The same things, really. He was incredibly sexy; I mean, *really* hot. And he was a great dive buddy. We spent the first seven or eight years going from one dive site to another, whenever we could scrape together the cash and get enough time off work. We had a lot of fun.'

'But you don't dive now?'

Her eyes shadow. 'One of us has to look after Milly.'

'You can't leave her with her grandparents?'

'Rob's parents are in their eighties, and mine are getting on. Mum'll be seventy-five next birthday. They can manage Milly for a day or so, but not for any longer without help.'

'What about friends? You know I'd have her.'

She sighs. 'It's too late now, Mia. I've been off the dive scene too long. I'm not even current any more. It's not about diving, anyway. I want to spend my free time with Milly, not a bunch of divers I barely know.'

'So,' I recap. She hasn't exactly given me much to work with. 'You fancied Rob because he was sexy and into diving. And you *still* fancy him because he's sexy and into diving.'

'Well, there's more to it, obviously . . .'

'What's changed?'

She looks confused. 'What d'you mean?'

'If he's still the same man he was twenty years ago, and you still like the same qualities in him, why is your marriage going off the rails?'

'Jesus. Why don't you come off the fence and tell me what you really feel?'

A silence falls between us, filled only by the gentle hubbub of laughter and conversation, the chink of china and the scrape of chairs.

'Look, I understand what you're trying to say,' she sighs finally. '*I'm* the one who's changed. He hasn't; and that's the problem. There's a reason most extreme divers are young, and it's got nothing to do with health or fitness. You know what it's like – when you're in your twenties, you have no real responsibilities. You can take risks, or drop everything and fly halfway round the world at a moment's notice. But eventually you have to grow up. Especially when you have kids.'

'It's why I stopped playing chicken with bullets,' I say. 'I couldn't risk it for Emmy's sake.'

'Exactly.' She pushes her plate away impatiently. 'When we first got together, diving was what we *did*. It defined our relationship. But I thought when we had Milly, *she'd* be what we had in common.'

'So apart from diving and Milly, what else is keeping you together?'

'History,' Charlie says simply.

'Is that enough?'

'Enough for what?'

'Enough for you for the next twenty or thirty or forty years.'

Another long silence.

'Not if it's going to be the same as the last twenty,' she admits at last. 'I've had enough of enabling him. I've done what Rob wants for half my life. I can't do it any more. Something has to give.'

'Have you told him this?'

'Of course. But as far as he's concerned, our marriage was fine the way it was. Sex every two days, holidays in places he could dive, dinner with friends he likes. He says I'm the one with the problem, and he's right.'

I suppress the urge to pile in and tell her what an asshole she's married to. I need to take myself out of the equation and be her friend. A friend would want the best for her. A friend would want her to be happy. I have to think of Rob as Charlie's husband, and put my own feelings about him aside.

'Look at it from his point of view,' I say carefully. 'You went into this relationship with him on certain terms, and now you're rewriting the rules. You've changed, and grown up, and decided you need a different kind of relationship, but he's still the same as he always was. I don't blame you, but it's no wonder he's hurt and confused. If someone married me for the qualities I had, and then decided later those qualities weren't what they wanted, I'd be hurt and confused too.'

'You're taking *his* side?'

I can't quite believe it myself. 'I'm just saying, instead of treating him like he's the enemy, maybe you could give him a chance to evolve too.'

'It's never going to happen.'

'So leave him,' I say bluntly.

'It's not that simple. Aside from what it would do to Milly, I do actually *love* him. I might not like him right now, but I do still love him.'

'You love who he is now, or you love who he was?'

'Stop badgering me, Mia. You make everything sound so cut and dried. If I leave Rob, I'd be walking out on half my life. It would be like a bereavement. All that shared history, gone.'

'So your future is held hostage to your past.'

'It's a compromise.'

'It sounds like you're the one who's doing all the compromising,' I say sharply. 'You can't expect him to change if you keep giving in to him. You're sending out mixed signals. As long as he thinks there's a chance you might quit trying and go back to the way things were, he's not going to move an inch in your direction.

'Rome wasn't built in a day.'

I give up. I'm not in the business of breaking up marriages, even to someone like Rob. You don't throw away twenty years lightly, and then there's Milly to consider. But at the same time, she *is* my friend, and she's obviously miserable. I wish she'd stand up to him more. I get that she wants to keep the peace, but all she's doing is enabling his bad behaviour.

We finish our tea and leave. Outside, it's started to rain, and Charlie produces a telescopic umbrella from her purse. Nearly a decade in this country and I still haven't learned.

'I'll see you to your car,' she says. 'You'll end up like a drowned rat otherwise.'

We link arms and dash out into the rain. There's something about the closeness, the schoolgirlishness of our laced arms, that makes me feel suddenly giddy and carefree. I deliberately splash in the puddles as we head up Turl Street, giggling at the disapproving expressions of my fellow pedestrians.

'Now who's behaving like a five-year-old?' Charlie says, laughing.

'Why do we stop skipping?' I ask curiously. 'I watch Emmy do it all the time. She never walks when she can skip instead. It's something adults never do. How old are we when we stop? Nine? Ten?'

'About that,' Charlie agrees.

'We're so buttoned-up. We forget how to have fun.'

'We don't forget. It just gets knocked out of us by life.'

'Skip with me,' I demand. 'Come on. Skip.'

'Mia.'

'Oh, come on. Live a little.'

She shakes her head, but when I start to skip, she keeps up with me. By the time we reach my car, we're both panting and out of breath and laughing so much we can barely speak.

'Better?' I gasp.

'Much.'

'Oh crap,' I say suddenly.

'What?'

I point to my front offside tyre. 'I've a flat.'

'Shit. Do you belong to the AA?'

'I take it you mean the car people, not Alcoholics Anonymous? Either way, the answer's no.'

'I'll give you a lift home,' Charlie says. 'You can come back with Kit later and he can change it for you.'

When she pulls into my driveway twenty minutes later, there's an awkward silence. She hasn't been inside the house since the night of her birthday, when Rob and I had that blazing row. I hesitate, my hand on the door handle. 'Look, do you want to come in?'

For a moment I think she's going to refuse. 'Oh, sod it. Why not?'

I make the two of us some tea, and we take it through to the sitting room. I throw open the French doors, savouring the smell of the rain-soaked garden, then sit next to Charlie on the sofa. I can't help but remember our previous encounters on this very sofa with a wistful erotic tingle.

'I've really missed you,' I say impulsively. 'I know we've been meeting up in town, but it's not the same as having you here.'

'I've missed you, too.'

Her eyes suddenly fill with tears. Surprised, I put down my mug, scooting over to put my arm round her. 'I'm so sorry this all happened,' she says thickly. 'If I'd just stood my ground in the first place . . .'

'It's my fault. I should never have written that blog. I made everything a thousand times worse.'

I take her tea from her shaking hands so she doesn't spill it on herself. She buries her head in my shoulder, just like Emmy does. I stroke her hair softly, trying not to think how good she smells, how much I like the warmth of her body against mine.

Suddenly she turns in my arms and kisses me, her tongue slipping between my lips. For a moment, I'm too taken aback to respond, but as her kisses grow more urgent and she starts to unbutton my shirt, scooping my breasts out of my lace bra, I kiss her back. She tastes even sweeter than I remember. I'd forgotten how good this could be. I close my eyes as she kisses her way down my neck, her hand working its way up my thigh.

We both freeze at the sound of the front door opening. Before we can straighten our clothes, Kit is standing in the doorway, his expression stunned. 'I didn't – I'm sorry, I should have knocked – I had no idea – '

'Come and join us,' Charlie says suddenly.

He shoots a startled glance at me. I give a tiny shrug, as surprised by all of this as he is.

It takes him only a moment to recover. 'Upstairs,' he says.

We follow Kit upstairs. The rain has stopped and motes of dust dance in the sunlight streaming through our bedroom window. Our next-door neighbours are out in their yard drying their plastic lawn furniture with a towel. It's the middle of the afternoon in suburbia, and I'm peeling off my clothes and climbing into bed with my husband and my best friend.

'It's OK,' I whisper quietly to him as Charlie slips between the sheets. 'You can make love to her. I don't mind.'

'You're my wife,' he murmurs softly. 'Only you. Only ever you.'

I offered Charlie to him with an open heart, no strings. But I'm indescribably glad he said no.

I lose all sense of time and place as the three of us move in perfect harmony, our pace urgent and yet unrushed. Every pleasure synapse in my body is firing at the mix of soft skin and hard muscle, rounded curves and thrusting masculinity. Afterwards, Kit leaves the bed first, disappearing downstairs as Charlie and I curl together, satisfied and at peace. When he returns, he has a bottle of good champagne and three crystal glasses in his hands. He opens it with a muted pop and pours, then climbs back into bed on the other side of Charlie.

'To us,' she says, raising her glass. She drains it in one swallow and smiles as she holds it out to be refilled. 'Sorry Rob couldn't make it, but this one was all for me.'

20

Charlie

To walk into Gerry and Lynda Brady's home is to understand instantly why Rob is the way he is.

Every surface, every wall, is covered with photographs. At first glance you'd think they were all of Rob, but on closer inspection you can see the pictures are actually of two different boys, so similar they could almost be twins. But one is a little taller, a little thinner. His hair is darker and more curly. There's a sense of mischief in his tawny eyes. The Brady household revolved around those two boys; you can tell that from the pictures. Lynda was forty-two when she had David, and an unheard-of forty-seven, in those pre-IVF days, when Rob came along. Twenty-odd years of trying, and then David, when they'd all but given up. Rob himself was put down to the menopause; Lynda didn't even know she was pregnant until she was six months gone. Miracle babies, the pair of them. No wonder they were the apples of their parents' eyes. Every smile, every step, was recorded for posterity. There's barely an inch of wallpaper visible beneath pictures of gummy babies grinning at the camera, toddlers on tricycles, little boys building sandcastles at Margate, competing in egg-and-spoon races, sporting plaster casts and Scout badges and huge, identical smiles.

Then they start to grow up. There's David with his arm around his first girlfriend, a pretty blonde; Rob scowling into the lens, all awkward angles and gangling teenage limbs. The two of them together, mugging for the camera. And then suddenly there's only Rob. Rob on his first day at university, Rob standing in front of the pyramids at Giza, Rob marrying me. Rob holding Milly when she was just a few hours old. Underwater pictures of Rob diving hundreds of feet down, taken by a photographer for *National Geographic* and carefully cut out and framed by his proud parents. One son, where there used to be two.

When Rob's brother was mown down by a drunk driver, his devastated parents focused all their love and attention on their one remaining child. Rob became the sun around which his parents revolved, the only reason for their continued existence.

I love Lynda and Gerry. They're good-hearted, decent, well-meaning people. But they've created a tyrant. Even before David's death, they spoilt those boys rotten. Afterwards, as the sole recipient of their devotion, Rob became a Little Emperor. But, paradoxically, one doomed to live forever in David's shadow. Who, after all, can compete with the martyred dead?

'Come in, son,' Lynda says now, ushering us into their crowded front room. It's almost impossible to move without tripping over a tapestry footstool or bumping into a nest of side tables. 'Gerry, get up. Rob's here.'

Gerry leaps spryly to his feet. Eighty-nine now, he's of the same generation as the Duke of Edinburgh and cut from the same hardy, uncomplaining cloth. 'Have my seat,' he says, clapping his son on the back. 'You must be tired after the drive.'

Twenty-five minutes down the A40, but Rob graciously takes his father's armchair as if ascending the Chrysanthemum Throne.

'What can I get you, son?' Lynda fusses. 'A cup of tea and biscuits? I bought some of your favourite Garibaldis. Or a beer? Would you prefer a beer? Dad got some in, didn't you, Dad? Those Budlikers of yours. They're in the fridge. Or are they supposed to be kept at room temperature? I can never remember.'

'Sit down, Gerry,' I say. 'If Rob wants a beer, he can get it himself.'

'No trouble, son, no trouble at all.'

Rob throws me a look: *see? This is how I should be treated*.

I join Lynda in the kitchen, where she's breaking the Garibaldi sheets into individual biscuits. Heaven forbid her son should have to raise a finger himself. 'Rob looks tired,' she says anxiously. 'Is he getting enough sleep? That job of his. So much responsibility. I worry about him.'

'He was away diving for a few days. Didn't get back till late last night.'

'Oh, you should have postponed!' Lynda exclaims. 'No need to drag him all the way to see us if he's tired!'

I take Milly to visit her grandparents at least once a week, but Rob comes with us no more than three or four times a year. His visits are the highlight of their calendar. 'I think he can manage a cup of tea, as long as he's sitting down,' I say dryly.

I watch her flap around her son, topping up his teacup, bringing him more biscuits, closing the curtains so the setting sun doesn't get in his eyes. I used to tell myself it wasn't Rob's fault he was the way he was. Given the way his parents doted on him, how could he *not* grow up with an inflated sense of his own importance? He was selfish and controlling because he'd never been taught not to be. He was insecure and narcissistic because he felt he couldn't live up to the older brother who'd been taller than him, a fraction better looking, more intelligent, more popular. He should have been the one who died, not David. He was the one who was supposed to buy the flowers for their mother that day, but he'd forgotten. David had gone instead, and David was the one who was killed. David was the Better Son. In Rob's mind, David was the one his parents would have preferred to live, if they'd had to choose.

I can't fix Rob. No one could fill the void created by his insecurities. I understand why he needs the constant affirmation and admiration of women, the endless reassurance and reinforcement. I'm not enough for him. No woman could be. He could have the adulation of millions and it would still never be enough.

For twenty years, I've loved him and made allowances, letting things pass and turning a blind eye. But at what point does a damaged child have to take responsibility for his own life? We don't permit an abused child to abuse the next generation because of what happened to them. We're all shaped by our upbringing, for good or ill. *They fuck you up, your mum and dad. They may not mean to, but they do.* Larkin was right. My parents fought like cat and dog, and still do, having passed their fiftieth wedding anniversary last year. I was the family peacemaker, the mediator, the pourer of oil on troubled waters. And I took that forward into my marriage. In that sense, I'm as responsible for the way Rob behaves as he is. My reasons for marrying were as complex and compromised as everyone else's.

Rob is forty-three years old. We've been married two decades. He has a child of his own now. But he hasn't evolved or grown up at all. If anything, he's more selfish than ever. Shorn of the novelty and passion and willingness to please that characterizes the early years of any relationship – and he *did* love me, I know that – he's become rigid and unyielding. And I can't do it any more. I can't spend the next twenty years of my life trapped in a relationship that's slowly suffocating me. I love Rob, and I don't want to destroy our marriage, but things need to change. We need to renegotiate the terms of our relationship. Otherwise . . .

Otherwise? There will be more Wednesday afternoons like the one I spent in bed with Kit and Mia.

I didn't plan it. It just happened. A mixture of anger and defiance and straightforward lust. All I know is that I refuse to feel guilty about it. A year ago I'd have been tormented and chewed up with remorse. Now it barely seems to matter. My indifference is what frightens me. I watch Rob now, lapping up the attention, shooting me unpleasant glances, and inwardly I shrug. It's as if I'm . . . *waiting*. Waiting for something to happen, to tip our marriage over the edge or bring it back from the brink of disaster. And I feel absolutely no imperative to push it either way.

We've barely spoken a word to each other all day, but when we get home, Rob expects me to fuck him. And because I still feel wrapped up in the same strange cocoon, insulated, separate from him, I acquiesce. After all, what does it matter? It doesn't *mean* anything. With no attempt at foreplay or even a modicum of tenderness, Rob pushes up my T-shirt and climbs on top of me, thrusting his way into me, heedless of the fact that I'm as dry as sandpaper. He comes within moments, rolling off and turning away.

I pull down my T-shirt, reach for my iPad and put on my reading glasses. Anita Shreve is a writer who knows precisely how to dissect a marriage like mine. I lose myself instantly in her pitch-perfect prose.

'It would be nice if you made an effort,' Rob says suddenly.

'Mmm?'

'In bed. It would be nice if you made an effort.'

I glance at him over the top of my glasses. 'I could say the same.'

'I'm not asking you to swing from the chandelier. It would just be nice if you didn't lie there like a bloody corpse.'

I shut my iPad. 'And it would be nice if you gave me a reason to turn up.'

'I'm not talking about how many pages of the *Kama Sutra* we burn through,' he says, and now I can hear the genuine hurt in his voice, 'but it's always me who initiates sex. You never come into my space and make me feel wanted. You don't even touch me. I feel like a leper sometimes.'

I don't meet his eyes. *I don't come into your space because I don't want to be close to you. I'm still too angry.* But is it really fair to tell him I've forgiven him for sleeping with Mia, for his previous infidelity, for all the many skirmishes of our marriage, if I secretly hold on to my grievances and allow them to fester? *I'm* the one undermining our relationship if I refuse to let the wounds heal.

He sits up against the pillows, ruffling his thick, dark hair with the flat of his hand. He looks like a model in *GQ*. I can *see* how sexy he is with that square Hollywood jaw and those come-to-bed eyes. It's just that I can't *feel* it any more. There's too much baggage, too much history, in the way. The realization shocks me to the core. The sexual chemistry between us was always our greatest strength – and my Achilles heel. Even when he's behaved badly, let me down, hurt me terribly, even when I've hated myself for it, I have always, *always* wanted him.

'Perhaps we should think about going to counselling,' I blurt out.

'*Counselling?*'

I didn't anticipate having this discussion now, though I've certainly thought about it over the past few weeks. Rob has always been implacably opposed to the idea of therapy in any form, though I've often thought grief counselling over his brother would have helped him. But suddenly it seems like the only way forward. If we could *talk* to each other, maybe we'd stand a chance of putting this right. 'Come on. You know things haven't been good between us for a while, Rob. I think we need some professional help to get back on track.'

'We don't need a bloody shrink telling us what to do. We're two intelligent people, we can figure this out ourselves.'

'We haven't managed it so far.'

'I don't know what you think the problem is,' he snaps defensively. '*You're* frigid, and suddenly *we* need marriage guidance?'

I wasn't frigid on Wednesday afternoon.

'Why do you have to be so hostile?' I ask, keeping my

tone reasonable. 'I'm trying to be constructive and find us a way out of this. Can't you at least meet me halfway?'

'First you lose interest in bed, and now you want *me* to see a shrink. You're the one with the problem, Charlie. You're having some kind of mid-life crisis, or whatever the fuck this is, and you're projecting it onto me. You need to get your head together before you really screw something up.'

'If either one of a couple thinks a marriage isn't working, *it isn't working*.'

'Our marriage is just fine, thank you.'

'Not for me, it isn't!'

'Then *you're* the one who needs therapy.'

'Are you really this dense?' I demand. 'We're sleep-walking towards *divorce* here! We can't just pretend it isn't happening. We need some serious help before it's too late!'

'Don't be so dramatic. We're not getting divorced. Go join a book group, hit the shops, whatever you need to get your mojo back, and we'll be fine.' He rearranges his pillows, punching them into position. 'If you spent a bit less time at that bloody school of yours, and a bit more at home, we wouldn't have any problems. You can't expect me to be all sweetness and light when you're never bloody here.'

I don't know whether to laugh or cry. *Stick a hormone patch on it, luv, and it'll be all sorted.* How do you reason with someone who doesn't even speak your language?

I almost start to wonder if he's right. Maybe I *am* the one who needs the shrink. I've lived with this man for twenty years, and he hasn't changed. *Insanity is doing the same thing over and over again, and expecting different results.* I knew what Rob was like when I married him. Watching him with his parents today was a timely reminder of just what I'm up against. I'm not sure Rob is actually capable of change.

The bedroom door opens. I glance up to see Milly silhouetted in the doorway, her thumb in her mouth. 'I had a bad dream,' she whispers.

I climb out of bed and scoop her up. 'Want to cuddle in Mummy's bed for a while?'

'Don't bring her in with us,' Rob says tersely. 'I need some sleep. I've got a long day tomorrow.'

'Come on. Just for a few minutes.'

'Milly, go back to your own room,' he snaps. 'There's no need for all this fuss. You're seven years old. It was just a dream. Go back to sleep.'

'I'll tuck you in,' I offer helplessly.

Milly buries her head in my shoulder. It breaks my heart the way her relationship with her father is falling apart. Every day, the gulf between them widens. Rob has never been a hands-on father; he hasn't changed a nappy or got up for a night feed in his life. But at least he used to play with her, even if it didn't take long to reach his boredom threshold. He taught her to ride her bike, and he used to love lying on his back and balancing her against his bare feet, swooping her around the room until she was almost sick. These days, he barely speaks to her except to tell her off. There are times when he actually seems to resent her even being here. She may be only seven, but she's not stupid. She knows when she's not welcome. She just has no idea *why*.

Of course he loves her. I don't doubt that. But, as with everything, it has to be in *his* way. And the older she gets, and the more she has a mind of her own, the more Rob is trying to grind her down.

If I leave him, she'll have to spend half her time with him, and I won't be around to protect her.

The thought forms in my mind before I can censor it. I try to push it away, hating that I'm even flirting with the idea of divorce like this. But Rob is already using Milly as a stick to beat me with. How much worse would it get if I actually left?

I tuck her into bed and snuggle next to her, stroking her hair and rubbing her back until she falls asleep. I'd fight till my last breath to protect my daughter. Somehow I have to get my marriage back on track for her sake.

As I cross the landing back to our bedroom, I hear my phone *bing* with a text message downstairs. I'm about to ignore it, but curiosity gets the better of me. I tiptoe into my office and pick it up. Kit's name illuminates the screen and I feel a tingle of anticipation. It's nearly midnight: this can't be about work. I open the message, butterflies dancing in my stomach.

Oh shit.

21

Mia

'You've been *suspended*?' I exclaim incredulously.

Kit nods.

'But *why*? What on earth did you *do*?'

'Thank you for assuming I did anything at all,' he says tightly.

'Well, you must have done *some*thing or they wouldn't have suspended you.'

'I had a row with Shelby,' he says, dragging out a kitchen chair and wearily sitting down. 'She went behind our backs to some of the trustees and talked one of them into leaking the proposed merger with Berwicks. It hasn't been agreed with the Sisters yet. With Wyatt underwriting the school, it's not even necessary any more. And she bloody blindsided us. We're going to haemorrhage parents panicking that the school is going to close, which will bounce us into the merger whether we like it or not.'

'When did all this happen?'

'Last night. The bitch fucking *emailed* me the news after dinner.'

'Why didn't you tell me?'

He rubs his hand across his face. 'I don't know. I had to get my own head around it first.'

'Does Charlie know?'

'I texted her before I went to bed.'

'And?'

'Look, Mia, do we really have to go into it now? I've had about three hours' sleep and I'm exhausted. My mother arrives from Edinburgh this afternoon. Before she gets here, I need to regroup and work out what my next move is going to be.'

'I still don't see why you got suspended,' I protest indignantly. 'Shelby can't fire you just for disagreeing with her!'

'She can if I then phone her and call her a fucking cunt.'

I gape at him. 'Christ on a bike! You're kidding?'

'Do I look like I'm kidding?'

Well, no. Now I think about it, he looks like he's been dead and buried about six months, then dug up and propped at my kitchen table. He's lost some weight recently, I realize suddenly. Quite a bit, actually. How did I not notice that before? And he has huge dark circles under his eyes. His mother's going to think I've been making him sleep in the basement when she gets a look at him.

'Can't you just call Shelby back and say you didn't mean it?' I suggest. 'Grovel a bit and promise to go on one of those anger management courses or something. I'm sure she'll get over it if you say sorry.'

'Say sorry?' Kit demands incredulously. 'You want me to *apologize* to the woman for shafting me?'

'What does it matter if you keep your job?'

'I'm not about to whore myself out for the sake of my bloody pension! I can't believe you're suggesting it! This woman's made my life a misery for the past year. She's practically driven the school into the ground and half the staff to the edge of a nervous breakdown. She's completely incompetent, Mia! Not only that, she's dishonest and vicious. Jesus!'

'OK, OK. No need to go postal on me,' I say hastily. 'I know the woman's a pain in the ass, but the moral high ground won't pay the mortgage, Kit. I'm freelance, remember? If I get canned, they owe me *bupkes*. And finding another job in this market . . .'

'I'm well aware of my responsibilities, Mia. Never let it be said you have to sacrifice your gilded lifestyle on the altar of my principles.'

'I pay for my own lifestyle, thank you very much. I'm not a WAG. All I'm saying is that jacking in your job without having another one to go to isn't exactly a smart career move these days.'

'I didn't jack it in. I was suspended, remember?'

'And whose fault's that?'

He shoves his chair back from the table. 'I fucked up, OK? I fucked up. I let my temper get the better of me after half a bottle of wine last night and said something I shouldn't have. Not something *you'd* ever do, obviously.'

I stare at him. Kit *never* loses his temper. Not at work, and not with me. I can count the times he's yelled at me on the fingers of one hand. One thumb, even. I flip out and throw things; Kit pours oil on troubled waters. That's the way it works. It's the way it's always worked between us.

'I'm sorry,' I say, bewildered. 'I didn't mean to take a shot at you. I'm just a little anxious, is all.'

'I could use your support right now, not a commentary

on all the things I should have done differently,' Kit snaps. 'It would have been nice if you'd just put your arms round me and told me it was going to be OK. A little reassurance would be helpful now and then. I get scared sometimes, same as you.'

'Kit . . .'

'Forget it. I need to talk this through with Charlie. It's going to affect her almost as much as me. Can you take Emmy to summer camp this morning? I'm going to be tied up on the phone here.'

'Sure.' I hesitate. 'Is there anything else I can do?'

'Just give me a little space, Mia. Can you do that?'

I nod. I've never seen Kit like this before, and I'm at a loss what to say to make things better. I hope Charlie can help. She knows Shelby. She'll have a better take on how to handle this.

I drop Emmy at her summer camp and decide to stop off at a small café in the village on the way home. I want to give Kit the space he's asked for, and anyway I'm not really in the mood to write this morning. My mind is running a mile a minute. I still can't get my head round the fact that Kit swore at Shelby. It's so out of character. It makes me worry there's something really wrong.

I order a coffee at the counter and go to sit down. With a start, I realize Rob is sitting at a table in the corner. Before I can even process what to do, he glances up and sees me. To my complete surprise, he gives a weary smile. 'Hi, Mia.'

'Hi,' I say warily.

'How're things?'

'I've been better.'

The server comes out from behind the counter with my coffee. 'Do you want to sit with your friend?'

I glance at Rob, who shrugs. I have no idea where this is going, but if he's game, I'm not going to be the one to wimp out.

'So,' he says as I sit down. 'How are you?'

We could keep dancing around each other for hours, but I'm not in the mood to play games. I cut to the chase. 'You're speaking to me now?'

'Do you think you can manage to keep that out of print?'

'Funny,' I say coldly. 'I don't think my readers are exactly panting for the latest update in our relationship.'

'That didn't stop you last time.'

OK, I'll give him that one. 'I've said I'm sorry for going public with our dirty laundry. But you're the one owes *me* an apology, and you know it.'

'Jesus Christ. You're not still banging on about *that*?'

'I'm going to keep "banging on" about it until you admit what you did,' I say, putting ironic quotation marks around the words with my fingers.

He mimics the gesture. 'I'll "admit" to a good fuck, which, let me point out, you were totally up for. You know the story. You came round to my house dressed to kill, and you got what you wanted. I've said it before, and I'll say it again: it's not my fault you feel guilty now and want to rewrite history.'

So nothing's changed. He has his version of events, and I have mine. The difference is, I've done a lot of soul-searching in the last five months, and unlike Rob I've shouldered my share of the blame. What happened that night was a direct result of the dynamic between all four of us in the weeks and months leading up to it. The flirting, the naked tubbing, the sex games, the foursomes. Playing with fire? We were zip-lining over an active volcano. Sooner or later, it had to blow. I'm not angry about what happened between Rob and me that night any more. Call it rape; call it a misunderstanding. It no longer matters. It's his attitude *since* then that's the problem. He can see how upset and hurt I am. He knows he played a part in that, whatever label you want to stick on it. Why can't he just say *sorry*?

I push back my chair. 'I can see I'm wasting my breath.'

I'm already halfway towards the door when Rob grabs my arm. 'Wait.'

I look pointedly at his hand on my coat. Quickly he removes it.

'Look,' he says uncomfortably. 'Clearly you and I saw things very differently that night.'

'Clearly.'

'If I did something you didn't like, I didn't mean to,' he says hurriedly. 'I was just reacting to the signals I was getting. You were coming on to me pretty strong. The boots and everything. I really thought you were up for it. I *swear* I wouldn't have gone ahead if I hadn't thought you wanted it, too. You said . . . you said once when we were playing Truth or Dare you liked it a bit rough. You said it was exciting. And it's not like it was the first slice of cake.'

'First slice of cake?'

He drops his gaze. 'What I mean is, we'd already done it once.'

'So you figured one more time was no biggie?'

'Well, obviously I appreciated it . . .' He stops, reddening. 'Not appreciated it, exactly – I mean, I *did*. Although that makes it sound like you were doing me a favour. Which you were, of course. Shit. What I meant was, we weren't breaking new ground. I wanted it. If you wanted it. Which I thought you did,' he adds hastily.

If this is Rob communicating, no wonder he and Charlie are in trouble.

The café door opens and a woman in a red sundress comes in. We both step back to allow her to get past.

'Mia, we can't talk standing here,' Rob says. 'Will you come back and sit down?'

For a moment I'm tempted to give him a taste of his own medicine and refuse, but then I relent. This is the first time Rob's even come close to admitting he might have got things wrong. I nod and follow him back to the table, reaching for my cooling cup of coffee.

'So,' I say.

He swallows hard. 'If we got our wires crossed that night, I'm sorry.'

Alleluia. A fucking apology – or as close as Rob is ever going to get to one. And miracle of miracles, he hasn't spontaneously combusted.

'Look,' I sigh. 'I'm not angry about it any more. I know I'm partly to blame for letting things get out of hand. But when you realized how upset I was, why in hell didn't you at least *apologize*?'

'Well, it was a bit bloody insulting, wasn't it? That you had such a lousy time you had to say I'd *forced* you. Anyway, I thought you were just feeling guilty. I honestly didn't know you were this upset. I swear to God, I just thought it was buyer's remorse. I didn't even know I'd done anything wrong.'

'If you'd said sorry in the beginning, we could have avoided all this mess.'

He sighs. 'You're right. I should have.'

'This isn't the schoolyard, Rob. You can't forbid your

wife to see me just because you and I fall out. We're not kids any more.'

'Charlie and I are a team. You attack me, we close ranks.'

'You know I sorted things out with Charlie. I told her how sorry I was about the blog, and she accepted that. If you didn't want to be friends with me again, fine, but the two of you aren't joined at the hip. You should have let her make her own decisions about whether to hang out with me or not.'

'Have you – have you told her about all this?'

'You mean, have I shared my version of events? Of course not. I'm not out for revenge, Rob. I never was. I just wanted you to take responsibility for what happened. An apology is all I was looking for.'

'So you won't say anything?'

'Why would I tell her now?'

'Please don't,' he pleads. 'Things are bad enough at home. If you tell her about this, she'll leave me.'

'I told you, I won't say anything to her.' I hesitate. 'It's really that serious between you?'

'We're fighting over everything,' he says tiredly. 'I can't make a cup of tea without her criticizing the way I squeeze the teabag. She's so down on me, she's starting to come between me and Milly. She's managing me right out of my own daughter's life. I can't seem to put a foot right these days.'

'It's been a tough few months,' I say awkwardly.

'Yeah, well. It's my own fault. I should never have played the heavy and stopped her seeing you.'

Here's a turn-up for the books. Two apologies in one morning.

'She's been under a lot of stress at work,' I say. 'I'm sure it'll get easier once things are sorted out at the school.'

'It's not just work. It's never been this bad between us before. She snaps at me all the time, and she never listens when I try to talk to her. She thinks she does, but she doesn't *hear* me. Jesus. If I didn't know better, I'd almost think there was someone else.'

I feel in no position to act as a marriage guidance counsellor, given our complex personal history. 'Maybe you should both sit down and talk with someone professional,' I venture.

'There's no point. We'll just go round in circles. Charlie will list all the things she doesn't like about me, and I'll have to sit there and take it. But it's not going to make her fall in love with me again, is it?'

I feel a surprising rush of pity. He doesn't always treat Charlie the way he should, but in fairness, she enables him. She's given in to him for twenty years, letting him get away with all sorts of bad behaviour. And now she's finally put her foot down – admittedly not before time – and he hasn't got a clue why.

'She loves you,' I sigh. 'No question. But you need to sort things out with her, Rob. It's not going to get better on its own.'

'I want to make things right,' he says earnestly. 'I love her. You have no idea how much. I know I'm not a walk in the park to live with, but I *need* her. She's my solid ground, you know?'

I do know. It's how I've always thought of Kit. No matter how many mistakes I make, it's having Kit to come home to that keeps me going. I literally can't imagine a life without him in it.

'I'm not the person you should be talking to,' I say softly.

I leave the café and get back in the car, winding down the windows as I replay my encounter with Rob in my head. I never expected to end up feeling sorry for him, but that's my overwhelming takeaway from our conversation. I actually believe him when he says he didn't realize how upset I was. And I believe he really does love Charlie. But unless he changes his game, he's in real danger of losing her, and that makes me sad for both of them.

I wonder where this leaves us all now. I think Charlie and I can see each other openly again, but the four of us? Can we truly be friends again after all that's happened?

I'm not surprised to find her car in our driveway when I get home. No doubt she and Kit are trying to sort out how to handle Shelby. It's going to make all our lives so much easier now that Rob and I have buried the hatchet. At least that'll be one crisis off the table.

I hear the sound of voices as I go through to the kitchen. I don't even stop to take off my coat, eager to tell them about my conversation with Rob. Opening the door, I find them exactly where I expected, at the kitchen counter.

I just hadn't expected them both to be naked.

22

Charlie

'Mia, wait! Please, wait!' I grab my shirt from the floor, struggling into it as I run down the hall. Mia is already yanking the front door open. 'Please, don't go! Let me explain!'

She spins round. 'Explain *what*? Even I can figure this one out! My so-called BFF is screwing my husband behind my back! What d'you think needs explaining here?'

'I know how it must look, but it's not what you think!'

'Seriously? People actually use that line?'

She slams the door so hard it bounces off the jamb and crashes against the wall. I want to go after her, but I'm completely naked beneath my shirt. I bolt back to the kitchen. Kit has vanished, presumably to dress and chase after his wife himself. I pull on my jeans, stumbling into my loafers as I button my blouse. How could we have been so *stupid*? Whatever might have happened between the four of us in the past, this was cheating, pure and simple. I've betrayed my husband and my best friend. What were we *thinking*?

Suppose Mia goes straight over to Rob's office to tell him? Or finds an Internet café and puts it up on her blog? I can hardly blame her if she does, but it'll destroy my career as well as my marriage if this comes out. Kit's too. The school will have no choice but to let us both go. Shelby will have a field day. She'll be able to push the merger with Berwicks through unopposed. Everything we've worked for over the past eight months will be swept aside . . .

I can't believe I'm even thinking about work. What about my *marriage*? Rob will never get over this if he finds out. He simply doesn't have it in him. He'll leave me, and our divorce will make the War of the Roses look amicable.

Milly. If my affair becomes common knowledge, sooner or later she'll find out. I wouldn't put it past Rob to be the one to tell her. *Daddy has to leave because Mummy wants to be with Emmy's daddy instead . . .*

I bury my face in my hands. It's been worse than ever at home recently and Milly's been caught in the middle of our fights more than once. But a child needs security, and even warring parents are surely better than divorce, with all the consequent shuttling to and fro between two homes. I don't want her to have to go through that. I don't want to go through it myself. It might not look like it right now, but I love my husband. How did I let this *happen*?

I only came over this morning to deal with the fallout from Kit's suspension, to calm him down before he committed career hara-kiri. When he swore at Shelby over the phone – and I still can't quite believe he did that – it was out of school hours, off school property. More importantly, there were no witnesses. There's a case to be made that it's a personal matter to be dealt with privately between the two individuals involved. Shelby had no right to verbally suspend him. She has no proof he even said anything. He could simply deny it. Except that isn't Kit's style, of course. He was all for falling on his sword and resigning when we spoke this morning, which is why I took the day off work myself and came here to try to talk him out of it.

He didn't answer the front door when I knocked, though I knew he was at home. I went round to the back of the house and let myself into the kitchen. He was sitting at the counter looking totally shell-shocked and just staring into space. I don't remember ever seeing him look so lost and rudderless.

'Kit? Are you OK?'

He started. 'What?'

'Are you OK? You were miles away.'

'If only.'

I pulled up a stool. 'Come on. We'll work something out.'

'I've let you down,' Kit said despairingly. 'I let her get to me. She baited me with that damn email, trumpeting her nasty little victory, and I rose to it. I should have known better. I *do* know better. I bet she couldn't believe her luck. I've handed my head to her on a plate.'

'She's an underhand witch,' I exclaimed vehemently. 'And come the trustee meeting on Friday, I'll make sure everyone knows it.'

He sighed. 'You can't do that, Charlie. You have to stay above it or it'll sink you too.'

'She had no right to send out that email before talking to the Sisters. The rumour mill will go into overdrive. We'll lose parents left, right and centre. I've already spoken to George Wyatt – he's furious. But he thinks that once he spreads the word Shelby was trying to bounce the board into the merger by jumping the gun on the announcement, at least one of her trustees will come over to our side. If we act quickly, we could scupper the Berwicks deal by the end of the week. She could end up having done us a favour.'

'I still should've kept my mouth shut. Mia's right: I've put my entire family's future at risk for the sake of my ego. It'll be almost impossible to get another job once word about this gets out.'

'Don't be so hard on yourself,' I told him firmly. 'I'd have been just as angry if I'd got that email. We can unpick this, Kit. Wyatt will see Shelby off, and once she's out of the picture, we can sort this out.' I touched his shoulder. 'Just hang in there a little longer. It'll be fine.'

His fingers covered mine. 'Thank you,' he said quietly.

Suddenly it was as if all the air had been sucked out of the room. We were barely touching, and yet somehow I knew how it felt to be inside his skin.

Calmly, as if it were the most natural thing in the world, Kit cupped my face in his hands and gently bent his mouth to mine. His tongue slipped between my lips. I snaked my arms around his back, pressing myself against the hard, warm length of his body, my fingers spread against his broad back. I didn't think of Rob. I didn't think of Mia. I felt as if I'd finally come home.

Just once, I promised myself. *Mia and Rob need never know. Just this one time, and then I'll go back to my marriage and* make *it work. Mia's borrowed my husband before, after all. More than once. The two of them have had freedoms Kit and I have never allowed ourselves. Don't we deserve this much, at least? I love Kit as Mia has never loved Rob. I understand him. If he were my husband, I would never have shared him. I'd never have needed to look outside my marriage.*

Just once.

Kit pulled me towards him. He unbuttoned my shirt and his fingers trailed a warm line of fire from my collarbone, between my breasts, past my navel. I unbuckled his trousers without taking my eyes from his face. We undressed each other slowly, taking our time, the erotic anticipation almost unbearable. When he entered me, his rhythm fast and even, taking me with him, the two of us soaring further and higher with every thrust, I'd never felt so *known*, in every sense of the word.

Even before it was over, I knew just once was never going to be enough.

I drive home slowly, fearful of what I'll find when I get there. But the house is deserted when I get inside. No aggrieved husband or bitter friend waiting to confront me. Just the usual breakfast chaos I left behind this morning.

Wearily I clean the kitchen and load the dishwasher, and then I call Kit. It goes straight to voicemail. So, too, does Mia's phone. I leave a message telling her again how sorry I am and beg her to phone me back.

Perhaps Rob deserved this, though I know keeping score in a marriage is a recipe for disaster. Two wrongs don't make a right, however much we might want them to. But I have no excuse for betraying Mia. She's never intentionally done anything to hurt me. I knew sleeping with Kit wasn't part of the complicated sexual game that's played out between the four of us this year. I can try telling myself it's just an extension of the Wednesday afternoon the three of us fell into bed, but it's more than that. Emotions are involved. I know it, and Mia knows it too.

I kill time pottering fruitlessly around the house, unable to settle. When it's time to collect Milly from summer camp, I half hope I'll see Mia, though I can hardly have a conversation with her there. But it's Kit's mother, Ruth, who picks Emmy up, nodding at me politely across the playground. Relief washes through me. Mia can't have said anything yet. Ruth would know about it if she had, and wouldn't have spared me her trenchant views on the subject.

Maybe she's not going to say anything, I think hopefully. She'll have it out with me, of course, but it'll stay between us. She's not going to want to break up two marriages over this, not after everything we've shared. Surely?

I wish Kit would return my calls. Or at least send me a text to let me know what's happening. Has he spoken to Mia? What did she say? Oh God, I have to *know*.

By the time Rob gets in from work at six, I'm so fraught with guilt I can't even look him in the eye. He's unusually solicitous too, which just makes me feel worse. He orders a Chinese takeaway so I don't have to cook, puts Milly to bed himself, and even makes an attempt to clean up the kitchen.

'We need to talk,' he says when we finally sit down together.

My heart speeds up. Has he been playing some sick game, lulling me into a false sense of security before confronting me?

'What about?' I ask nervously.

'About Mia.'

'Mia?'

'I think – maybe I've been a bit harsh. Perhaps it's time to bury the hatchet.'

I don't know whether to laugh or cry. 'What's brought about this change of heart?'

'I ran into her at the café this morning. We had a bit of a chat.' He shrugs. 'Sorted a few things out.'

My husband was having a reconciliatory coffee with Kit's wife while we – oh God. I can't bear thinking about it. 'I see,' I say faintly.

He looks peeved. 'I thought you'd be pleased.'

'I am. It's just been a long day.'

'Would you like me to run you a bath?'

'What?'

'I said, would you like me to run you a bath?'

I stare at him. Rob hasn't run me a bath since . . . I don't think he's *ever* run me a bath. It's like I've fallen down a rabbit hole into a parallel world where I cheat on my husband, who has suddenly transformed from Neanderthal into New Man.

'Why don't you open a bottle of white while I go upstairs and start it?' he offers.

Curiouser and curiouser. I pour myself a large glass of Pinot Grigio, knock it back and refill it. Any minute now, the Mad Hatter is going to want his dormouse back.

'Bath's ready!' Rob calls down the stairs.

He leaves me alone in the bathroom 'to have some space', and I sink into the hot water, resisting the urge to drown myself. Bubbles, too. Clearly he is leaving no stone unturned in his light-some-candles, give-her-a-foot-rub quest to reignite our sex life. It may be a little clichéd, but nonetheless I'm touched. It's the first time Rob's made any effort to please me for as long as I can remember.

I splash some water over my face. In fairness, I can't recall the last time I tried to please him, either. I've been going through the motions, cleaning the house, caring for Milly, performing for him in the bedroom, but there's been no generosity of spirit. I've given nothing to him willingly. I hug my knees in the cooling water, my heart aching with regret. How did Rob and I go so wrong? We've been through so much together. Twenty years! And I put it all at risk today.

Enough, I vow suddenly. I climb out of the bath and start to towel myself dry. I don't know why Rob's suddenly holding out an olive branch – whether it was something Mia said to him this morning, or if he's just grown as tired as I have of the constant domestic strife. To be honest, I don't really care. Home is supposed to be a refuge. We're meant to be holding each other up, not dragging each other down. I don't want to keep fighting. If he's willing to call a truce, so am I. No more keeping score. No more looking outside our marriage for distraction. From now on, it's just Rob and me.

I expect him to make a move on me when I get into bed, but to my surprise he simply pulls me into his arms and cradles me against his shoulder. Perhaps he really *is* trying to put things right. I know we have a very long way to go. We can't fix our marriage overnight. But if he's willing to meet me halfway, maybe we have a sporting chance.

I wake to the sound of hammering in my head and sit up, my neck aching from the way I've slept in Rob's arms all night. I realize the hammering isn't in my head at all. I nudge Rob. 'Someone's at the door.'

He glances at the bedside clock. 'At seven on a Saturday morning?'

The pounding intensifies. Rob staggers out of bed in his T-shirt and boxers. I pull on my dressing gown and follow him downstairs. A large shadow looms on the other side of the frosted window in the front door.

'Don't open it,' I say nervously. 'It could be anyone.'

The shadow disappears and a moment later the letterbox flips open. 'Let me in, you fucking bastard!'

'Kit!' I gasp.

We glance at each other in confusion.

'Open this fucking door or I'll break it down!'

'Rob, wait—'

Too late. Rob doesn't even see the blow coming.

'Stop it!' I scream, running to my husband as he reels back against the wall, blood pouring from his nose. 'What d'you think you're doing? What the hell is going on?'

'Ask him,' Kit snaps.

Rob backs away. I recognize the expression in his eyes as they flick from me to Kit and back again. It's not fear. It's guilt.

23

Mia

I find a view of water strangely comforting. Maybe it's from being raised in Boston, where you're never far from either the Charles River or the Atlantic Ocean. When I flee from the house, the image of Kit and Mia naked on the kitchen floor burned on my retina, I end up where I always do when I need to think: sitting on a bench in Christ Church Meadow, gazing out across the Cherwell. Which is where Kit finds me, as I knew he would.

'Are you going to run again?' he asks warily.

'I'm done running,' I say without looking up.

He sits on the other end of the bench, giving me space. 'Are you ready to talk about it?'

'I'll listen.'

He rests his hands on his knees, his head bowed. The leather patch on one of the elbows of his blazer has come unstitched, I notice idly. I wish he'd buy a new jacket. He's had this shabby one years. He refuses to replace it, just takes it to a seamstress in the village whenever it needs repair. His car is clapped out, too. Kit's not one to discard something just because the novelty and shine have worn off. When I married him, I thought it was for life.

'I have reasons, but no excuses,' he says heavily. 'Nothing can excuse what I did.'

'Something we agree on.'

'I am deeply, deeply sorry for hurting you. That was never my intention. I hope you believe that.'

'So I'm just collateral damage?'

He sighs. 'I don't blame you for being bitter. I would be, in your place. You may not believe me, but I love you very much. I've let you down appallingly. I can only imagine how you must feel right now.'

'I'm sure you can. I'm a bit of a cliché, after all. Wife discovers husband and best friend getting it on behind her back. Not exactly original, is it? Couldn't you jazz it up a little? Have an affair with Rob instead? Now that'd be worth a blog or two.'

'Don't joke, Mia. It's not funny.'

'Hey, I'm the injured party here. If I want to lighten things up with a little black humour, indulge me.'

'We're not having an affair,' Kit says.

'What would you call it, then?'

'It only happened *once* . . .'

'Did you know you need to commit three separate murders over a period of at least a month, with downtime in between for "cooling off", to be considered a serial killer?' I dig in my jacket pocket for the bag of stale breadcrumbs I've brought from my car, kept there for my weekly trips with Emmy to feed the ducks. Standing up, I throw a handful towards some mallards at the edge of the water. 'If you kill a bunch of people all at once, like at Columbine, you're a mass murderer. Kill a bunch of people in more than one place, but without any downtime, you're a spree killer. There's a hierarchy, you know.' I glance at him. He hasn't moved or raised his head. 'Do you think it's the same with adultery? Three separate fucks over a month makes it an affair, but just a couple and it's only a fling. And then there's the one-night-stand—'

'Would you stop?' Kit pleads finally. 'This isn't helping either of us.'

'*Au contraire*, my love – I find it rather a diversion. But please, I'm interrupting. You were explaining your reasons for screwing my best friend. Do go on.'

'Do you really want to know?'

'I want to know if it's going to happen again,' I say, suddenly dropping the tough-guy act. 'I want to know if you're leaving me. I want to know if you love her.'

'Will you believe me if I tell you?'

I search his face. He's never lied to me, not in all the years we've been together. 'Would you have told me about this if I hadn't caught you?'

'Yes,' Kit says, his gaze unwavering.

Call me naive, but I believe him. He doesn't lie. Not even by omission.

But then again, I thought he didn't cheat, either.

'I love you,' he says, gripping my arms, his eyes blazing with intensity. 'More than you can imagine. I'm not leaving you. I'm not having an affair with Charlie, and it's not going to happen again. I love *you*, Mia. With all my heart and soul.'

'Then why did you do it?' I ask miserably.

He sighs and lets me go. 'I don't know. I didn't plan it, Mia. The last few months at work have been the worst of my life. I've had my back against the wall, I don't feel like

I've had a decent night's sleep in weeks. *Months*, even.'
Briefly, he closes his eyes. 'I'm tired, stressed, and angry. I
come home every night and I'm so filled with rage I want
to punch walls. I'm not making excuses for what I did.
There are none. I'm just trying to explain.'

'You could've talked to me about it . . .'

'No, I couldn't. You've made it plain you don't want to
hear about work. Look, I don't blame you. Of course you're
bored of hearing me bang on about what a shit day I've
had. *I'm* bored by it.'

'But you can talk about it to Charlie,' I say bitterly.

'We work together. We do little else *but* talk about work.'

'This is why you slept with her?' I say scornfully. *'Work?'*

His jaw tightens. 'I needed some support. And yes, she
was there. But it's not just that, Mia.' He take off his glasses
and pinches the bridge of his nose. 'The line was already
pretty blurred. It didn't take much to cross it.'

'What line?'

'That afternoon Charlie came to the house and the three
of us went to bed. We've all been pushing the boundaries
for months. How many rules have we broken already?'

'This was totally different!' I exclaim. 'I was *part* of what
happened before. This was just some sordid little fuck
behind my back!'

'Hold on. If you're going to open that box, let's be honest
for a moment, Mia. I've been sold a raw bill of goods when
it comes to the fun and games between the four of us. You
and Rob got what you wanted. I haven't tried to stop you,
or intervened. I wanted you to have fun. But I've spent the
last six months on the outside looking in.'

'It was your choice not to take things any further with
Charlie.'

'I know that.'

'So this was about evening up the score?'

'You know it's not that simple.' He glances out across the water. 'We all thought we were able to handle colouring outside the lines, didn't we? The four of us in bed together, the threesomes, we all signed up to it. We went into it with our eyes open. Except none of us were really ready for the consequences. I should have stopped it a long time ago when I realized how jealous and insecure Rob was. I knew Charlie was getting over-involved. I knew *you* were.'

'Why didn't you stop it then?' I demand thickly.

He turns to face me. 'You get your own way with me a lot of the time, Mia. I let you stamp and tantrum and play the diva. But it's not because I'm weak. I *choose* to let you get your own way. I can't shower you with diamonds. I've never earned big bucks. The one thing I *can* do is make you happy. That's all I've ever wanted. As long as you're happy, I'm happy.'

His voice cracks on the last word. He puts his glasses back on, but I can see his eyes are bright with tears. I've never seen Kit this vulnerable. He's always been the one I've leaned on, drawing comfort from his strength.

'I'm only human, Mia,' he says gruffly. 'Sometimes it would be nice if I could drop my guard and show it when I'm scared or anxious or just don't know the right thing to do. But you always need me to be strong. And so I can't let you see what's really going on inside my head. Do you have any idea how *lonely* that is?'

I look away, shamed. Kit is absolutely right: for ten years, he's reassured and supported me, no matter how wrong-headed I've been. How hard would it have been for me to put my arm round him when he told me about the suspension from work and tell him I was there for him? To let him voice his fears and admit he doesn't have all the answers? 'I'm so sorry,' I say, my cheeks wet with tears. 'I didn't realize.'

'I didn't want you to realize. My job is to protect you.' Gently he thumbs my tears away. 'Where do we go from here, Mia? Are you going to come back home with me now? Can we get past what happened?'

'I want to,' I begin.

'But?'

'Look, I understand why you did it. Everything you said is true. But it's not that easy, Kit. You cheated on me. How can I trust you after that?'

'The same way I trust you,' Kit says softly. 'You slept with Rob and I forgave you.'

'I didn't want to!' I burst out.

Instantly I wish I could bite off my tongue. Kit stares at me. 'What do you mean by that?'

'Nothing.'

'Mia. What do you mean?'

'Only that I never intended it to happen,' I say lamely.

His voice hardens. 'What do you mean, *you didn't want to*?'

And so, finally, I tell him.

'Please, Kit! Wait!' I cry, running down the towpath after him. 'If you confront Rob now, you'll destroy everything! Think about Charlie and Milly! It's not fair on either of them! You don't need to stir it all up again now. I've forgiven him! I've gotten over it!'

He whirls round to face me, his expression a mask of pain and fury. '*I* haven't forgiven him! *I* haven't got over it!'

'You can talk to Rob when you've calmed down. But don't tell Charlie!' I beg. 'Think how much it'll hurt her! There's no need for her to ever know, unless Rob wants to tell her. It won't change anything.'

'Why do you even care about upsetting Charlie now?'

I shrug helplessly. 'I wish I didn't, but I can't just switch my feelings off. I don't want to see her hurt, and especially not Milly. It won't make me feel any better to make them as miserable as I am. Please, Kit. You don't want to break her heart either, I know you don't.'

'I can't just pretend nothing happened!'

'I'm not asking you to. I'm just asking you to think before you go rushing off half-cocked.'

'You're my *wife*,' he cries in anguish. 'I'm supposed to *protect* you.'

'Why d'you think I didn't tell you before?'

'How could you keep it from me?' he demands furiously. 'You let me sit down with that man and eat at his table! After what he'd done to you! Christ, you had me *apologizing* to the bastard after you tore into him on your blog! You should have damn well *told* me, Mia!'

'I know . . .'

'All this time, and you never said a word!'

'I didn't think you'd believe me!' I cry.

He recoils. 'Of course I believe you! Mia, I love you. I will *always* have your back, no matter what. Why would I think you were lying? I gave you permission to sleep with him. You had no reason to lie.'

'I just felt so guilty, like it was all my fault . . .'

'If a man forces you to have sex when you don't want to, it's *never* your fault,' he says fiercely. 'It doesn't matter what you were wearing, how much you'd had to drink, whether you led him on or not – once you say no, it's all over. There's *no* excuse for what he did. Do you understand me? *No excuse.'* He pulls me into his arms, hugging me like he'll never let me go. 'Oh, Mia. You should never have kept something like this to yourself. I'm your *husband*. You can tell me anything.'

'I'm so sorry,' I sob. 'I wanted to. I thought I could handle it on my own.'

'Look how much damage keeping it secret has caused.'

'I know. I'm so sorry . . .'

'Stop saying that, Mia. I told you, it's not your fault. I'm sorry, too.' He tilts my head up and drops a soft kiss on my lips. 'Come on. Let me take you home. I have to collect Mum from the station. She and I can pick Emmy up from summer camp on the way back and save you a trip. You go to bed and get some rest. We'll talk about everything tonight.'

'You promise you won't go over to Rob's?'

'I promise. It's not going to help either of us if I end up in jail.'

I suddenly realize how exhausted I am. I feel as if I'm made of glass: one more blow and I'll shatter. Is it really only a few hours since I dropped Emmy off at camp? It seems like half a lifetime. This is the kind of drama that happens in soaps, not real life. Except real life is far less civilized and restrained; things rarely work out by the end of the episode.

I'm too tense to do as Kit suggests and go to bed when I get home, so I spend the rest of the afternoon cleaning the house, bringing order and clarity to my pantry and closet in a way I wish I could do with the rest of my life. I stumble through an evening with my mother-in-law as if feeling my way underwater, too preoccupied to pay any attention to her usual acerbic comments. By the time Kit and I finally climb into bed, I'm too tired to talk.

I lie awake long after we've turned out the lights, though. It's not the thought of Kit with Charlie that's keeping me up, painful though that is. It's not even anxiety over whether he'll say anything to her about Rob. What has me tossing and turning until the small hours is the truth of everything my husband said to me today. For ten years, I've behaved as if the fact that I gave up my homeland, my job, my family and my friends all meant Kit owed me in some way. I've taken him for granted and assumed his good nature and willingness to compromise was bottomless. The surprise isn't that he finally did something for himself in sleeping with Charlie; the miracle is that I didn't lose him long ago.

Eventually I fall into a fitful sleep filled with dark and troubled dreams. I wake early, but Kit's side of the bed is already cold and empty. I push myself up on one elbow. It's not even seven yet. Maybe he couldn't sleep either.

He's not downstairs. I put on a pot of coffee, a faint anxiety gnawing at me. His car has gone, but Ruth and Emmy are still upstairs fast asleep. Everywhere will be shut this early on a Saturday morning. I suppose he could have gone for a run, but then why would he take his car?

I check my phone for messages. There are half a dozen missed calls and texts Charlie sent yesterday which I haven't had the strength to open yet, but nothing new from Kit. Suddenly the phone rings in my hand and I jump and drop it on the kitchen table. Charlie. I stare at it as it goes to voicemail. I can't ignore her forever. She listened to me when I screwed up. She has the right to be heard.

Moments later, a telltale *bing* informs me I have a new

text message, quickly followed by another. With a sigh, I click them open.

Is it true?

Mia, is it true?

Oh God. Bile rises in my throat. Kit must have brooded about Rob all night and gone over to confront him this morning before I could talk him out of it.

Bing.

Tell me you made it up to get back at me.

Bing. Bing. Bing.

Tell me you made it up.

Is it true?

Mia, is it true?

24

Charlie

Twenty years, and I find I've never really known my husband at all.

The man I thought I'd married would never have raped a woman. Mia can put all the spin on it she likes – and she has: she's told me over and over it was as much her fault as his, she led him on, they were both drunk, things just got out of hand – but if a woman says no and you go ahead anyway, it's *rape*.

As Rob cowered on the floor holding his bleeding nose, Kit standing over him like an avenging angel explaining with bitter clarity *why*, it didn't even occur to me to question whether or not Mia's story was true. And then I realized – what did that say about my marriage? My best friend was effectively accusing my husband of *rape*, and I wasn't protesting. I wasn't crying 'he couldn't *do* something like that!' because deep down I knew he could.

All the months – *years* – I've spent running from the truth. I've bent over backwards to avoid facing it. I've allowed him his other women, enabling his adultery by joining him in bed with them and telling myself I wanted it too. I've pursued a career that allowed me to be at home and be the wife he wanted. I followed him from one dive site to another so he could break world records while I kicked my heels and stewed with the other dive widows. I've let him dictate our friendships. I've parented Milly pretty much single-handedly since the day she was born. I've accepted a narrow, confined, *lesser* life because I was too cowardly to break free. Our marriage has been dead for years, but I carried on trying to revive its corpse because I didn't want to take the responsibility for divorce. I didn't want to *fail*.

I should have left him when he asked me to turn down Khartoum, when he invited other women into our bed. I should have left when he made it clear he didn't want a child. The writing was on the wall, as plain as day, but I refused to see it. If he didn't love me enough to want to create a child with me, he was never going to love me *more* when that child arrived. Deep down, he never forgave me for pushing him into having Milly, turning the spotlight of my attention away from him and creating a rival for my affections. And deep down, I never forgave him for not wanting our daughter as much as I did.

We've been stumbling along in the dark ever since. Milly's arrival heralded the end of our marriage, and yet it's because of Milly that we've limped along as long as we have.

But what he did to Mia puts an end to everything. I don't care if she led him on. I don't care if she put a damn pole in the sitting room and did the Dance of the Seven Veils. She told him *no*, and she meant it. I don't need to have been there to know she's telling the truth. I've lived with the man twenty years. He takes what he wants and to hell with anyone else. How could he do that to her? And how could he do it to *me*? He wanted another woman so much, he was so bloody randy, that he *had* to have her, no matter what? How could I possibly stay after that and be able to face myself in the mirror? Sex had become so divorced from love in Rob's mind, I couldn't even bear to be in the same room as him now, never mind the same bed.

Even so, I still didn't want to believe Mia. I texted her: *Tell me you made it up to get back at me*. Still running away from the truth. I didn't need her tearful phone call confirming everything Kit had said, but it gave me just enough courage to go through with what had to be done.

When Rob came back from casualty, his broken nose splinted and taped, I met him at the front door with two suitcases and his dive gear. 'Take your things,' I said, thrusting his wetsuit at him. 'Take it all and go. I've booked you into the Randolph. Go there, or don't. Go anywhere you like – I don't care – but you're not staying here.'

'You're throwing me out?'

'You didn't seriously expect me to let you stay?'

'But didn't you speak to Mia?' he cried, his voice nasal and distorted from his injury. 'She'll tell you – we sorted it out! Come on, Charlie, let me in. We can talk about this . . .'

'This has nothing to do with Mia. This is about you and me, Rob.'

'Let's just sit down and—'

'I've been trying to talk to you for months. *Years*. Every time, you shut me down. We never actually have a conversation because you're too busy telling me I'm using the "wrong tone" or arguing the "wrong way". For twenty years, I've been your emotional switchboard. I've cleaned up your messes and done whatever you wanted to keep you happy, and I've had enough of it.' I looked him straight in the eye. 'I can't keep doing it. I've changed, Rob. I've given up expecting you to change, but I *do* expect you to let me have some say in my own life. And you won't even do that.'

'So you're ending it?' he said incredulously. 'Just like that, you're walking away?'

'Not just like that,' I said painfully.

For the first time, it dawned on him I was serious. 'It doesn't need to be like this,' he said persuasively. 'Come on, Charlie. We've survived worse. If you really want us to see a therapist, fine, I'll do it. I'll see whoever you want. I know you don't want to throw away twenty years of marriage without even *trying* to fix it.'

'I've been trying to fix it for God knows how long, Rob. But according to you, our marriage doesn't need fixing, because I'm the one with the problem. Well, maybe you're right. My problem is *you*, so I guess the only way to fix that is to stop being married to you.'

He dropped the conciliatory smile. 'But I'm on the same page as you now! I want to sort it too!'

'A week ago, you didn't even accept it needed sorting.'

'Look, I can see you're a bit upset – I get that. So why don't we go and see someone, this therapist of yours, and sort it all out?' he offered. 'Maybe we can get away for a break. We could leave Milly with your mum and dad, go to Paris or something. You've been saying for years you want to go back to Paris . . .'

I felt a brief and unexpected stab of pity. *Too little, too late.* 'I've been where you are, Rob. Unable to go back, too scared to go forward. But one of us has to be brave enough to make the break.'

'You don't really want that. You're not thinking straight. You don't want to break up our family any more than I do. And think what it'll do to Milly,' he added quickly. 'She's my daughter as well as yours. I'll go for joint custody. She'll be with me half the time. You'll spend Christmas morning on your own every other year. Is that really what you want?'

My sympathy evaporated. *Bastard*. As if he gave a damn about Milly. She was only ever a stick to beat me with. 'Don't make this any harder than it has to be, Rob.'

He grabbed the suitcases. 'This is a mistake. You'll be begging me to take you back in a week. You just want to hope I'm still waiting when you come to your senses.'

'Oh, I've come to my senses,' I said bitterly. 'It may have taken me twenty years, but I've finally managed it.'

I pull up outside Milly's primary school, noting with dismay the parked cars jamming the playground and sports field, where autumn leaves are already blowing around in the late afternoon sun. I have to drive round three times before I find a parking space at the end of a line of vehicles on the grass verge outside the school. It's my own fault for letting my staff meeting run over and cutting it so fine. It'll be standing room only inside the auditorium. I hope Mia's saved me a seat or I'm going to need binoculars to pick Milly out on the stage.

I never thought I'd say it, but the school play has been nothing short of a godsend. Milly's been so excited about costumes and rehearsals she hasn't had time to ask too many questions about why Daddy isn't living with us any more. Although in the six weeks since Rob left he's spent more time with her than in the previous six months. He's entitled to fifty per cent custody, and he's made sure he's got it. I know he's only doing it to get back at me, but either way, Milly's loving the attention.

It doesn't make it any easier for me, though. On the weekends that she stays at Rob's newly rented flat in Oxford, the house seems desolately empty. I have all the free time I used to long for: I can lie in, watch movies, read a book – and I can't bear it. Without Milly, the time between Friday evening and Sunday afternoon passes glacially slowly. Over the past few weeks I've cleaned the house from top to bottom, sorted out the garage (three-quarters empty, now that Rob's collected the rest of his diving equipment and gadgets and tools), cleared the attic, and even tidied the cupboard under the stairs. I'm fast running out of DIY projects. If I don't find something more productive to do soon, I'll have to take up knitting.

I spot Rob's car now, neatly parked in pole position near the school gates, perfect for a quick getaway. Clearly he arrived here in plenty of time. He hadn't been to a single event at her school before we separated; not one carol concert, parent–teacher conference or sport's day since Milly started nursery school. Now, of course, he has time for them all.

I wish I'd had a chance to go home and change, and then hate myself for caring what Rob thinks. My grey suit skirt is crumpled, and I've spilled coffee on my cream blouse. My hair could do with a wash, too. I'm barely keeping my head above water these days. The sooner Kit comes back to work, the better. Thanks to pressure from George Wyatt, the school board has convened an emergency meeting next Friday to discuss the merger with Berwicks and Kit's suspension. I think we'll win both, by the tiniest of margins, but in the meantime I'm not only having to handle Shelby's attempted putsch, I'm having to cover Kit's classes as well as my own.

I slip into the back of the auditorium. There are still another twenty minutes to go before the play starts, but it's already packed. I search the rows of seats for Mia and spot her sitting with Kit about a third of the way from the front.

My heart thuds painfully. How long before I can see him without reacting like a lovesick teenager? I realize what happened between us was a mistake, a one-off lapse of judgement never to be repeated. I knew that going in. I knew he loved Mia. I just hope that one day the message will finally reach my poor, wayward heart.

Mia spots me and stands up, waving madly. How we're still friends after the events of the past year I have no idea, but I don't think I could have survived the collapse of my marriage without her. There can be very few women who could not just forgive me for sleeping with their husband, but truly let it go and put our friendship first. 'I'd have said yes if you'd asked to borrow him,' Mia told me during our first painful conversation two days after Kit came round and broke Rob's nose. 'I love you, and I'd have trusted you. It's that you went behind my back. That's what really kills me.' But since then, she hasn't reproached me once. She's sat up with me when I've needed to talk into the small hours, and patiently tolerated my churlish silences when I've retreated into myself like a hermit for days on end. She's invited Milly and me over for dinner on numerous occasions, and at the weekends when Milly's been with Rob, she's made sure I haven't spent the entire time alone.

I will get over Kit, I tell myself fiercely a hundred times a day, because if I don't, I will lose Mia too; and I couldn't bear that.

'Charlie!' she calls. 'Over here! I've saved you a place!'

Apologizing repeatedly as I tread on toes and bang knees, I squeeze down the row and sit next to her. 'I got caught up in another bloody meeting at school. Couldn't get away.'

'Anything I should know?' Kit asks, leaning around his wife.

'Nothing earth-shattering. I'll fill you in later.'

'Have you seen Rob?' I ask Mia.

'Couple of rows in front of us, on the other side,' she says, discreetly pointing him out with her play programme. 'He's brought some girl along.'

Despite myself, my stomach flips. 'A *date*?'

'I guess. She's hardly here for the quality of the acting.'

I digest this in silence. I knew Rob wasn't the type to stay single for long, but a date after just *six weeks*? My bed's still warm!

Rob and the girl stand up briefly to allow someone past them, and I get a better look at her. 'I know her,' I say, shocked. 'She works with him. I've met her a couple of times at office parties. She's not even twenty-five!'

'You're well rid of the asshole,' Mia says firmly. 'When you're ready, you'll find someone wonderful, and it won't be a teenager who doesn't know any better.'

I've found someone wonderful, I want to say. *He's decent and kind and perfect husband material. The only problem is, you're already married to him.*

The lights dim. For the next sixty minutes, I forget about Rob and his new girlfriend, or the fact that the man I'm in love with is sitting there holding hands with my best friend. My daughter has a starring role as a pink stick of rock in *Hansel and Gretel*, and nothing else matters.

When the curtain comes down, I go backstage to collect Milly. Her face is as pink as the corrugated cardboard tube encasing her from neck to ankles, forcing her to walk like an emperor penguin. 'Did you see me?' she squeals. 'Did you see me?'

'You were absolutely marvellous,' I say. 'So pink! So – so rocky!'

'Mummy,' Milly scolds, but she's laughing.

'I thought you were brilliant,' Rob says behind me. 'The star of the show, in fact.'

I busy myself picking up Milly's clothes and shoes from the muddled heap against the wall. Rob and I haven't really spoken since he moved out, other than to confirm pick-up and drop-off times for Milly over the phone. This is the first time since our break-up we've attended anything together as Milly's parents. We'll have to get used to it, I think sadly. This is what the future looks like.

'I need to say goodbye to Mrs Law,' Milly says. 'We're supposed to tell her when our mums and dads are here.'

She shuffles away as fast as her pink cardboard straight-jacket will permit. Rob and I hover awkwardly where she's left us.

'So how are—'

'What are you—'

We both stop, and laugh nervously. 'After you,' I say.

'No, you go first.'

'I just wanted to ask how you were.'

'Fine. Yes. Getting there. You?'

'I'm fine too.'

We lapse into silence. 'What happened to your friend?' I ask finally. 'Julia, isn't it?'

'Yes,' Rob says, surprised. 'You remember her from work? She's decided to quit the company and go back to college to train as a primary school teacher. I said I'd introduce her to Doug Hamill. She wanted to see if she could do some shadowing before her interview, and a reference from a primary school head would be great for her CV.'

I suppress a rush of relief that's neither fair nor logical. I don't want him, so why shouldn't he find someone who does? But emotions aren't logical, and you can't just jettison twenty years overnight.

Milly returns with a pink and gold helium balloon given to her by her teacher, and the three of us join the crowd thronging towards the auditorium doors. Outside, Kit and Mia are ushering Emmy – a hot-looking gingerbread man in orange towelling – across the playground not far in front of us, discreetly keeping their distance to give the two of us some time together.

'Why don't I help you to the car?' Rob asks as I struggle to keep Milly upright. 'Where are you parked?'

I lead the way, Milly wobbling unevenly between us, clutching her balloon. It feels very strange to be this close to him again: familiar and dislocating at the same time. Rob deliberately adjusts his pace to ours instead of striding ahead and telling us to hurry up as he would normally do. If only he'd been this considerate when we were together, perhaps we wouldn't be leaving now in separate cars.

'It's been good spending so much time with Milly,' he says suddenly. 'Thank you for letting it happen. I know you could have made life difficult for me.'

'You never have to ask to see your own daughter.'

'I've had more fun with her the last few weekends than I have for years,' he admits.

'I'm so glad,' I smile. 'I know some of the schlepping back and forth can be a pain, but she's so much fun to be around. She's so smart, and so funny—'

'I know,' Rob says quietly.

We exchange a look of understanding. I suddenly feel a little spring of hope. If nothing else comes out of this, that Rob has rediscovered his relationship with Milly will make all the pain and loneliness worthwhile.

I unlock the car boot and pile Milly's things into it. 'She's joined the junior cross-country team, did she tell you? They have a meet every other weekend. I scheduled those as my weekends with her because I didn't want to cramp your style, but if you'd like to come and cheer her on, I wouldn't mind.'

'That would be great. I'd love to.' He hesitates. 'Charlie. You and me. Do you think – is there *any* chance . . .?'

A week ago, I'd have said no. But Rob and I have travelled further in the last ten minutes than we have in ten years. There's so much still wrong with our marriage, I can't yet see how it can be repaired. But that doesn't mean I never will.

'Let's just see how things go, shall we?' I say, opening the passenger door.

I turn to help Milly climb into the back. As she reaches for my hand, she lets go of the string of her balloon. Before I can stop her, she's wobbling after it as it floats across the road, hampered by the cardboard tube around her legs.

'*Charlie!*' Rob shouts urgently.

I whirl. Behind me, a car is coming around the bend, heading straight towards us. It's going way too fast; it'll never brake in time. Milly's seen the car, but she can't move quickly enough in her restrictive costume to get out of the way. She tries to run, and then trips and falls. I can see the panic in her eyes as she lies on her back in the middle of the road, beached by her costume, unable to get up. She's screaming. Screaming for me to help her.

I don't know what to do. I can't move. I don't know what to do!

There's a blur as Rob runs past me. He doesn't have time to pick Milly up, or pull her out of the way. He dives towards her, trying to push her clear. I can't see what happens next: the car is upon them. When it's passed, I can no longer see my husband or my child.

'*Milly!*' I scream, finally coming to life. 'Milly! Milly!'

There's a movement in the ditch by the road. Rob raises his head, our daughter in his arms, and I rush towards them.

'Milly! Are you all right?'

'Mummy?' Milly asks shakily.

Rob struggles to his feet. Between us, we pull Milly out of the ditch. I rip the cardboard costume away from her, standing her up and running my hands up and down her small, warm body. 'Are you OK? Does it hurt anywhere?'

'I don't think so,' Milly says, too stunned even to cry.

Our eyes meet over her head. 'I froze,' I choke out. 'I couldn't move. I just froze. If you hadn't been here—'

'But I was,' says Rob simply.

I swallow hard. Every bad thought I've ever had about his parenting, every nappy he didn't change and feed he didn't get up for and school concert he missed – all that means nothing now. As I stand there, the slate is wiped clean. For seven years I've loved and nurtured and cared for our child, but when it mattered, Rob was the one who saved her.

I suddenly realize he's holding his left arm awkwardly. 'Your shoulder!' I exclaim.

'I think the car clipped me,' he says. 'Bloody hurts, if you must know.'

'We need to get you to hospital. Milly too. I want her properly checked out.'

Behind us, a small crowd has gathered, murmuring quietly. Kit and Mia run over with a warm picnic blanket from their car to wrap around Milly, who's shivering in the T-shirt and underwear she was wearing beneath her costume. 'Let me drive Rob and Milly to the hospital,' Kit urges. 'You can come with us. Mia can take Emmy back home in your car, if you don't mind giving her the keys. You shouldn't get behind the wheel after a fright like that.'

We help Rob into the back of Kit's people carrier and then strap Milly into Emmy's booster seat. Rob's looking a bit green about the gills now – a combination of pain and delayed shock. Kit opens the front passenger door for me to get in, courteous even in a crisis.

I glance into the rear seat, where Rob and Milly are pressed together.

I smile. 'I think I'll go in the back with them,' I say.

25

Mia

One year later

I glance up as Charlie lets herself in the back door. I'd get up to give her a hug, but I'm firmly wedged between my stool and the counter.

'Stay there,' Charlie admonishes as I start to push my stool back.

'I can't. Need to pee. Give me a hand, would you?'

She takes my arm and hauls me upright. 'God, you look like you're going to pop any minute. You sure you're not due for another fortnight?'

'Everyone keeps saying that. I'm beginning to wonder if it's twins after all. Those cheapo damn NHS scans. I'll sue the ass off them if I end up with a matching pair. I swear to God I was half this size with Emmy.'

I waddle down the hallway to the bathroom for my fifteenth potty break of the day. Either I've suffered almost total memory loss regarding my pregnancy first time round, or it really is way tougher when you get older. Last time I breezed through the whole nine months like a walk in the park: no morning sickness, no heartburn, no swollen ankles, no haemorrhoids, no backache, no stretch marks. This time I've got the lot. Could be my age; or could be because this one is a boy. They're nothing but trouble from the moment sperm meets egg, as Lois has pointed out more than once. Naturally, she thinks this entire situation is hilarious, and no more than I deserve after having had the perfect pregnancy and perfect child first time round. But she's already volunteered to be godmother, and I'm betting she'll be on a plane over here the minute my waters break to check up on me.

It wasn't planned, obviously. I've always reckoned I scored the jackpot with Emmy: healthy, smart, beautiful and a girl. I had no intention of chancing a second roll of the dice, but Mother Nature thought otherwise. Or, to be more accurate, having come off the Pill nine months ago because my doctor felt it unwise to continue beyond age forty, Kit and I played Vatican roulette and lost. Except I can't think of this baby as *losing*. He may be unexpected, but I couldn't be more thrilled, and Kit's like a dog with two dicks at the thought of a son and heir. The only person more excited than either of us is Ruth, who has become my number one fan since learning I'm carrying a child who will continue the family name. She's already knitted him enough blue booties to carpet the sitting room.

'So is Emmy getting excited?' Charlie asks, handing me a cup of tea as I come back into the kitchen.

'She was until she found out it was a boy.' I heave myself back onto my stool and sip the tea gratefully. 'But she's been very sweet, going through all her old baby clothes with me to pick out the ones she thinks a boy can wear, and helping me decorate the nursery. I think she'll be great with him, actually. My biggest problem will be her mothering him too much and giving him a God complex. The last thing this world needs is another man who thinks the world revolves around him.'

'Say what you like about Ruth – and you have – she did a good job with Kit.'

I nod. I know Charlie will always be a little in love with my husband. But that's OK, because a part of me will always be a little in love with her.

Of course I forgave her for sleeping with Kit. How could I not? She forgave me when she thought I'd slept with Rob. She stuck by me against his wishes when I wrote that snippy comment about him on my blog, even though she had no inkling of the mitigating circumstances. And I'd already forgiven Kit. I've never been one to blame the Other Woman rather than the husband. He's the one who makes the vow to you, after all. So how could I hold Charlie to a higher standard than I held him? Three may be a crowd in most marriages, but not in mine. Kit and Charlie and me: a perfectly balanced triangle of friendship and love and loyalty. During the last twelve months, there have even been a handful of occasions when the three of us have ended up in bed together again. We don't plan it; and we don't talk about it afterwards. There's no need. One day soon, when the baby comes, it'll just stop happening. I'll miss it, but I won't mind. It won't make any difference to the way the three of us are together. Our trust in each other is absolute.

'Talk of the devil,' Charlie says as Kit staggers through the back door laden with shopping bags. 'Here, let me help.'

'Cheers. Couldn't find any ripe avocados, Mia,' he puffs,

dumping the bags on the counter. 'I did the best I could, but you'll probably have to put them on the windowsill for a few days.'

As Kit unpacks, Charlie automatically starts putting things away. She and Milly lived here for several months last year; she knows where everything goes better than I do. Kit opens the fridge and starts reorganizing the crammed shelves to make room for the fresh produce. 'You'll never guess who I bumped into at the supermarket,' he says over his shoulder.

'Surprise me.'

'Shelby Grade. She was standing in a queue at the fish counter. Acted like butter wouldn't melt when she saw me. "Ooh, Kit, how lovely to see you! How are things? I hear the school is going from strength to strength!"'

'No thanks to her,' Charlie mutters sourly.

'I'd have slapped her face with a wet haddock,' I say. 'No, on second thoughts I'd have turned it sideways and—'

'Mia,' Kit warns.

I subside crossly. After the trustees voted Shelby off the school board and reinstated Kit last fall, he insisted we had to put it all behind us and not rake over the past. As he pointed out, it had all come right in the end: Shelby had gone, Charlie had been appointed head teacher, and he'd been promoted to her old job as Head of Humanities. Still, things were pretty tough going for the rest of the school year; quite a few parents pulled their kids out because of all the uncertainty, and several trustees who'd supported Shelby quit mid-year. Most of the staff stayed loyal, but a few troublemakers had to be let go and replacements sought. It's taken Charlie a full academic year to turn things round, but the proof of the pudding came in the enrolment figures this September: up almost twenty per cent.

In an ideal world, Shelby would have slunk away with her tail between her legs, but like most useless managers, she was actually booted sideways and up, rather than out. She's currently on one of the many quangos advising the government on education reform. Doubled her salary, too, but at least she's out of our hair.

'You want to stay for dinner?' Kit asks Charlie now.

She stacks the last of the tins in the cupboard. 'I can't.' She blushes. 'I've got a date.'

'A date?' I exclaim. 'Oh my God! You've played that close to your vest! Who is he? Do I know him?'

'No. At least I don't think so.'

'So where'd you meet him? Is he nice? What's his name? How old is he?'

Kit laughs. 'Spare the poor girl the third degree.'

'His name's Ben Greenwood,' Charlie says, and I can tell just from the way she says his name she's got it bad. 'I met him on a bus. Sorry to be so prosaic. And of course he's nice! I wouldn't have agreed to go out to dinner if he wasn't. He's a doctor at the Radcliffe – '

I giggle. 'A *doctor*!'

' – and five years younger than me.'

'A toyboy! You go, cougar!'

Charlie rolls her eyes. 'God, you can be such a child.'

'Can I help it if I'm excited? This is your first First Date!' I rub my belly with the palm of my hand as the baby joins in my enthusiasm with an energetic kick. 'What are you going to wear? You can borrow something of mine if you'd like.'

'I was hoping you'd say that. The black Alaïa?'

'Help yourself. I'm not getting into it anytime soon.' I give her as warm a hug as my belly allows. 'I'm so glad, Charlie. You really deserve this.'

She smiles again. Her blue eyes are sparkling with something I haven't seen in more than a year, not since she threw Rob out: hope.

No matter how many times Charlie has told me the split had nothing to do with me, I know finding out what Rob had done was the tipping point. If I'd kept my mouth shut, maybe she and Rob wouldn't have broken up. Or maybe it was always inevitable, part of their story, from the moment they met.

Even though the break-up was her decision, it broke her heart. I can't count the number of times I stayed up with her all night those first few weeks, holding her hand as she sobbed her heart out. As she saw it, it wasn't just that her marriage had ended; every memory she had of Rob had been corroded and tainted by what he'd done to me. It didn't matter how many times I tried to explain it hadn't been that black and white. Every time she looked at him, she saw a man she didn't know, a stranger with whom she'd shared her bed for two decades.

Which was why I was surprised to see them talking the night of Milly and Emmy's school play. Rob had turned up with a girl in tow – not a date, it turned out, but a colleague who wanted an introduction to the school head – and I could tell it had thrown Charlie. Love is a habit, like any other. You don't just quit cold turkey after twenty years and not have a few nostalgic pangs. Maybe that's why she accepted the olive branch he held out to her when they went backstage to collect Milly. Maybe she did it for their daughter. Or perhaps she just couldn't get him out of her system.

Every moment of that afternoon is etched on my memory. I close my eyes and it's as vivid as if it were happening again in front of me. Kit and me in the playground with Emmy, just ahead of Charlie and Rob as they come out the auditorium with Milly shuffling between them in that stupid damn costume. We're standing chatting to some other parents near the school gates, deliberately giving Charlie and Rob some space, as Milly wanders out into the road after her balloon. I didn't actually see the accident; it all happened too fast. But I heard Charlie screaming Milly's name over and over, and I saw her frantically ripping the cardboard costume off her daughter afterwards to see if she was all right. The sound of those panicked screams will stay with me forever.

Kit got a picnic blanket out the back of our car and wrapped it around Milly, who was only wearing a sleeveless T-shirt and some panties under her costume. He offered to take Rob to the hospital to get his shoulder checked out, and Charlie gave me her keys so I could take Emmy back home while she went to A&E with Milly and Rob. She got in back with the two of them; I'll never forget the look on Rob's face, crystal clear despite the pain he was in. *Gratitude.* He knew he'd been given that rarest of things: a second chance.

I drove Emmy home and hugged her extra close when I put her to bed, still pretty shaken myself. I was just about to pour myself a large glass of wine when Kit called from the hospital. 'Can you ask Annie next door to babysit Emmy for a bit?' he asked, sounding distant and strangely unlike himself. 'I need you to come to the hospital.'

'Oh God. Is Milly—'

'Milly's fine,' Kit said in that new, strangled voice. 'It's Rob.' He hesitated and my heart chilled. Suddenly I knew what he was going to say. 'He died, Mia. Rob's dead.'

I laughed. 'He can't have done. He only hurt his shoulder! They've made a mistake, confused him with someone else . . .'

'You have to come,' Kit said, cutting through my babble. 'Charlie needs you.'

Rob was dead before they even reached the hospital. A traumatic aortic rupture: the blow from the car had only been glancing, but had delivered enough force that when his heart decelerated inside his chest, his aorta did not. Apparently Princess Diana died from something similar, only in her case it was a pulmonary vein. Rob's aorta didn't rip away entirely, which would have killed him more or less instantly; it took a number of minutes for his chest to fill with blood, but he was doomed from the moment the car hit him. He died sometime on the way to hospital, with his wife and daughter beside him, filled with hope and optimism.

Afterwards, we brought Charlie and Milly home to us and insisted they stay as long as they needed to. It was four months before Charlie felt strong enough to go back to her house and pack everything up. She couldn't bear the thought of living there again without Rob, so she sold the house and used the proceeds to buy a small cottage a couple streets away from us. We helped her organize the funeral, and we listened when she needed to vent, or rage, or grieve, or weep. We became her family, and we closed ranks around her.

For a while, I thought the guilt would consume her. She blamed herself for panicking the night of the accident, for not being the one to rescue Milly, for not being the one who died. She tormented herself with what ifs: *what if I'd got to the school earlier? What if I hadn't parked on such a dangerous bend? What if I'd watched Milly a little closer? What if I'd reached her in time?* If only she hadn't thrown Rob out. If only she'd realized he was hurt. But eventually the guilt receded, leaving in its wake a healing sense of grief and loss.

I don't know if she'd have taken him back if he'd lived. I suspect she would: he was her addiction, and addicts nearly always relapse. But in the aftermath of his death, what mattered to Charlie was that he'd believed she would. Their last conversation had been friendly and optimistic. And the last thing he ever did for her redeemed all the bitterness and hurt that had gone before.

That single act of thoughtless courage was the best and bravest thing Rob ever did. Perhaps it's what he was born to do. Maybe his entire life led up to those few split seconds on a chilly fall afternoon when he threw himself in harm's way to protect his daughter.

That's how Charlie saw it, anyway. 'That day, he was the man I married again,' she told me months later. 'He gave me back all my memories, clean and uncorrupted. How could I not love him after that?'

Last week marked a year since his death. We visited his grave with Milly and Emmy, and remembered him that night at dinner. Milly knows her daddy was a hero; that he loved her so much he went to heaven to look after her. Unlike most children, she'll never have to discover he had feet of clay.

I waddle upstairs now and pick out the Alaïa dress for Charlie's date tonight. They say the first year of grief is always the hardest. The first Christmas alone, the first birthday, the first anniversary. Charlie's survived it. It's time for her to be happy again. Kit puts his arm round me as we wave her goodbye, wishing her luck and making her promise to call us for a full debrief tomorrow. His hand rests on my belly, and I feel my son's strong kick inside me.

We've already picked out his name.

Acknowledgements

My thanks, as always, to Carole Blake, the most brilliant agent in the business and an entertaining and loyal friend (here's to the next fifty years).

Thanks, too, to my editor, Wayne Brookes, who fights for his authors like a tigress protecting its cubs. I owe him, and the entire team at Pan Macmillan, especially Louise Buckley, Laura Carr and Emma Bravo, a huge debt for making this book the best it can possibly be. I have adored working with you.

Melis Dagoglu and Daisy Way at Blake Friedmann, for always being there to handle any questions with speed and charm.

Juliet Van Oss, my copy-editor: thank you for picking up my many dropped stitches.

For reading this book in a single sitting in its unedited form, and her insightful feedback, Tere: I owe you a Dark and Stormy.

For providing boltholes to edit and write: Michèle in

Devon (I highly recommend a stay at the elegant Knapp House, an Arts and Crafts-style retreat in the heart of the Exmoor countryside: www.knapphouselodges.co.uk), Fabio in Rome, Georgie in London and Barrie in St Petersburg. Love you all.

And thank you to my husband, Erik, who read this book at least a dozen times in its various forms, and heroically critiqued every stage. I couldn't have done it without you.

Burlington, Vermont
February 2014

If you enjoyed

an open marriage

you'll love these other books by

there are some
things we are never
meant to know

tess
stimson

the
lying game

**There are some things we are
never meant to know . . .**

Harriet Lockwood has never really bonded with her
daughter, Florence, the way she has with her three sons.
Then one day, she discovers why. The girl she's raised
for the last fifteen years is not her biological child.

Zoey Sands is a single mother with a chaotic lifestyle.
The one constant in her life is her daughter, Nell.
Nothing can ever come between them – can it?

When Harriet turns up on Zoey's doorstep demanding
to see her biological daughter, the two families are
plunged into a storm of bitter rivalries . . . and
unexpected alliances.

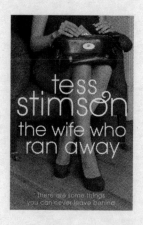

tess
stimson
the wife who
ran away

There are some things
you can never leave behind

Can she ever truly escape the ties that bind?

Kate Forrest is invisible . . . Ned, the husband she adores, doesn't seem to know she's alive, and her two charming children have grown into stroppy adolescents. Her boss is suddenly shunting her towards career Siberia, and her demanding mother is never off the phone. With her fortieth birthday fast approaching, all Kate wants to do is run away from the lot of them.

And so she does. On impulse, Kate walks out of her job, her family and her life, and gets on a plane to Italy. With no ties and no responsibilities, she soon finds herself deliriously caught up in La Dolce Vita – and the arms of a man barely half her age. But when the unthinkable threatens her family, Kate is brutally forced to choose between her past and the future.

**A story of sisters who share
just a little *too* much . . .**

Like a princess in a fairytale, Grace Hamilton has been
showered with blessings: professional success, a happy
marriage – she even lives in a beautiful castle. But the
only thing she really wants – her heart's desire – is
the one thing she can never have.

Her sister, the gorgeous Susannah, has made a mess
of her life. Like a reverse Midas, everything she touches
turns sour. But Fate puts Grace's future in Susannah's
hands, changing the balance of power between
the sisters forever.

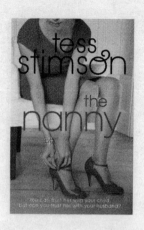

**You can trust her with your child,
but can you trust her with your husband?**

Clare Elias has always known the risks of being
married to a rich, handsome, younger man like
Marc. When she gives birth to two gorgeous babies,
she discovers motherhood isn't quite the cinch she'd
expected, yet Marc takes to parenthood like a duck to
water. Desperate to regain her independence running a
successful chain of boutique flower shops, Clare hires
Jenna, a confident, efficient nanny keen to escape
a relationship that is going horribly wrong.

But before too long, a deadly rivalry emerges, and
as events spiral out of control, Clare finds herself
forced to make painful decisions about love,
loyalty and motherhood.

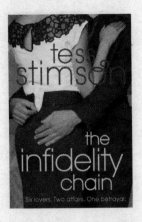

Jackson is married to Ella, who's sleeping with William, whose wife Beth is falling for daughter Cate's boyfriend Dan . . .

Ella Stuart has worked hard to achieve the perfectly balanced life. She has a high-flying career as a paediatric doctor, a charming husband in Jackson Garrett and a passionate lover in William Ashfield.

But when tragedy strikes out of the blue, Ella's carefully ordered life spirals out of control and she is forced to question the one thing she holds dear.

William is happy to have his cake and eat it too, but as his wife Beth emerges from the illness that has plagued some of her most precious years, it's her turn to rediscover passion – and not with her husband.

And for William and Beth's daughter, Cate, the transition from girlhood to womanhood is suddenly set to be a baptism of fire.

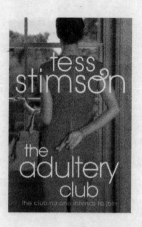

A wife, a husband, a mistress.
Whose side will you be on?

Life couldn't be happier for Nicholas Lyon,
a divorce lawyer and contented husband of the
beautiful Mal, a successful cookery writer and
mother to their three gorgeous daughters.

And then Sara Kaplan, a bright, vivacious young lawyer,
explodes into his life like a sexual hand grenade. At first
stunned and horrified by the extent of his attraction to her,
a catastrophic event soon forces Nicholas to recognize
his own mortality and throw caution to the wind.

For Sara, what started as a harmless fling swiftly
deepens into a painful battle with Mal for Nicholas's
heart, who is not quite as preoccupied in her world of
food and school runs as Nicholas had believed. But as
Mal faces temptations of her own, she realizes she has
to decide what she wants – and whether it's worth
fighting for.

extracts reading groups
competitions books new
discounts extracts
competitions
books new
events books
extracts new reading groups
events books
extracts new titles reading groups
interviews events new books
new books events
discounts extracts discounts

www.panmacmillan.com

extracts events reading groups
competitions books extracts new